MECH

Heart & Soul

KEN DEEPROSE

 FriesenPress

Suite 300 - 990 Fort St
Victoria, BC, V8V 3K2
Canada

www.friesenpress.com

ISBN
978-1-03-910646-8 (Hardcover)
978-1-03-910645-1 (Paperback)
978-1-03-910647-5 (eBook)

1. JUVENILE FICTION, SCIENCE FICTION

Distributed to the trade by The Ingram Book Company

For Jason

The best son a dad could ever ask for.

1

"Watch where you're going!" Orin yelled at the truck that had just side-swiped him, sending his hoverbike careening through the middle of a sidewalk café. There had been less traffic on the roads the last couple of weeks, but those drivers that remained were understandably distracted. Fortunately, the café was deserted. There weren't many pedestrians around these days either.

Orin had to admit that the incident was partially his fault. Being late for work, he may have been travelling a little faster than he should have been. He had come to the city yesterday to pick up a few things from the apartment he shared with his father. Fearing it might be his last chance to sleep in a real bed for a while, he decided to spend the night and had slept a little longer than he intended. Oh well – he'd just have to blame it on a faulty alarm clock.

Unlike most kids his age, Orin couldn't get away with using his youth as an excuse for irresponsible behaviour. For better or worse, he had already taken on far more responsibilities than was typical of someone his age. His father, who was also his boss, was the most brilliant and respected scientist on the planet and expected a high level of excellence and maturity from his young son. Thinking about it now, he might have to come up with something a little better than a faulty alarm clock.

Taking a moment to regain his composure after the near-miss with the truck, Orin removed his helmet and stepped away from the bike. Sweat soaked his short dark hair and trickled into his intelligent brown eyes. He rubbed it away with the back of his hand and checked his reflection in the café's plate-glass window. The image he saw was familiar, but not particularly impressive. Tall for his age, but a little on the skinny side, he always felt his appearance projected an image of someone smart but boring, like a kid who spent more time reading books than roaming sports fields. At this particular moment, he also had the jittery look of a kid who almost got hit by a truck, so he closed his eyes and took a few deep breaths to calm his nerves. He looked at his hands – steady as a rock. Feeling ready to go, he put on his helmet, mounted the hoverbike and continued on his way.

As he cruised along Main Street, Orin was saddened to see the current state of the city he called home. At this time of day, the streets would normally be bustling with activity. Merchants would be out selling their wares, street vendors would be at their food carts filling the air with the aromas of savoury delights and customers would be out searching for the latest bargains. Today however, the streets were nearly empty, the food carts were gone and the only merchants he saw were out nailing boards over their store-front windows.

Turning onto the highway heading out of town, he was met with a much welcomed, but somewhat ridiculous, exception. Leaping Lano's Furniture Emporium was alive with the colour of balloons and banners promoting his latest sale. According to his overly enthusiastic advertising campaign, Lano had hired a local mystic to place an enchantment on his entire store, protecting it from any potential disaster. Fortunately for his customers, this protection extended to everything in the store as well, so by simply buying a sofa and matching coffee table, your home could also be protected from any possible harm. It wasn't the craziest promotion Lano had ever come up with, but Orin had to admit, it was one of his more creative ones. Judging from the empty parking lot, however, it didn't seem destined to become one of his more successful endeavours.

Returning his focus to the road, he soon found himself climbing the steep hill out of the valley that held the entire city of Volara. When he reached the top of the hill, he pulled over to the side of the road to look back over the city. It was a wonderful sight. Even though he was late, Orin never missed an opportunity to admire the view from the rim of the valley.

It was a beautiful day. The sky was a perfect shade of amber, so typical of a pleasant mid-summer morning. The city itself stretched all the way to the horizon. The tall buildings at its core were surrounded by houses, shops and parks with large factories and warehouses dominating the southern fringe. Beautiful estates lined the walls of the valley where the city's wealthiest citizens lived in luxury. Looming in the distance was Mount Volaris, with the sun glinting off the spires of the Royal Palace near its base. It was a glorious sight and he hoped this wouldn't be his last opportunity to appreciate the beauty of this place.

An image of his father scolding him for his tardiness brought Orin back from his thoughts. Firing up his hoverbike, he continued down the highway with the accelerator pinned to its upper limit. He knew that he really should be more careful – technically, he wasn't even old enough to operate a motorized vehicle on public roadways, so getting pulled over might pose a bit of a problem. However, on those few occasions he had been stopped by the police, he had managed to convince the officer that, because his hoverbike didn't actually touch the road, he wasn't really breaking any laws. That, combined with his rather famous last name, had kept him out of trouble so far.

But today, there was no traffic on the road and little chance of encountering the police, so he didn't worry too much about his excessive speed. People would be leaving Volara from the other end of the city, heading west to one of the smaller towns near the coast. Up here on the high desert to the east, he felt like he had the whole world to himself. The highway wound along a rocky ridge to his left, and on his right, a view of endless sand rushed by in a blur, interrupted only by the gnarly outline of an occasional marspike tree. The morning sun reflected waves of heat off the jet-black road that stretched before him as far as he could see. The hum of his hoverbike provided the only sound in this desolate place.

As he rounded the final bend in the highway, Orin finally spotted his destination. In the distance, he could see the vast cluster of buildings that made up the Cambrian Defence Force Mechanized Artillery Depot, or as everyone who worked there simply called it, The Depot. The Depot was the largest military base on the planet of Cambria, encompassing more than two dozen buildings. There were barracks, laboratories, administration and support buildings and, at its heart, a huge assembly building that housed the mechanical fighting machines responsible for the security of the planet. It was the home of the Mechs.

Suddenly, an armorat darted across his path, snapping his attention back to the road. The large rodent had four stubby legs with interlocking bands of armoured shell covering the length of its body. When it saw the bike's high-speed approach, it tucked into a perfect sphere and awaited impact. Orin swerved, very nearly avoiding a collision, but he clipped it on the way by and sent it skittering back into the ditch. He felt guilty for his speeding, but he knew the animal would be OK. Those things were tougher than rocks when they got themselves rolled into a ball.

Reducing his speed, he turned into the entrance of the high-security facility. Rolling up to the main gate, he held up his ID card for the guard to check. Not even glancing at the card, the guard simply lifted the gate and waved him through. Everyone at The Depot knew Orin, so he never got questioned at the gate. There certainly were perks to being the boss's son.

Manoeuvring his bike through the narrow corridors between buildings, he pulled up to the Central Assembly Building, coming to a stop in his assigned parking spot right next to the main entrance. Ah, yes – there certainly were perks to being the boss's son. As he approached the entrance, he drew in a deep breath knowing this might be his last chance to breathe outside air for a while.

Orin practically grew up in the Central Assembly Building, so had entered it thousands of times, but it still took his breath away every time. It was spectacular! The ceiling soared over sixty feet above the ground and the space it enclosed was so large you could barely see the wall at the far end. Enormous gantry cranes rumbled overhead and the place buzzed with the activity of hundreds of workers and dozens of assembly drones.

And, of course, there were the Mechs. The Mechs were gigantic robots that served as mechanized war machines for the protection of Cambria. The very first Mechs had been designed and built by Orin's grandfather, Professor Orin Umbra, his namesake. There had only been three of the steam-powered behemoths, but they proved to be the heroes of the First Maran War. His grandfather passed away the year after the war, long before Orin was born, and the steam-powered Mechs were deemed obsolete. That meant the task of building the next generation of Mechs fell to Orin's father, Professor Darin Umbra, or as everyone simply called him – The Professor.

The new Professor Umbra embraced the challenge and created a formidable fighting force. First, he created a series of diesel-powered units. Next came Mechs powered by an internal hydro-electric generator and, finally, a solar-powered series. By the time the Marans returned, ten years after the first war, Cambria had nine of the most powerful fighting machines ever conceived to assist in its defence.

The Second Maran War dragged on for weeks. The Marans had arrived with a much more powerful force themselves. Dozens of Satellite-Controlled Unmanned Drones, or SCUDs as they came to be known, landed on the plateaus of Mount Volaris and attempted to overrun the Royal Palace, the seat of Cambria's political power. Ultimately, the Mechs prevailed and the Marans retreated for what everyone had hoped was the final time. The end result was two heroic victories for the Mechs and the name Umbra now featured prominently in Cambrian history books. Orin didn't care about being famous, but it was nice to get out of paying the occasional speeding ticket.

His thoughts returned to the present when he looked up to see one of the Mechs heading in his direction. Gigahertz. Gigahertz was one of the Hydro Mechs and was considered the greatest hero of the Second Maran War. Even in a room full of giant fighting robots, Gigahertz was impressive. As he approached, the light bounced off his shiny titanium armour, all trimmed in blue. He was nearly twenty feet tall and weighed over fifteen tons. Despite his immense size, his movements were graceful and his footfall was as soft as that of a targacat.

Orin's mother died when he was very young and his father was obsessed with his work, so much of Orin's childhood was spent here at The Depot. With no siblings and no other children around, his youth could have ended up very lonely. But it didn't. This monstrous machine now heading his way was much more than a ferocious fighting machine. Much more than a war hero. He was Orin's best friend.

"Hey Gig, how's it hangin'?"

"Good morning Master Orin. As is the case with so many of your questions, I am having trouble formulating an appropriate response."

"That's OK Gig – you'll get it eventually."

"That is what you keep telling me. I *do* hope you are correct."

Most of the Mechs were shaped like people, with all the same basic body parts. Two arms. Two legs. Head at the top, feet at the bottom. Just like people – only bigger and more menacing. Generally, when a person was introduced to a Mech, they tended to yell up towards the head to be heard. In reality, each Mech had a comm panel with a microphone and speaker down at person height, so having a conversation with a Mech was quite comfortable. Of course, the degree of comfort did vary from Mech to Mech.

One thing that both Professor Umbras insisted on was including an individual artificial intelligence, or AI, in each Mech. They did not want their creations to be mere machines following commands from a control centre, miles from the action. They wanted the Mechs to be true warriors, observing the battlefield, reacting and improvising as required. Having individuality enabled different points-of-view to be considered during the battle. With the Mechs able to discuss, deliberate and decide on the best course of action during a fight, they became a true military unit rather than a bunch of machines running around shooting at stuff.

As a result, each Mech now had a unique personality. Some were quite talkative and friendly, while others were much less so. For instance, Carnage, Mayhem and Havoc, the Diesels, rarely responded to questions with an answer longer than one word. Unless, of course, you got them on the topic of how to break stuff – then they could go on and on all day. Orin knew all of the Mechs, but it was always Gigahertz with whom he could talk about anything. His one true friend.

"So, what's on the agenda for today?" Orin asked Gigahertz.

"New shield arrays are being installed in the Bio units and the prototype fusion reactors are being replaced in the Atomics."

Despite having their research budget slashed to nearly zero, Professor Umbra had managed to develop two new series of Mechs over the last few years. One was powered by an exotic bio-fuel he had developed and the other by an atomic fusion reactor. The new units weren't battle-ready yet, but everyone at The Depot was hoping there would be six new Mechs added to the team very soon.

"Your father has been looking for you," Gigahertz informed Orin. "He's over by the coolant tower talking with the General."

"Thanks Gig. I guess I better get over there and find out how mad he is."

As Orin headed across the facility to meet his dad, he passed Solitaire, the largest of the Solar Mechs, carrying a large bin of hydraulic cylinders.

"Hey Sol, can I give you a hand with that?"

"No. I do not require assistance at this time," Solitaire replied as he stomped off.

The offer was a joke of course – a completely wasted joke as Solitaire had no sense of humour at all. He was probably the most appropriately named of all the Mechs – he preferred to do everything by himself.

Approaching the coolant tower, Orin noticed his dad in a heated discussion with the General. Professor Umbra was the lead scientist, chief designer and overall leader of the Mech program, but the tactical genius responsible for turning them into a true military unit was General Aldin Zatari.

Orin couldn't help but notice the contrast between the two men locked in conversation. They were about the same height but the similarities ended there. The Professor was a tall, thin, almost skeletal man. His arms and legs seemed far too long for his body and his greying hair seemed to point in every direction at once. Throw in a pair of round wire-rimmed glasses and he looked every bit the geeky professor that he was. General Zatari, on the other hand, looked solid. He had a large chest, flat stomach and square shoulders. His dark hair, greying at the temples, gave him a distinguished look. You could almost see an aura of authority surrounding him. The men and women under his command didn't just obey him, they adored him.

The General gave Orin a nod as he approached. "Good morning Orin. I was just telling your father how important it is that we get the Bios and the Atomics battle-ready as soon as possible".

"And I was just telling the General that some things simply can't be rushed," the Professor urged.

"I'm not trying to be difficult here, but we do have a fixed deadline and there's nothing we can do to change it," the General countered.

The Professor released a heavy sigh and ran his fingers through his thinning hair. "All we can do is our best," he finally replied.

"Find a way to make it happen, Darin," the General said as he turned to leave. "I suggest that you gentlemen have a *very* productive day."

With the General gone, the Professor turned to address his son. "Ah, Orin. Good afternoon. How nice that you could join us today."

Realizing honesty was likely his best course of action, Orin stood up straight and looked his father in the eye. "Sorry Dad. I slept a little late. I also stopped at the rim and had a look at the city."

The Professor wasn't very good at being mad at his son, so he returned a gentle smile. "That's OK, Orin. It's probably for the best. It might be some time before you can get back to the city, so I'm glad you took a few moments to enjoy it."

"Thanks Dad…," Orin started, but before he could continue, they were interrupted by a soft voice.

"Excuse me Professor, do you have a moment?" The question came from Diara, one of the Techs on his dad's team. Techs were the people responsible for supporting the Mechs before, during and after their missions. They were in charge of designing and implementing hardware and software upgrades, communicating battlefield conditions and providing anything else the Mechs required to increase their effectiveness. They were basically the technical geeks of the Mech team. It was a great job and Orin desperately wanted to be one, but any time he mentioned taking the training, his dad told him he was destined for bigger and better things. Orin had a hard time imagining anything bigger or better than being a Tech.

Diara was the youngest of the Techs, being only a few months older than Orin. The Professor had commented several times that, despite her youth, she was one of the smartest and most innovative members of his team. As Orin watched her there, with her short blond hair and striking blue eyes, he caught himself thinking that she was one of the prettiest too.

"What have you got there, Diara?" the Professor asked.

"It's a change I think we can make to the SIMs, Professor," she said, handing him a datapad. "I think a small modification to the transceiver would allow us to change the output frequency on the fly. We could do harmonic matching with the SCUD's shields and increase the disruptive power by a factor of five."

Professor Umbra stared intently at the datapad, looking over the design. Soon, a broad smile formed on his face and he turned to Diara. "This is brilliant," he said. "I will see to it that this gets implemented right away. Truly a gold star idea!"

As Diara turned to leave, her face glowing with a proud smile, Orin couldn't help but feel a pang of jealousy. A "gold star" was the highest compliment paid by his father – he did not hand them out idly. Orin couldn't remember the last time he had received one. Well, the day *was* just getting started – he might find some way to collect one for himself before it was over.

"So, what's up for today?" he asked his father.

"I will be supervising the installation of the new fusion reactors in the Atomics. As for you, why don't you report to Dorel down on the assembly floor. I've briefed him on a special project I'd like you to take on. He'll fill you in on all the details."

"Thanks Dad," Orin said excitedly as he turned to go meet Dorel. Dorel was the foreman of the assembly mechanics, or "Wrenches" as they preferred to be called. He was a giant of a man and had a huge heart to go along with his oversized body – Orin really enjoyed working with him. He thought it was odd that his father wanted Dorel to tell him what the project was all about. Maybe it was actually something good this time.

Making his way through the assembly building, he could sense a nervous energy in the air. People were moving more quickly than usual and there was a look of fierce determination on every face he saw. The building always felt busy, but this was something different. Fear, maybe? Even the Mechs seemed a little off. According to his father, Mechs weren't technically capable of feeling emotions, but today their movements had an urgency about them and they seemed particularly focused. It did make sense, after all. War was coming. The Third Maran War. And it was only six weeks away.

2

"Princess Juna. Put. That. Down."

Ah, Mister Stotz. Things always got worse whenever he walked into a room. Juna had been caught red-handed, carrying a box of her belongings from the closet to a large pile forming near the door. "Sorry Mister Stotz. I certainly didn't mean to be helpful," she replied with more than a hint of sarcasm.

Mister Stotz, who was the manager of the palace and one of her father's favourite lackeys, returned one of his familiar smug smiles. "Princess, we have had this conversation a thousand times. There are people who do things and there are people who have things done for them. You were fortunate enough to be born the latter, so I suggest you remember your place."

Juna's temper flared. Oh, how she wanted to tear that smirk right off his face. And would everyone please stop calling her Princess! But before her thoughts could turn to action, Pom, her personal servant, approached with eyes lowered and shoulders bowed, to retrieve the box. "I can take it from here m'lady," she said softly as she took the box and carried it over to the pile.

"There, do you see how much easier that is," Stotz gloated. "Someone will be coming to pick up all of your things in one hour. Do you want me to send more help?"

"No, it's almost done. I'm sure Pom can finish the rest by herself."

"Very good, Princess. I shall return in one hour to make sure nothing was missed," he said as he rushed off to ruin someone else's day.

When he was gone, Pom squared her shoulders, stood up straight and looked Juna in the eyes. "Yes Princess. We wouldn't want you putting out the royal back now would we," she said playfully.

"Oh, shut it Pom. By the way, if you call me Princess again, I *will* make you do the rest by yourself. And where did that m'lady come from?"

"I thought you might like that one," Pom teased.

"No, I really didn't."

"Oh Juna, we really do need to work on that sense of humour of yours."

"If you don't mind, I think I'll save my sense of humour for things that are actually funny."

The two girls shared a laugh. Pom was so much more than a servant to Juna – she was the best friend she had ever had. Pom originally came to the palace when she was barely old enough to walk, as an assigned playmate for the young Princess Juna. Others had come and gone over the years, but Pom had been the one constant in Juna's life. When they got older and Juna was forced to take a servant, she had insisted that Pom take on the role. Now, Juna loved her like a sister. Not like her real sister – she didn't even like her real sister. No, it was more like she always thought love between sisters should really be.

The girls were always very careful to keep the closeness of their relationship a secret. There were three distinct classes of people on Cambria. There were the Elites, a group that included the royals and all of the political players on the planet. Next came the commoners. They were the doctors, merchants, teachers and all the other people living what should be considered a normal life. Making up the lowest class were the hods, essentially slaves, who spent their lives serving the Elites and doing all the other unpleasant jobs that no one else wanted to do.

Juna was an Elite. Pom was a hod. Any sort of friendship between them was simply not permitted. To Juna, it had never made any sense. The hods looked exactly the same as everyone else. At some point in history, some powerful people, likely Juna's ancestors, decided that some people would, from that moment forward, be hods. Now, if your parents were hods, then you were one too. It was just wrong. When she was younger, Juna recalled telling her father that she didn't think it was fair that the hods worked so hard to receive so little, while the Elites did nothing but were given so much.

"Fair?" he had replied. "Of course, it's not fair. It's not supposed to be fair. They were born to their place in life and we were born to ours. You are a princess, my dear. Just accept it and maybe even learn to enjoy it once in a while."

Princess. Oh, how she hated that word. Juna was simply not cut out to be a princess. They say, an apple doesn't fall far from the tree, and that certainly was the case with her brother and sister. Juna, however, preferred to picture her family tree perched atop a steep hill. She imagined her apple falling from the tree, bounding down the hill and rolling away so far that she could scarcely see the tree anymore. No, the life of a princess was not for her. She wanted a life where she and Pom could be friends and every-one, even the Elites, could just do things for themselves.

Just as she started getting mad again, Pom interrupted her thoughts. "So, what do you think is really going on with this move? It just doesn't make any sense."

Juna agreed. Absolutely everything in the palace was being packed up and shipped to their summer palace in Alderae, a small city on the western coast. Everyone knew the war was coming and assumed that the Royal Palace would be the focus of the attack, but moving every article of clothing, knick-knack and stick of furniture seemed a bit much.

"I don't know Pom," she replied. "Maybe I'll go talk to Father and see if he can shed some light on things."

"That's a good idea," Pom urged. "And while you're there, please tell his lordship that if I have to spend any more of my time lugging his precious things around, I'm going to have to put in for a raise."

Juna knew, of course, that Pom was kidding. Hods did not actually get paid for their efforts and even making a suggestion like that would get her thrown into a prison she would never walk out of.

"Well, he never tells me anything, but I suppose I'll go try anyway," Juna replied. "And let me see what I can do about getting you that raise."

Juna helped Pom move the last of the boxes and then set out to wander the corridors in search of her father. The Royal Palace was a beautiful place. It had high ceilings with rough timber rafters towering overhead. There were windows everywhere, so the late-morning sun filled every corner with light. Intricate mouldings bordered every window and each of the massive wooden doors. The stone floors felt so solid, you could not help but feel safe. She truly loved it here and did not look forward to an extended stay in Alderae.

It was no secret that her father did not share her love for this wonderful building. He felt it was old and outdated and not worthy of housing a family as distinguished as theirs. Seeing it with all of the furniture gone, Juna had to admit that the place was showing its age. Paint was peeling, there were some holes in the walls and the floors had a few cracks, but to her, that just added to its charm.

As Juna rounded the corner approaching the Great Hall, she spotted her sister Lacee with a gaggle of her servants, in obvious distress. When Lacee spotted Juna, she rushed over.

"Oh Juna, have you heard? Daddy is only letting us bring three servants each when we go to Alderae. I need someone to dress me, to do my hair, to run my bath. Why, that's three already! Who is going to do everything else?"

Juna was having a hard time mustering any sympathy for her older sister, but she knew an explanation of the potential hardships of war would be completely wasted on her. Like Juna, she had grown up in a life of privilege, where anything you could possibly want was given to you and every task, no matter how trivial, was done for you. Unlike Juna, however, Lacee just accepted it, truly embracing the life of an Elite. It wasn't really Lacee's fault – she was just very good at being a princess.

Juna plastered a fake look of compassion on her face and attempted to console her sister. "I know Lacee, it's terrible," she said. "But, you know, I will only be taking Pom, so why don't you tell Father and see if he will let you take two extras."

"Oh Juna, you are such a gem," Lacee gushed as she kissed Juna twice on each cheek. "I knew you would find a way to fix everything. What would I ever do without you?"

Juna was the youngest of the royals, but sometimes she felt she was the only one in the family who had managed to escape childhood. "My pleasure. Now, go make sure you have everything ready for the move. Mister Stotz is on the prowl," Juna warned as she turned to continue the search for her father.

Making her way through the bustling halls, she frequently had to dodge passing carts laden with boxes and furniture. The place was teeming with hods, trying their best to complete the arduous task of gutting the entire palace. Juna thought, not for the first time, how much easier things could be if they were to utilize machines to do some of the back-breaking labour that, instead, got delegated to the hods. Technology, however, was not something the Elites readily embraced.

The people of Cambria had once actively pursued technology in all its forms. They had built drones to assist with manual labour, launched satellites and even built a starship to explore the heavens. All that changed on one fateful day. The Starchaser, Cambria's lone starship, was loaded and ready to embark on the planet's greatest adventure. Almost every scientist and engineer on the planet was onboard for its maiden flight. This turned out to be a very bad idea, as three days into the flight, something went terribly wrong and the ship crashed into their own sun. After that, with the grief for all that was lost and with almost all of their technical people gone, the pursuit of science was all but abandoned. The emperor at the time, ordered all plans and data regarding the mission destroyed and forbade any further scientific research – an order that limited technological advancements for several generations.

Today, there was a small scientific community on the planet still dedicated to keeping the dreams of progress alive, but they were generally considered eccentric rogues and held little status in society. The University of Cambria did have a small science department and her father had actually commissioned some sort of research facility shortly after his coronation. There was also Professor Umbra's team out in the desert, or as her father liked to call them, "those crazy robot guys." Juna never understood why her father had such disdain for the people who had already saved the planet twice and were their only hope for doing so again.

Juna's wanderings finally found her at the door to her father's office. Knocking gently, she pushed the door open and stepped inside. And there he was in all his glory – Emperor Zoban Volara, the most powerful man on Cambria. The Emperor was flanked by his two most trusted advisors, Colonel Pavic and her brother Jakol, who would likely be emperor himself one day.

Emperor Volara was a formidable man. He was tall and muscular for an Elite. With dark hair and piercing brown eyes, he had the look of a man who expected to be obeyed. He was fairly new to the job, having replaced his now-deceased father only five years ago. Juna's grandfather had been a ruthless man. His treatment of the hods had been appalling and his support for the Elites, above all others, had been relentless. Unfortunately, the new emperor had proven to be quite a bit worse.

The two men standing beside the Emperor were cut from the same cloth. Her brother was every bit his father's son, having the same look, bearing and attitude. Jakol was an exact copy of her father, only thirty years younger. There was no love lost between Juna and her older brother. When they were younger, Jakol endeavoured to make her life as unpleasant as possible. Wanting everyone to know that he was next in line to be emperor, he would push his younger sisters around thinking this was the best way to show it. The worst part was that his near-constant harassment was actually encouraged by her father, feeling it was preparing him for a life of wielding power. Now that they were a little older, they came to an uneasy truce and, for the most part, simply ignored each other.

The best word Juna could think of to describe Colonel Pavic was evil. He had the posture of a military man and the look of a tyrant. You could almost see the scheming going on behind his eyes whenever he looked at you. Juna knew that her father was an unpleasant man, but sometimes she felt Colonel Pavic was even worse. When a new idea arose to improve the lives of the Elites or make things worse for the hods, she often wondered which one of them came up with it first.

The Emperor finally looked up to acknowledge her presence. "Juna," he said, a hesitant smile crossing his lips. "What a lovely surprise. Do come in."

"Thank you, Father. I was hoping I might speak with you about the move."

"What is it, my dear?" he asked, trying his best to seem concerned.

"I just don't understand why we have to take everything. By the time we leave, there will be nothing left but the walls. It almost feels like we're never coming back."

"Come back? To this drafty old eyesore…," he began, but was cut short by a subtle shake of the head and icy stare from Colonel Pavic. "I'm kidding, of course," he continued. "I assure you we will return victoriously as soon as those treacherous Marans have been expelled from our glorious empire. I would never allow any harm to come to this wonderful place. My only concern is for the safety and welfare of you and the rest of our family. But all this should be of no concern to you. Leave worries like this to the adults. I promise you that everything being done is necessary for the well-being of all Cambrians. But we are very busy. Please leave us to our important work."

"Well, that was useless," Juna mumbled to herself as she exited her father's office. If anything, she felt even worse about the prospect of ever returning to the only home she had ever known. Those three scoundrels were definitely up to something, but she couldn't think of a way to find out what it was. As she neared her room, she decided to spend some time in her quiet place trying to sort it all out.

Knowing what to expect when she swung the door to her room open, still did not prepare her for the scene she faced now. The room was empty. Really empty. The only items that remained in the cavernous space were her mattress sitting on the floor, a box with a few clothes inside and a candleholder with two silver candles that she had insisted Pom leave behind.

It really did look deserted, but everything that was truly important to her was still there.

Juna's room was more than just a princess's bedroom, it was her training room. Juna had always thought the Elites were weak and flabby and was determined to never let that happen to her. Performing a demanding exercise routine every day, she soon outgrew the equipment available to her. She then decided to turn her room into a training facility and no one, not even the people who built it for her, had any idea it was there.

One day, Juna told her father that she wanted to redecorate her room. The Emperor was so pleased to hear that his youngest daughter was finally interested in something frivolous, that he immediately dispatched a team of tradesmen to help her with the project. Each request brought an odd look from the foreman, but she was a princess, so he did just as she asked. "I think a sturdy wooden panel twenty-five feet high would look great here," she would say. "Oh, and drill a bunch of holes in it." Or, "I think iron bars between the rafters would be lovely. And how about some wooden rings on leather straps hanging high up in the ceiling. Maybe even some thin, decorative ledges installed here, here and here."

When the work was done, Juna had to admit that the room looked beautiful. Even her mother and father dropped by to see it and both said it was wonderful. They would proudly tell all their friends what a keen eye their youngest daughter had. Yes, everyone loved the new room, but only Juna, and Pom of course, actually knew what it was.

Juna walked over to the candle holder and retrieved what everyone assumed were silver candles. They were, in fact, polished steel rods. Juna took one in each hand and walked over to the enormous wooden panel. She plunged one of the rods into a hole at the highest point she could reach. The muscles of her thin, but powerful arm strained as she pulled herself off the ground and stabbed the rod in her other hand into a hole higher up. Again, her muscles tensed as she pulled, lifting herself higher and then stabbed again. She continued this process until she was at the top of the panel, over twenty feet off the ground. The whole trip took her less than twenty seconds.

Once at the top, Juna stood and lunged at one of the wooden rings hanging from a strap attached to the ceiling. She swung from ring to ring with the grace of a dancer and, with the final swing, threw herself at the wall, catching herself on one of the narrow decorative ledges. She climbed from ledge to ledge until she reached one of the iron bars in the rafters. From there, it was an easy swing up into the base of the dormer window at the very peak of the room. Her quiet place.

Juna loved it up here. The view from the window was beautiful, but more importantly, it was so private. No one else even knew this place existed. This was the place she always went to when she needed to think. And right now, she desperately needed to think. Wanting to see things change in this world, she simply felt powerless to do anything about it. Her father was still a young man and would be ruling for years. After that would come Jakol. She held out little hope that things would get any better when he took over. And now, she was faced with the mystery of what this move was all about. She wanted to do something, but didn't really know what was going on, let alone what she could possibly do to fix it.

No sooner had Juna settled in, when the creak of the door opening interrupted her thoughts. She peered over the edge, curious to see who it was. Mister Stotz – no doubt here for his final inspection. Juna heard him picking something up and muttering some nonsense about children not being able to do anything right. The candleholder, Juna realized. Oops. At least the pegs were still at the top of the panel, so she would be able to make her way back down to the floor. Finding a new hiding spot for the candles wouldn't be too much of a challenge, so it was all good – nothing to worry about. Suddenly, Juna ducked down when she heard the voice of another person enter the room and close the door behind them. That sounded like Colonel Pavic, Juna thought.

"Stotz, I've been looking all over for you," the Colonel grumbled. "I have an urgent matter to discuss with you."

"Certainly, Colonel," Stotz replied eagerly.

"We are working on a project and your involvement will be required," the Colonel stated. "There is a meeting tonight at midnight in the emperor's office. You *will* join us."

"Certainly, Colonel," Stotz repeated.

"And, Mister Stotz," the Colonel said firmly. "The nature of this meeting is highly secretive. It is imperative that you not share even the existence of this meeting with anyone. Are you absolutely sure that you understand?"

"Certainly, Colonel," Stotz said for a third time.

"Good. I'm glad we're clear on this," the Colonel concluded. "I *will* see you at midnight. Don't be late."

When the two men were gone, Juna slowly peered over the edge to make sure she was alone. "Hmm, a secret meeting," she said to herself, sporting a devious smile. Eavesdropping on secret meetings was one of her favourite things to do. Well, she knew where she was going to be at midnight. Maybe, she might finally get some answers.

3

"Inventory! Are you kidding me?"

Orin had just been informed of the nature of his father's "special project" and he was not impressed with the news.

"Let me get this straight," he continued. "The fate of our planet is at stake. The very survival of our species may be at risk, and I'm supposed to spend my time counting things!"

Dorel, who had been the bearer of the bad news, could only shake his head, shrug his immense shoulders and hand over the clipboard.

"Sorry kid. You know if it was up to me, you'd be helping out on one of my crews, but when the boss speaks, you gotta listen."

Scanning the stack of papers on the clipboard, Orin let out a resigned sigh. "That's OK," he finally moaned. "It's not your fault."

"It is an important job," Dorel replied, trying hard to put some enthusiasm into his words. "A little boring maybe, but certainly important."

"Yeah, I guess. It would just be nice to get something a little more exciting once in a while."

"Hang in there kid," Dorel said as he turned to leave. "Your time will come."

Giving the list one more look, he squared his shoulders and began making his way to the armoury. Oh, well. It wasn't exactly the job he wanted to be doing at the moment, but at least he could give it his best effort and do it well.

The reason Orin was always so disappointed to get assigned such trivial tasks was that he was capable of so much more. Everyone, including his father, knew that Orin was a genius. He had been taking university-level courses in mathematics, physics, engineering and programming since his peers were in grade school. He knew that, given the chance, he could have come up with that modification Diara proposed. "Harmonic matching of the shield frequency," he muttered to himself, "I could have come up with that one in my sleep." But now was not the time. Apparently, today was a day for counting, so he mustered all the enthusiasm he could for the project and set to work.

When Orin reached the armoury, he used his key card to unlock the door and stepped inside. Not having been down here for a while, he immediately noticed that things had changed a great deal. He remembered this room as a huge, empty space but what he saw before him now was row upon row of missiles. Orin knew that if there was one item that needed an accurate count, it was these missiles. His father had designed them himself and knew that this weapon would be the key to their victory over the Marans.

They were called Shield Implosion Missiles, or SIMs for short. They were quite small, about the length of Orin's forearm, and were designed specifically for the battle with the Marans. One of the reasons the Second Maran War had dragged on so long, was that the Marans had developed a shield technology to protect their SCUDs with an invisible, energy-based armour that could not be penetrated by conventional artillery. In the war, Mechs had to fire dozens of traditional missiles before the shield would finally fail, leaving the SCUD open to a direct attack. The SIMs were designed specifically to implode an energy shield by attaching themselves to the shield itself and draining the energy from it. The Professor was confident that one or two SIMs would be sufficient to completely collapse one of the SCUD's shields and then one additional hit from the explosive tip of another SIM would blow it apart. It was a truly lethal weapon. Everyone at The Depot hoped that the Marans would not be prepared to deal with a device so specifically designed to eliminate their greatest advantage.

Orin completed the count of the SIMs and moved to the next item on his list. Tucked in the back corner of the armoury, he found his next target – a single row of Time-Release Implosion Pods, or TRIPs. This was another recent invention of his father's. They were a disk-shaped projectile that, like the SIMs, would attach themselves to an energy shield. Once attached, the TRIP would draw energy from the shield and then use that energy to pulse the shield every thirty seconds, weakening it further. A single TRIP would, given time, implode any energy shield, regardless of its initial strength.

The morning passed quickly as he worked his way through the list, so by early afternoon, he had completed every item but one. Checking everywhere he could think of, he was unable to find any of the hydrostatic field generators. They just didn't seem to be anywhere. He was reluctant to ask for help. The last thing he wanted was for his dad to hear that he couldn't do something as simple as an inventory count without assistance.

He began wandering the hallways in search of the elusive storage location and soon found himself standing in front of a door marked "Authorized Personnel Only". Guessing he had walked past this door a thousand times, it seemed odd that he had never really noticed it before. He had no idea what was behind it or if he was, in fact, authorized to open it. Scanning his key card, he smiled at the satisfying click of the lock disengaging.

As Orin pushed the door open, he could sense the immense size of the room before him, but it was too dark to see anything. Feeling along the wall until he found the light switch, he turned it on, revealing a small office area near the door. When he rounded the corner to check the rest of the room, his heart stopped. Feelings of shock and disbelief flooded him. His eyes were seeing something that his brain was unable to process. Oh, he knew exactly what he was looking at – it just seemed so improbable that he found it hard to imagine it could be real. Standing before him were three gigantic Mechs. And not just any Mechs – it was Spanner, Torque and Clank, the steam-powered Mechs that had been the heroes of the First Maran War.

There was not a person on the planet who would not have recognized these machines on sight. When he was a little kid, the Steam Mechs were the stars of countless stories and comic books, their exploits re-enacted on every playground on Cambria. Almost every T-shirt Orin owned growing up was emblazoned with their images. He even had a Torque lunchbox when he was barely old enough to walk. And now, here he was, staring up at the real thing.

Orin walked around, looking them over from top to bottom, admiring every detail. They were a little dusty, but totally intact. He could imagine them engaged in battle, launching missiles and sending dismembered SCUDs flying through the air. Orin's brain went into overdrive, plans forming, details coming into focus. All thoughts of locating the missing hydrostatic field generators left his head and he rushed out of the room to find his father.

"Dad," Orin yelled when he spotted his father on the assembly floor, "I found the Steam Mechs!"

"Well, it's not like they were ever really missing," the Professor replied calmly. "I haven't thought about them in years. What were you doing in the archives vault?"

Orin completely ignored the question. "I want to get them running again. They can still fight. I just know it!"

"Orin, those machines haven't been powered-up in fifteen years," the Professor said doubtfully. "It would be a monumental task just getting them to move again, let alone fight. I'm afraid those Mechs' best days are behind them."

"But Dad, I have a plan. We leave the boiler in, but strip out the furnace and replace it with one of the prototype fusion reactors you just pulled out of the Atomics. It's just a new heat source, everything else stays the same."

"And how are they going to survive a battle with a modern SCUD?" the Professor challenged.

Undeterred, Orin continued. "The reactors are only a third the size of the furnaces. I can use the extra space to install shield generators and SIM storage. We have the prototype shield arrays from the Bios and there are six SIM launchers in the armoury. I just counted them."

Orin could see his dad thinking, analyzing the viability of his plan. "What about the AI's?" he asked. "Fifteen years could cause some degradation and, as I recall, one of them was a little crazy to begin with."

"I don't think that will be a problem," Orin urged. "Everything on them must be military spec. The electronics should be good for a *hundred* years."

The Professor was silent, obviously considering the proposal. Orin knew he was close to making his case. "Dad, I can do this. I know I can," he pleaded. "All I need is two Mechs to help with the heavy lifting. How about Gigahertz and Carnage? They're both battle-ready so they have nothing to do for the next six weeks."

"Carnage!" the Professor scoffed. "What exactly is it you need broken?"

Orin thought his dad was probably right about that one. Carnage was extremely strong but he was much better suited to destruction than construction. Just as he was considering his next counterproposal, his dad spoke.

"You can have Gigahertz and Diode."

Orin beamed. "You mean it, Dad?"

"Yes," he replied with a smile. "But you only have four weeks. The General wants two weeks with the team to get everything ready. If the Steam Mechs aren't battle-ready two weeks before the Marans arrive, they get left behind."

"Thanks, Dad. You won't regret this," Orin yelled over his shoulder, sprinting away before his dad could change his mind.

Orin did not sleep well that night. He laid on his cot, staring at the ceiling, waiting for tomorrow to begin. At first, his inability to sleep was the result of excitement, but that slowly turned to dread as the night progressed. What was he thinking? He had no idea how to do all the things he had proposed to his father. He had never actually worked on a Mech before. There were going to be countless challenges that he would have no idea how to resolve. Oh well. There was no turning back now. He would just have to figure it out as he went along.

The alarm clock rang as the first light of day came in through his tiny bedroom window. Orin got up, put on some clothes and prepared himself for the day. Making a quick stop at the canteen for some breakfast along the way, he made his way to the archives vault and opened up a huge overhead door on the far side of the room that the Mechs could use to get in. Then, sitting down at the desk, he began drawing up some sort of plan that might possibly save him from the inevitable embarrassment of total failure.

Just as he was getting started, he noticed Gigahertz enter through the overhead door.

"Hey Gig, what's shakin'?"

"Master Orin, I have been assured by the Wrenches that all of my bolts have been torqued to within acceptable tolerances. There should be nothing shaking."

"Thanks for the update, Gig. Come on in. We've got a lot of work to do."

Following closely behind Gigahertz was Diode. Diode was another one of the Hydro Mechs, looking very much like a slightly smaller version of Gigahertz with his gleaming titanium armour trimmed in blue. Oh – and he had two heads. Diode had been an interesting, if somewhat unsuccessful, experiment of his father's that involved installing two separate artificial intelligences in one Mech. The theory was, having two distinct thought processes would force him to arrive at a consensus, and therefore, make better decisions. In reality, it meant he spent half his time arguing with himself. Orin worried that this would make him a less than ideal addition to the team, but at this point, he was just thankful for any help he could get.

When he was designing a Mech, Professor Umbra always made sure to include some special features that would give it civilian uses in addition to its primary military function. He had provided all of the Hydro Mechs with detachable arm extensions that included precision fingers for gripping and a torch that could be used for both cutting and welding. Orin noticed that both Gig and Diode had their extensions attached. Ready for work.

Orin knew that the first step in the process of rebuilding the Steam Mechs was going to be getting the furnaces removed, so he had Gig and Diode start to work on that while he went back to the office to figure out what the next step might be. He hadn't been at it very long, when he was interrupted by a knock at the door. Looking up, he saw Annu.

Annu was Dorel's wife and a fine Wrench in her own right. Her short dark hair framed a delicate face that was at odds with her imposing presence. She was a head taller than Orin and had shoulders broader than the

General's. "The Professor sent me down here," she said. "I'm supposed to be helping you out with something for the next four weeks."

Orin's initial excitement about receiving much-needed help was tempered when he realized Annu's ever-present smile was conspicuously missing today.

"I got pulled off the team installing TRIP launchers on Tortuga," she continued. "This had better be good."

Orin couldn't help but smile. "Have a look for yourself," he said, hooking a thumb over his shoulder. Hearing her gasp as she rounded the corner, he stood and went back to join her. It was obvious that her initial reaction to seeing the legendary machines was every bit as powerful as it had been for him.

"They're amazing," was all she could say.

"Dad says that if we can get them battle-ready in four weeks, they can join the team," Orin informed her.

"Well, let's get to it then," she whooped, as she dashed off to get started.

The next week was a blur. Orin and Annu worked tirelessly, taking only short breaks to eat and nap. Gig and Diode worked continuously, causing Orin to worry about how his father would react to the number of fuel cells they were burning through. He kept telling himself that it would all be worth it if they could just get these machines running again. It was this goal that kept them motivated during the long days and numerous setbacks.

Their little group became minor celebrities as word of the project spread through the building. Everyone was calling them "Team Steam". There was a near-constant flow of spectators as people from all corners of the facility dropped by to monitor their progress. Every person in the building revered the first-generation Mechs and were excited by the possibility of seeing them in action again. The crew at The Depot was understandably nervous about the upcoming war and this project played an important role in keeping everybody's spirits up.

"Things sure would go faster if we didn't have so many visitors all the time," Annu complained to Orin as another group of gawkers left the archives vault.

"Oh, who are you kidding?" Orin scoffed. "You love the attention as much as anybody. I saw you giving the General a tour the other day and you were loving every second of it."

"Yeah, I guess I was," Annu chuckled. "These machines are just so amazing! Your grandfather was a genius building something this advanced. I can't wait to see them running again."

Orin had to agree. They were still early in the project, but this was already the best thing he had ever worked on. And Annu was amazing! Her passion for the project was as unwavering as his and her knowledge of the inner workings of a Mech was unparalleled. Despite the age difference between them, they got along so well. They would joke and kid around with each other like they had been working together for years.

"Hey kid," Annu added. "Why don't you get that big brain of yours working on a way to solve our Diode problem?"

"And what problem might that be?"

"You're kidding, right?" she replied in disbelief. "Yesterday, I asked him to get me some wrenches and he didn't come back for ten minutes. It turns out his right head wanted to bring me a set of wrenches and his left head wanted to bring me one adjustable wrench."

Orin just laughed. Dealing with Diode did have its challenges. "Alright, I'll see if I can come up with a software upgrade to help him a bit with his decision making."

Happy to finally have a coding project to work on, Orin set down his welding torch and headed for the office to get started. He was physically exhausted. His skill set was better suited to working on the software upgrades the Steam units would eventually require, but until they were powered up, there was little work to do on that front. So, for now, he spent his days helping Annu and the Mechs with the demanding physical work of assembly. It was tiring, but rewarding too. Something about seeing the pieces come together made him feel like they were really accomplishing something.

By the end of the first week, Orin knew the team needed a break. He sent Annu off to spend some quality time with Dorel and he went to interrupt Gigahertz from his work. "Hey Gig, let's take a break. Meet me at the hill in five."

When your best friend is a giant robot, you have to find creative ways to have fun together. Playing ball sports was out of the question and a game of hide-and-seek with someone the size of a small building was just too easy. Orin's favourite memories of his time spent with Gigahertz were of the two of them sitting on the hill, looking at the stars and talking, long into the night.

The hill was out behind the barracks at the eastern edge of The Depot's boundary. Orin sat down in the grass, facing east, away from the lights of the city and stared out into space. He knew the exact spot on the hill on which to sit – the two friends had spent so much time out here that there was an indentation in the ground that would fit Gig's butt perfectly when he arrived to sit down next to him. Just as he was getting comfortable, Gigahertz arrived and settled into his spot.

They talked about the project for a while but soon drifted into a comfortable silence. As Orin looked at the stars, he couldn't help but think about the three points of light that would be joining them in the night sky in five short weeks. Interstellar warships from Mara.

"Why do they hate us, Gig?"

"The Marans?" he surmised. "That is another one of your questions that I am unable to answer. It is hard to know what is in the heart of another person. Perhaps, they do not hate us."

"Well, I hate them," Orin said softly.

"I know they have taken more from you than from most, Master Orin," he replied. "But be careful with hate. Nothing good can come from hating another person."

During the Second Maran War, dozens of stray missiles left the battle-field and fell on the city. One of them hit the hospital where Orin's mother was helping to care for the wounded. He never saw her again after that.

"I wish they would just leave us alone," was all he could think to say in return.

As they sat on the hill, staring at the stars, Orin could feel his eyes starting to close as a wave of exhaustion washed over him. He stood up to leave. "I need some sleep. You coming?"

"No, I think I will stay a little longer."

"OK, good night Gig."

"Good night Master Orin."

As Orin turned to go, he noticed the small engraving near the bottom of Gig's shin plate. He softly ran his hand over it. It said, "O + J Forever" enclosed in a heart. It had been scrawled there, with a screwdriver, in the shaky handwriting of a child. He always felt a little sad when he saw it. He didn't know if it was because he still missed her or if he felt guilty for vandalizing his best friend's leg. Deciding it must be the latter, he whispered a quiet apology and headed off to get some sleep.

4

Juna had some time to kill before the big meeting, so she decided to wander the halls of the Royal Palace. Almost everything was gone now. Walls once covered with beautiful paintings, now lay bare and rooms that had held magnificent collections of ornate furniture, were empty. A few hods still roamed the halls, picking up the last remaining pieces, but the building was so much quieter than she was used to. Her wonderful palace had become an empty shell. She could hear the echo of her own footsteps as she moved from room to room.

Making her way through the Great Hall, she stopped in front of the towering window at the far end of the room. The view outside featured sculpted hedges framing rows of flowers in every colour you could imagine, all surrounded by a wall of towering barcuti trees. It was the loveliest view from anywhere inside the palace. As she gazed out onto the beautifully manicured gardens, she heard footsteps approaching from behind.

"Why do you ask so many questions?"

She turned to see Jakol, his icy stare focused solely on her.

"Why is that any concern of yours?" she replied.

"That's another question."

"So it is. Maybe I just like to know what's going on."

"You don't need to know what's going on. Father and I do and that's all that matters. All these questions just upset him. He doesn't need that right now."

"Why now?" she asked. "Are you guys up to something?"

Jakol's expression gave away nothing. "He likes you, you know. I've never understood why, but he does. For years, I've tried to open his eyes to how much trouble you are, but he refuses to see it. You need to know that you will never take my place by his side."

"Do I threaten you, brother?"

"That's another question, but I'll answer it if you'd like. No. You do not threaten me. I know my place. It's time that you learned yours. Be careful," he warned her as he turned to leave. "I'll be watching you."

Juna was shaken by the encounter with her brother. That, combined with her anticipation of tonight's meeting had her buzzing with energy. When she returned to her room, she flew through her personal obstacle course a half-dozen times, but it didn't provide her the release she required. She needed to hit something.

Juna's desire to train went far beyond not wanting to be flabby and weak. Years of being tormented by her brother had given her an unquenchable desire to learn how to fight. She used to watch the Royal Guard cadets training in the courtyard beneath her quiet place, scrutinizing and memorizing every move they made. One day, she got up the nerve to go down there and ask to join in.

Sergeant Danto, the head of the cadet program, was initially reluctant. Girls on Cambria, particularly Elites, were simply not allowed to partake in such aggressive behaviours. Juna, however, was persistent and the Sergeant finally relented. She had never had so much fun! Kicking, punching, throwing people around – it was like she was born to do this. Her hours of observation had prepared her well, so she excelled right from the first day. But when she arrived for her second week of training, Sergeant Danto pulled her aside and told her she was no longer welcome to join the group. Apparently, getting beat-up by a girl was having an adverse effect on the morale of his squad. She ran back to her room, crying all the way, and buried herself in a pile of pillows. Pom tried to console her, but had little success.

The next day, Pom arrived at the door carrying a large bag and wearing an even larger smile. "Oh Juna, I have brought you the most wonderful surprise," she said as she scampered into the dressing room. Emerging a few minutes later, she was wearing the most ridiculous outfit Juna had ever seen. Pom and her mother, a seamstress at the Royal Palace, had stayed up all night and made a padded suit that she was now wearing along with a mischievous grin.

"Now you can fight me!" she exclaimed.

At first, Juna was reluctant. She didn't think it was right to use her best friend as a punching bag. But it would be fun. And the whole thing was Pom's idea. Soon the two girls were locked in combat. She was right – this was fun! Pom loved it too, giggling with glee every time Juna sent her flying through the air or tumbling across the floor.

As the girls grew older, the padded suit was enlarged and their battles intensified. Pom would make cardboard weapons and use them to lunge at the defenceless princess. Juna would skillfully dodge the attack, disarm her foe and toss her across the room. They kept their game a secret, always locking the door and making up silly excuses whenever someone would knock and ask about the racket they were making.

Unfortunately, there would be no training with Pom today. The padded suit would be halfway to Alderae by now and Pom was busy helping with the move. Juna decided to spend her day as she spent so much of her free time – locked in hand-to-hand combat with a horde of imaginary Marans.

No one had ever seen a Maran. Juna pictured them being seven feet tall with bulbous heads and tentacles for arms. The one before her now was particularly menacing, with six-inch fangs and armed with a spear. She dove to her right, rolling to avoid the spear, then sprang to her feet to ready herself for the next attack. She held her imaginary dagger high, then swept it down quickly, slicing through a tentacle as it reached out to grab her. As she rolled to her left preparing for the killing blow, she sensed a movement near the door. She stopped her attack and turned to see Mister Stotz staring at her with an incredulous look on his face.

"Princess Juna. What *are* you doing?"

"I…I'm working on a new dance," she stammered. "What do you think?"

"It looks like you're being attacked by an alderbeast."

"Yeah, I'm still working on it."

Mister Stotz just rolled his eyes and returned his attention to the clipboard he was holding. "We leave for Alderae first thing in the morning," he said as he turned to leave. "Do make sure you're ready."

The encounter with Mister Stotz soured Juna's mood. She flopped down on her mattress and stared at the ceiling. All her training was just a waste of time anyway. When was she ever going to fight anyone? It's not like they were going to let her join the Royal Guard. Not that she would join them even if they asked. Colonel Pavic and his goons were just a bunch of bullies who spent their days hassling hods when they made outrageous demands like asking for more food. No, the palace was perfectly safe and did not require the services of a lethal princess to protect it. Besides, if anyone ever did attack the palace, the Mech at the front door should be enough to turn away any threat.

Since the last war, the emperor had insisted that a Mech be stationed in the courtyard in front of the palace at all times. Juna had always thought it was just a machine, but when she was much younger, her brother told her it could think and talk, just like a real person. That made her very sad. Surely, it must be lonely, standing there all the time with no one to talk to. She decided to go meet it. As she first approached, she nearly changed her mind. It was really big and kind of scary, but she mustered all her courage and confidently knocked on his foot.

"Hey, are you really just like a real person?" she yelled up at the massive machine.

"Well, I am a lot bigger," he replied softly.

And that was the first moment in what became a wonderful friendship. His name was Helion and he was really nice. They could talk about anything. She learned that he got all his power from the sun and that his friends lived in a place called The Depot, but he didn't get to see them very often. She asked him if he ever got lonely. He told her he did not. He could go into something called a "wait state" where he didn't experience the passage of time until his external sensors alerted him to activity in the area and woke him up.

Even so, Juna made sure she visited him often, telling him about her day and all the dumb things her brother and sister did. Then he would tell her about what it was like to be a Mech and what fighting in a war was like. Once, when she had just returned from a two-week vacation in Alderae, she rushed to see him as soon as she could.

"Hi Helion. Sorry I've been away so long."

"Don't be sorry Juna," he replied. "I do not feel time pass while I am waiting. No one ever attacks the palace and you are my only visitor, so you are always with me."

That made her feel a little better, but she still went to see him whenever she could. She would have loved to visit him right now, but he had been recalled to The Depot to train with his team when the Maran fleet was first detected.

"No time for visiting anyway," she said to herself after noticing that night had fallen. Time to get ready. Retrieving her "candles" from their new hiding place under the mattress, she zipped up to her quiet place.

The view from the window was dominated by Cambria's two moons: Nandoo and Aradoo. It was an awesome sight. They looked like giant iridescent pearls that were so large and felt so close, it seemed at any moment they might fall from the sky and crush the planet and everyone living on it. Constant storms raged over the moons' surfaces, creating ever-changing bands of noxious clouds that would peel the skin from your bones if you ever set foot on one. Despite having such an imposing presence and hostile environment, their beauty was undeniable.

The moons were one of Cambria's most stunning features, but also its greatest curse. Because the moons orbited the planet at the exact same rate, they always appeared in the sky together. The larger, Nandoo, was behind and to the left, with the smaller, Aradoo, slightly overlapping to the right. The gravitational pull was immense. Alderae was considered a seaside city, but that was only true during high tide, when the moons were overhead. As the planet rotated, placing the moons to the side, the sea retreated so far that it was no longer visible from Alderae.

Juna always thought it was funny when her father referred to his "empire". The reality was that the land surrounding the base of Mount Volaris was the only place on the planet that did not spend at least part of the time underwater. With half of that area being taken up by the high desert, the amount of habitable land was only a tiny fraction of the surface area of the planet. Every one of the thirty million people living on Cambria lived within a thousand miles of the Royal Palace.

It was getting late and Juna knew from experience that she had a lengthy trip ahead of her. Not wanting to be late for the big meeting, she started getting ready. There was a special outfit she always kept up in her quiet place that, fortunately, she had decided not to pack for the move. It was a simple black bodysuit and a thin black scarf she could wrap over her face. Tying her long dark hair into a ponytail, she pulled on the suit and smiled at her reflection in the window. Wearing the suit gave her such a powerful feeling of invincibility – she felt like a shadow. Slipping on her climbing shoes, she set off in the direction of her father's office.

None of the walls in the palace extended all the way to the peak of the roof, so once you were up in the rafters, you could move about freely any-where in the building. Juna stepped carefully from beam to beam, trying not to make any noise or kick up too much dust. Wearing her shadow suit made her almost invisible up here, but a poorly timed sneeze would give her away in an instant.

Juna had made this trip several times before. Her father's inner circle was like a bunch of children when it came to keeping a secret, so it was pretty obvious when a clandestine meeting was being planned. She would usually journey through the rafters to find out what was going on, but it almost always turned out the same. "There is a rumor so-and-so is plan-ning a coup," someone would say. "There's no proof but it seems like it may be a real threat," someone else would add. "We can't take the chance – we have to do something," her father would insist. It was all very boring, but she did notice that after one of these meetings, she never did see so-and-so again.

It was by spying on these meetings that Juna first realized the people of Cambria did not necessarily love their royal family. She recalled the celebration following their victory in the Second Maran War. A parade was planned and she was so excited to be riding on the royal float. Her brother was wearing a miniature replica of her father's uniform and her sister looked like a cupcake. The people were cheering as the float passed by, but she remembered looking at a boy in the front row. He was smiling up at her, but his hand was directing an obscene gesture in her direction. At the time, she thought it was funny. This poor boy must have seen an adult make the gesture and didn't realize it was a bad thing. It was listening in on her father's meetings when she realized that the little boy knew exactly what that gesture meant. He, and probably most of the other people on the planet, hated her and everything she and the Royal Family represented.

These meetings also showed Juna *why* everyone hated the Royal Family so much. They treated the hods like dirt and made everyone else pay exorbitant taxes. The Elites had life so easy and her father wanted to make sure it stayed that way. The only thing more important to him than wielding his power was making sure no one ever took it away from him. Every action taken, no matter how cruel, was warranted if it meant the Elites remained in charge and everyone else did what they were told. That was why she didn't want anything to do with being a member of this family. That was why she hated being a princess.

Juna had been moving through the rafters for almost an hour by the time she reached the space above her father's office. She was a little early, but there were already three people in attendance: Mister Stotz, Mister Nardo and a woman Juna didn't recognize, who didn't look at all happy to be there.

Mister Nardo was the Royal Interpreter. He was the only person on the planet that had succeeded in translating the Maran language. Juna never understood how he had been the one to do it – he really didn't seem that smart. Spending his days lounging around the palace, ordering hods to bring him things did not inspire a great deal of confidence in his intellectual abilities. She had not seen him do a single thing since the last time the Marans showed up.

Juna did not understand much of what was happening the last time the Marans attacked. She remembered hearing that these evil beings had arrived and wanted to destroy their planet. Her grandfather, her father and Mister Nardo then locked themselves in a room with a radio and tried to talk them out of it. An hour later they emerged with very sad faces and showed everyone a transcript of the discussions. Basically, it was the Marans threatening to burn Cambria to the ground and the emperor responding with various versions of the phrase "please don't kill us." In the end, the Marans attacked anyway and everyone in the palace hid in the basement until word of their victory reached them several days later.

The sound of more people entering the room below her brought Juna's attention back to the present. It was the Emperor, along with Jakol and Colonel Pavic. It was when her father addressed each of the people already in the room that she realized who the grumpy-looking woman was. It was Professor Aeva Oletta.

Professor Oletta was a brilliant scientist whom some people said was even smarter than Professor Umbra. She had developed some way of opening a portal through space that would allow you to see what was going on at the other end. Juna didn't really understand all the details of it, but she heard it was like being able to place a camera anywhere in the galaxy and see what was going on there. It was the device that had first detected the current Maran incursion. "What is *she* doing here?" Juna whispered to herself.

The Emperor instructed everyone to take their seats and started the meeting. "Mister Stotz," he began. "Starting tomorrow, there will be a team of experts moving through the palace installing explosives in the walls. It is very important that no one be made aware of this activity, so it will be your job to ensure the team does not encounter anyone while they go about their work. Do you understand?"

"Certainly, Your Highness," Stotz said hesitantly. "But I am a bit confused. Why would we be putting explosives in the walls? Doesn't that seem a little dangerous?"

"Stotz. It is not required that you know all the details of the master plan, but I will tell you what I can," the Emperor replied calmly. "We do not expect the war to go well. The Marans only sent one warship in each of their previous attacks – this time they are sending three. We are expecting them to defeat the Mechs this time around. We anticipate they will then send down a landing party and overrun the palace. Once they have established a base of operations here, we will trigger the explosives and turn this place into a smouldering crater, putting an end to this Maran nonsense once and for all."

"Ah, yes. A very fine plan, my liege," Stotz began cautiously. "But do you not think the Marans might get suspicious when they find the palace abandoned?"

"The palace will not be abandoned," the Emperor countered, obviously losing his patience. "We will dress up a few dozen hods in fancy clothes and have them roaming about the place when the Marans arrive."

"Again, brilliant, my lord," Stotz said with all the sincerity he could muster. "But is all hope really lost? Surely, there is some chance that the Mechs will be victorious."

"Do you think us fools?" the Emperor thundered as he hammered the desk with his fists. "We have thought of every possible contingency! If you really must know, the Mechs will not even be here. The Marans will be arriving three days earlier than we have been telling the public. The Mechs will still be back at The Depot when the Marans attack. If we're lucky, when

43

the Mechs do finally show up, they will storm the palace trying to drive the Marans out and blow the place up themselves. It is a perfect plan and I do not appreciate it being questioned. I simply do not have the time to explain all this to idiots! Just do as you are told and leave the thinking to people who are qualified."

As everyone filed out of the room, Juna sat in the rafters in a state of stunned disbelief. It took all of her self-control not to cry out as each level of the plan was revealed. She had despised her father for years, but that word no longer seemed adequate to describe how she felt about him now. He was trying to lose the war. He was going to blow-up her beautiful palace. He was going to murder a few dozen hods.

Juna knew that she had to stop him but didn't know how. Confronting him was obviously not the answer. She had information, but no way of using it. Just then, an idea sparked in her head. She couldn't use this information but she knew someone who could. The whole family would be packing up and leaving for Alderae in a few hours – she better get moving.

5

Orin was extremely pleased with the progress Team Steam had made over the last few weeks. Tomorrow, he would be handing the three steam Mechs over to the General for final inspection and he was confident they would be declared battle-ready. He just needed to install a couple more software upgrades and they would be good to go.

It had been two weeks since the installation of the fusion reactors was completed and the first power-up tests were run. Orin had never been so nervous. The first test was on Spanner. When Annu threw the switch, Spanner's eyes lit up and you could see an awareness begin to take control. He looked around to assess his surroundings, then focused his attention on Orin.

"Who are you?" he asked.

"My name is Orin."

"I was built by a man named Orin."

"He was my grandfather."

"Ah. I have been away for some time then."

"The Marans are back. We could use your help."

"It would be my honour."

By the end of the next day, all three units were powered-up and initial testing was underway. Spanner was definitely the leader of the group. He had a calm wisdom about him and was totally focused on doing everything he could to prepare for the impending battle. Torque was the most aggressive of the trio. He reminded Orin of a slightly friendlier version of a Diesel. Clank was... well, Clank was Clank.

There was no question in Orin's mind that the "crazy one" his father had alluded to was in reference to Clank. When he was first powered-up, he began speaking immediately, finishing a sentence that had begun over fifteen years ago. He rambled on continuously, sometimes blurting out an answer to a question that had been asked three hours earlier. He also started shuddering and making a high-pitched wheezing noise, in what Orin could only assume was the Mech equivalent of a giggle, whenever someone said the word "cheese". But he wasn't crazy. Orin preferred to think of him as eccentric. Besides, who was going to say cheese in the middle of a battle?

All three of the Steamers, as everyone was now calling them, were extremely curious to know what had happened in the world while they had been turned off. Disappointed that they had not been able to help during the second war, they were looking forward to contributing in the third. They asked questions constantly, so Gigahertz spent as much time answering questions as he did working. Orin's decision-making software upgrade had not been entirely successful, so Diode spent most of his time debating with himself about how best to answer each of the questions directed his way.

Fortunately, the task of answering all these questions did not fall solely on the members of Team Steam. The Steamers were revered by all of the

Mechs and each one of them made numerous visits to talk to the oldest, but newest, members of the team. Even the Diesels were frequent visitors.

During the first war, Torque had developed a reputation for picking up first-generation SCUDs, lifting them high over his head and tearing them in half. To the Diesels, he was a legend. Orin thought Carnage had summed up their feelings the best when he introduced himself to Torque by saying, "your unwavering commitment to destruction has been an inspiration to us all." It was a touching moment indeed.

With the power systems up and the AI's fully functional, the next challenge was to get the Steamers physically prepared for the rigours of war. Each of them received two detachable SIM launchers, Torque's mounted on his shoulders, with Spanner's and Clank's on their forearms. All of them had looked intimidating before, but with their missile-launching cannons installed, they were truly terrifying.

Orin had grown very fond of his new steam-powered friends and he found it was affecting some of his design decisions. When it came time to allocate space to SIM storage or shield arrays, he tended to lean towards providing as much shielding as possible. He felt responsible for them and wanted to keep them as safe as one could during a war.

Shields were something new for the Mechs. While Professor Umbra was attempting to design weapons to counteract the Maran shielding systems, he was able to not only replicate their shields, but improve upon them. In the previous wars, the Mechs used advanced systems to detect incoming missiles and quick reflexes to try to avoid them, but when a missile hit, it was only the strength of their armour that kept them from being blown to bits. Mechs were often severely damaged in battle, but with shields now installed in every Mech, Orin hoped serious injuries could be avoided.

He had first met Gigahertz when he had been damaged during the last battle with the Marans. Orin spent the duration of that war at The Depot.

He remembered his parents arguing about whether he would be safer there or with his mother at the hospital. I guess his dad had been right about that one.

Prior to the war, a rail line had been built between The Depot and the Royal Palace for moving the Mechs to and from the battle. A near-constant flow of trains brought damaged Mechs to The Depot for repair and then returned them to the frontline. Orin still remembered Gigahertz limping onto the assembly floor with his left arm completely missing. To a young boy, it was an intimidating sight, but something about the way the huge machine carried himself made Orin feel safe.

"Does that hurt?" he yelled up at the giant Mech.

A soft voice returned from the machine's leg. "No. It doesn't hurt, but I would prefer to have two arms."

"What's your name?" Orin asked.

"My name is Gigahertz."

"That's a big name. Can I call you Gig for short?"

"Yes, you can. Shall I call you Master Orin?"

"If you want. How'd you know my name?"

"You are the Professor's son. Everyone knows your name."

"I guess. Where'd your arm go?"

"I was fighting in the war and a missile blew it off."

"Wars are stupid."

"Yes, they are. You are very wise for someone so young."

As they talked, Gigahertz was swarmed by a team of Wrenches. A huge gantry crane brought in a new arm while another team removed his right leg so the knee joint could be replaced. The whole process took over six hours and Orin stayed with him for all of it, chatting the entire time. When the work was done and Gigahertz was leaving for the train that would return him to the battle, Orin asked him one final question.

"When you get back, can we be friends?"

"I would like that very much."

Thinking about that conversation now, Orin was glad he had installed so many shield arrays on the Steamers. He imagined how he would feel if Spanner came back without an arm and he didn't like it at all. As it turned out, he had the whole thing figured out when he was just a little kid – wars *were* stupid.

Orin installed the last of the software upgrades and ran a final series of diagnostics. They were ready. He had never been so proud of himself. Walking over to Annu, he gave her a big hug, hardly able to wrap his arms around her powerful frame. They tried to tell each other how much they enjoyed working together, but were so emotional neither of them could speak, so they settled for an awkward high-five and walked away before anyone noticed the tears. Once recovered, he set out in search of his father to let him know the Steamers were ready.

The assembly floor was humming with activity as everyone was putting the finishing touches on the Atomics and Bios, getting them ready for the General's final inspection. In the three closest bays were Tortuga, Armorat and Scarab, the Bio Mechs. The design of the Bio Mechs was very different from that of the other units. They were built to roughly resemble the animals for which they were named and had tires or tracks instead of legs. They looked more like vehicles than they did traditional Mechs. Each of them had a massive internal storage compartment for transporting things and fully functional AI's with a full armament of missile launchers and shield arrays. They were also much faster and more maneuverable than the other Mechs being built so much lower to the ground. The General was very excited about adding them to the team for the versatility all these features could bring to the battlefield.

The next three bays held the Atomics: Isotope, Fallout and Geiger. They were the most modern-looking of all the Mechs. They were white and shiny with soft curves instead of angles and ridges. They also differed from the other Mechs in that they did not need to touch the ground when they moved. The Professor had developed a way to use a powerful force field to levitate a Mech three feet off the ground. Altering the angle of the force field created a propulsion system that could move the Mech over any terrain, including water. The very first prototype for this revolutionary technology was turned into Orin's hoverbike.

As Orin passed the last of the assembly bays, a soft woman's voice directed a question at him. "Hello Orin. How is work on the Steamers progressing?"

It was Isotope. Orin had met her over two months ago, but was still getting used to hearing a woman's voice coming out of a Mech. His dad had created two female AI's for the latest batch of Mechs – one for Isotope and one for Scarab. The Professor felt that adding a little diversity to the group would make for a more well-rounded, analytical fighting force. So far, he had been proven correct – they were both excellent additions to the team.

"Hi Isotope. I just finished up. They're doing great and can't wait to join you guys."

"I look forward to it too," she replied. "I would love to hear more of Clank's wonderful stories."

Orin hoped she was serious about that – sometimes Mech sarcasm was a little difficult to pick up on. Maybe he should start working on an Annoyance Suppression algorithm for Clank just in case.

Rounding the corner leading away from the assembly floor, Orin spotted his dad, staring intently at a data terminal. "Hey Dad, what are you doing?"

"I'm just reviewing the results of your latest diagnostics run on Torque," he replied. "Splendid. Simply, splendid. I must say Orin, I was skeptical when you first mentioned reactivating the old Steamers, but the results have been spectacular. That was a gold star idea, my boy. Truly, a gold star idea."

Orin was momentarily unable to speak. That may have been the single greatest moment of his life. "Thanks Dad," he finally managed. "Of course, I couldn't have done it without a lot of help."

"There's nothing wrong with needing help with something. It's when everyone works together towards a common goal that we are at our best."

It was at that moment that Orin realized it was all worth it. All the menial tasks. All the cleaning up, the tool sorting and even the inventory counts. He was part of the team and that's what mattered. Everyone had worked together and done their best on every task assigned to them so they could defeat the Marans and send them home for good.

A piece of friendly advice from his dad interrupted Orin from his daydreaming. "I think you should go get some sleep, young man," he said. "Tomorrow is a big day. The General's final inspections. I believe, by the end of it, he will be declaring eighteen Mechs ready for battle."

"Thanks Dad. I think I'll take you up on that," he replied as he turned to go. The exhaustion that had been building for the last four weeks hit him like a hammer as he realized his work was done. He really did need to get some sleep. Making his way through the maze-like hallways of the Central Assembly Building, he headed for the small room in the services wing that had served as his bedroom for most of his life. His father had kept the small apartment in the city, even after his mother died, but they spent less and less time there with each passing year. Orin spent most of his nights sleeping in a closet-sized room with little more than a cot, a small wardrobe for his clothes and a tiny window.

As he slid the door open and entered the room, he noticed something outside his window. It couldn't be. He looked away and returned his gaze to the window to make sure he wasn't hallucinating. Yup, still there. Sitting on his window sill was a small bird. But it wasn't just any bird – it was Mister Feathers. It was certainly not the first time he had seen this very bird sitting in his window, but it had been such a very long time.

Orin first met Mister Feathers five years ago. The emperor had just died and everyone was preparing for the coronation of the new one. He didn't recall anyone being very excited about the big event. No one much liked the old emperor and the new one seemed like he was going to turn out about the same. Orin would probably have ignored the whole thing, but about a month before the ceremony, a royal emissary arrived at the gates of The Depot and demanded to see the Professor.

A spectacular parade was being planned and, much to the Professor's dismay, the Mechs were going to be there. The royal event planners had choreographed an elaborate series of movements that the Mechs would perform during the ceremony, but that plan was quickly squashed when the Professor simply said "Mechs don't dance." A compromise was reached where the Mechs would line the parade route and salute as the new emperor passed.

Professor Umbra was angry about the whole fiasco but Orin was very excited. Preparations were to take a week and they would be guests of the Royal Family for the duration. Orin had never even been to the Royal Palace and now he was going to live there for a whole week. He made a point of agreeing with all of his father's grumblings, but on the inside, he could hardly wait to go.

When the big day arrived, each of the Mechs was loaded onto a train car for the trip to the Royal Palace. A passenger car was added to the train for carrying support staff, but his dad allowed Orin to ride with Gigahertz on his flatcar. He could still remember the feeling of the wind whipping through his hair as the train sped through the desert and into the city. Gig lifted him up so he could ride on his shoulder. It seemed like he could see to the end of the world. When they reached the city, the tracks were lined with thousands of cheering people. He felt like the most important person on the planet.

As they rounded the final turn, Orin got his first close-up look at the Royal Palace. Wow! What an amazing place. It was bigger than any of the buildings back at The Depot and so much prettier. It was built with white stone and had more windows than he had ever seen on one building. A black tiled roof soared into the sky and each corner held a towering turret capped with a gleaming copper spire. The building was already hundreds of years old, but looked solid enough to last a thousand more.

Upon arriving at the palace, the train shuddered to a stop and all the Mechs wandered off to visit with Helion while everyone else was ushered into the Great Hall. The place was amazing! The ceiling was nearly as high as the one in the Central Assembly Building and the room was lined with tables covered with the finest linens and set with scores of shiny dishes. Each plate was surrounded by so many pieces of silverware that Orin couldn't imagine how anyone could possibly use them all. Dozens of well-dressed servants circled the room carrying trays of fancy drinks and delectable treats. Orin had no idea that people lived in this much luxury.

The meal was the best he had ever eaten. The food was so exotic that he didn't know what half of it was and no matter how much he ate, people kept bringing him more. He didn't know Cambria even had this much food. After the meal, his father and the Techs were taken to a meeting with the event planners, leaving Orin to wander the palace on his own.

That was when he met Juna. She was sitting on a bench just watching people go by. When she spotted Orin, she stood up and walked over.

"Hi, I'm Juna. Are you here with the Mechs?"

"Yes," he said, almost too softly to be heard.

She was the prettiest girl he had ever seen. At the time, Orin mostly thought that girls were kind of icky, but she definitely was not. She had dark brown hair that stretched almost to her waist. Her eyes were the most beautiful green he could imagine and her warm smile reminded Orin of his mother's. When he found out she was a princess, he became completely tongue-tied, but she told him it was no big deal and that she hated being a princess anyway.

Soon they were talking and laughing and telling each other about their lives. He had never met anyone who was so easy to spend time with. She was even friends with a Mech! Juna told him how she liked to climb on Helion's back and go running through the fields. Orin told her that he and Gig did the same thing and that they should race sometime. He also got to meet her best friend Pom, who was really nice too.

One day, when the adults were all in meetings, Solitaire took Helion's post in front of the palace so Orin and Juna could sneak off with their Mechs and race through the fields. It was the best day of his life – he never wanted it to end.

The day of the parade was not nearly as much fun because Juna had to ride on the royal float. Her brother and sister looked ridiculous but she wore a simple sundress and had a flower in her hair. She was so beautiful. When the parade ended, the team from The Depot packed up the Mechs to take the train home. Just as they were about to leave, Juna came up to him to say goodbye. She was carrying a small cage with a bird in it. She said his name was Mister Feathers and he could carry messages between them in a little tube strapped to his foot. All Orin had to do was put in a message and then release the bird out his window. As soon as Orin got home, he wrote a short note on a small piece of paper:

I had fun. Hope I see you again soon. O.

He rolled it up and stuffed it into the tube and sent Mister Feathers soaring out his bedroom window. Regrettably, his next move was to rush down to the assembly floor and carve up his best friend's leg.

Orin exchanged notes with Juna for the next couple of months. It wasn't like being there with her, but at least it was something. One day he anxiously opened Mister Feather's tube to find a note that read:

Father found out. Have to stop. J.

Orin almost burst into tears. He thought so hard about what to write for his reply. He wanted to beg her to change her mind. He wanted to tell her it wasn't fair. He wanted to tell her that she was the nicest girl he had ever met and he wanted to see her again more than anything else in the world. Unfortunately, what he came up with was:

OK. Have a nice life. O.

There was not a day that went by that Orin didn't regret sending that note. The worst part was that he never got a chance to come up with something better. Until now. His hands were shaking as he opened the tube and read the note. Not understanding, he read it again. It still didn't make any sense, but he knew it was important, so he sprinted out of the room to show the General.

6

Juna tossed and turned all night. Despite not getting any rest the night before, sleep still eluded her. She tried to let the darkness sweep her away, but she was just too worried. Her brain was spinning with all of the horrible things she had learned and images of exploding palaces and screaming hods flooded her mind every time she closed her eyes. It seemed like her whole world was coming apart and she felt powerless to stop it from happening. Her only hope was Orin.

Her life had been in constant motion since learning of her father's treacherous plans. As soon as the meeting had ended, she scurried through the rafters, straight to the royal aviary to find Mister Feathers. Along the way, she racked her brain, trying to think of the perfect thing to write in the note. The first challenge was coming up with something that could fit on a tiny piece of paper. Next, the message had to be vague enough that it would not be understood if it was intercepted along the way. Mister Feathers had not been to see Orin in over five years, so there was a good chance he would simply deliver it to someone else. Lastly, the message needed to be specific enough that Orin would know what to do when he got it. It had to be just right.

Juna finally settled on the perfect text for her note as she dropped to the floor outside the door to the aviary. Quietly sliding the door open, she stepped inside. There were always small slips of paper kept on the desk near the door, so she quickly wrote her message and went to search for Mister Feathers' cage. Finding it, she opened the small door and pulled him out. He seemed a little annoyed to be bothered at this time of the night, but she calmed him with a few soft words. When he was settled, she rolled up her note and slid it into the tube attached to his leg.

"I know it's been a long time," she whispered to the bird, "but you have to remember. Go to Orin. Do you understand? Go. To. Orin."

Mister Feathers returned a look of total confusion. She repeated Orin's name several more times, but the expression on the bird's face never changed. Realizing she had done all that she could, she took the bird to the small exit chute and released him into the night. Convincing herself that the look on his face was simply what birds always looked like, she stepped out of the aviary with at least a tiny bit of optimism. After all, it was her only hope.

The trip back to her room would be much faster using the palace hallways, but she realized she would not be able to explain her odd choice of clothing if she was caught, so it was back up into the rafters for the return trip. The first light of dawn was just showing on the horizon when she finally arrived back at her room. Changing out of her shadow suit, she made her way down to the floor of the bedroom. Pom had spent the night on Juna's mattress to cover for her absence just in case someone decided to check in on her during the night.

"Pom, you have to wake up right now," she said softly as she gave her friend a gentle nudge.

"Juna!" she exclaimed as she woke with a start. "Where have you been? I've been so worried."

"No time to explain. Get up. We have to go see your mother."

Pom's mother was to stay behind in the palace when the Royal Family departed for Alderae, which made her one of the people her father clearly intended to blow up. Juna was careful not to provide too many details – hods with information they should not have did not tend to stay alive very long. She told Pom's mother that she, and several other hods, would be asked to wear some fancy clothes and wander around the palace while the Royal Family was away. Juna told her that they should go along with the plan, but as soon as the last of the Elites had left, they were all to sneak out and get as far away from the palace as they could. They were to hide away with family or friends until the battle with the Marans was over and they were certain it was safe to return. Pom's mother was confused by the request, but she promised to make sure the building was empty before the Marans arrived.

With that task completed, Juna felt a little better. Maybe her father was going to vaporize the palace, but at least she had managed to save the lives of the people he so callously planned to exterminate along with it. She would miss the palace, of course, but at least it could be rebuilt. Knowing that lives could be lost was not something she was willing to accept. They said their goodbyes to Pom's mom and raced back to Juna's bedroom so they would be there waiting when Mister Stotz came to collect them for the trip to the train station. Sitting on the mattress, they waited for the inevitable knock on the door.

"Oh Pom, it's just so horrible," Juna seethed, barely able to keep her anger in check. "I wish I could tell you more about what's going on, but I don't think it would be safe for you to know."

"Yeah, don't you worry about me," she replied, dismissing the idea with a wave of her hand. "From the bits and pieces I've been able to pick up so far, I think I'm glad I don't know any more. I trust you and I know that you're doing something important. If you need me to do anything, anything at all, you only need to ask."

Juna squeezed Pom's hand and returned a loving smile, but before she was able to respond, there was a knock at the door and Mister Stotz came in to escort them to the train station. Juna fumed all the way there. Leaving her bedroom. Passing through the hallways she knew so well. Walking past the Great Hall and out into the beautiful courtyard in front of the main entrance. Everything she saw, she knew she may never see again and it made her *very* angry. The journey on the train was miserable. Everyone seemed so excited, like they were on their way to a vacation at the beach. But she knew. She knew that this was a one-way trip and that their lives would never be the same.

Light was now pouring in through her bedroom windows, the moons dominating the golden morning sky. Juna heard the surf pounding the cliffs below and the call of gulls in the air. Her first full day in Alderae. She would not let herself believe that this was her new home. No. Mister Feathers would get the message to Orin. General Zatari would understand and know just what to do. The Mechs would be there in time and they would turn back the Maran assault.

And if they won, then what? The General would learn that there was a second enemy – an enemy within. He would stop the evil plans and he would need her help to do it. Juna sprang out of bed and got herself ready for the day. Now was not the time to be weak and feel sorry for herself. She would learn everything she could about what was really going on and, when the time came, she would be ready to fight.

59

Orin, his dad and General Zatari were sitting in the Professor's small office near the assembly floor. They read the note for what must have been the hundredth time.

O. They are lying. Be there three days early. J.

For the first message he received from her in five years, he would have hoped for something that made a little more sense.

"Do we even know the message is for me?" Orin asked the room. "I mean, I haven't heard from her for a long time."

"She did start the message with an 'O'," the Professor responded. "Did she always do that?"

"No," Orin replied. "She never did that before, but 'O' is the most common initial for a boy's name. Maybe she has a boyfriend and it was supposed to go to him instead."

"And who exactly is it that is lying," the Professor muttered to no one in particular. "And where is it you are supposed to arrive early?"

"I know the messages have to be short," Orin said with a note of frustration, "but would it have killed her to just tell us exactly what she wants me to do."

"She's too smart for that," the General said from the back corner of the room. He had been quiet for so long, Orin almost forgot he was there. "The message was definitely for Orin. She would only have included the 'O' if she was sending it to someone not expecting the arrival of a message. I think it's quite obvious. Somehow, your royal friend has learned that the Marans will be arriving three days early and she wanted to make sure the Mechs were there to greet them. Her only way to get that message through was to send the bird to Orin. She couldn't provide too much detail just in case the note ended up in the wrong hands. This Juna is a clever girl."

"But why?" Orin pleaded. "Why would anyone lie about something like that?"

"The why is not important right now," the General replied as he began to pace the room. "We will sort that out when the time is right. For now, we focus on when, and when is apparently three days early. So, let's continue with our preparations but advance the schedule so that the Mechs are in a position to defend the palace three days earlier than we had originally planned."

"We better get to it then," the Professor said, his frustration obvious. "There is a lot of work to be done and we just lost three days in which to do it."

The entire team kept up a hectic pace the following week. The General reviewed the battle plan with the Mechs, running through every conceivable counterattack the Marans could employ. Orin and the Professor spent their time fine-tuning the missile targeting systems. With a finite number of missiles available to them, it was crucial that each one hit its mark. Once they were gone, the war was lost. The Techs reviewed strategies and ran simulations while the Wrenches ran practice sessions for repairing battle-damaged Mechs to get them back to the fighting as quickly as possible.

Two days prior to the new ship-out date, the General walked into the Professor's office. Orin and his dad looked up from the schematics they were reviewing and noticed the look of concern on his face.

"I think we may have a problem," he informed them. "I'm starting to think that victory in this war is not what our political leaders are hoping for."

"Why?" the Professor asked, taking a moment to slide his glasses back up the bridge of his nose. "What is it?"

"I informed Colonel Pavic that we wanted to get the Mechs training on Mount Volaris as soon as possible to familiarize themselves with the local terrain. I requested that the train for transporting them to the battlefield be sent here earlier than originally scheduled. He has informed me that this will not be possible."

"But the train cars that carry the Mechs are always kept here at The Depot," the Professor replied, not understanding the issue.

"I realize that," the General countered. "The problem is that every locomotive on the planet has already been assigned to emergency evacuation tasks. Pavic has refused to send one to us until the day before the announced arrival of the Maran fleet and that, according to our friend the princess, will be two days *after* their actual arrival."

"Well, if that's your only problem," the Professor replied, an ear-to-ear grin on his face, "then you do not have a problem."

"And why is that?"

"As you both know, I like to give each of my Mechs a little bonus feature," the Professor beamed. "I had a set of retractable rail bogies installed on Scarab. I think you will find that she has the pulling power of all the locomotives on Cambria put together."

A smile slowly appeared on the General's face. "You *are* full of surprises Darin," he said, slapping the Professor on the back. "If our illustrious leader really does want to lose this war, let's make sure he ends up disappointed."

Two days later, the Mechs were loaded on their flatcars, ready for their journey to the Royal Palace. Scarab took her spot at the front of the train and coupled herself to the first car. The Mechs were arranged by their power type. Gigahertz, Vortex and Diode were in the first three cars, followed by the Steamers and the Diesels. Solitaire was in the lead for the Solars, with Helion and Rayzor able to share the next car due to Rayzor's small size. The Atomics were next and, right at the back, were Armorat and Tortuga. Seeing them all together like that filled Orin with a sense of awe.

They had assembled a fighting force so powerful, he almost felt sorry for the Marans.

The General wanted to have the whole team get a feel for the layout of the battlefield, so he and the Professor, along with all the Techs, were riding inside Scarab to make the trip to the palace. Orin was tagging along with Gig in the car right behind them.

"OK Scarab, take it nice and easy," the General instructed. "We don't want anyone thinking we're in a big hurry." He wanted to make sure that their unexpected arrival appeared to be only for advanced training and not the result of being tipped off to the Marans' early arrival. Not knowing how Juna had received her information, he did not want to endanger her should the emperor decide to go looking for possible leaks in his inner circle.

The rumble of Scarab's engine filled the air and the train began to inch forward. Soon, they were steaming along the tracks, through the high desert, on their way to Mount Volaris. An hour into the trip, they reached the end of the desert and the eastern edge of Volara. Orin immediately noticed the lack of activity in the city. There was no traffic on the streets or people on the sidewalks. It appeared that everyone had heeded the warnings and evacuated the city.

As they were rounding a corner, Orin could feel the train slowing. It seemed a little too early for their arrival at the palace, so he climbed onto Gig's shoulder to get a better look at what might be wrong. Off in the distance, he could see a man standing in the middle of the tracks. Scarab continued to slow until she came to a full stop directly in front of the man. Her side access door opened and the General emerged. Dropping down the ladder, he went to talk to the person responsible for halting their progress.

"Colonel Pavic," the General said in his most pleasant tone. "How nice of you to come out to greet us."

"General," the man responded in a much less pleasant tone, "we didn't expect to see you for another couple of days."

"Well, it sounded like you were all extremely busy out here, so we decided to save you the trouble of sending us a locomotive. As you can see, we didn't even need one. I thought it would be good to get the team out early, learn the lay of the land, dig in a few trenches, that sort of thing. Every battle is won in the planning, I like to say. I promise we won't get in anyone's way. I hope it's not going to be a problem."

The two men stared at each other. The Colonel's mind obviously churning, the smile never leaving the General's face.

"No, of course not," the Colonel finally replied, now sporting a smile of his own. "An excellent plan. I just wanted to come out and make sure everything was alright. Please, carry on. And good luck with your preparations."

"Thank you, Colonel," the General said, his stare never wavering. "All of us working together is what will help us repel this invasion and drive the Marans off this planet for good." With that, he turned on his heels and climbed back up the ladder and through Scarab's access door.

As the train started moving again, Orin's attention remained on Colonel Pavic. He was watching the passing train, obviously surprised by the amount of firepower rolling by. He looked unhappy, like a man whose plans had just been ruined. Not even the friendly wave he got from Clank seemed to cheer him up.

The train finally came to a stop when it reached the plateaus that surrounded the base of Mount Volaris. Orin had forgotten how impressive the Royal Palace was from this close. It was such a magnificent building! The sun was shining off the spires, making it look like the entire structure was lit from within. He scanned the windows, wondering if Juna was in there somewhere. He hoped she wasn't. When the Marans arrived, this was going to be a very dangerous place to be. He could only hope that the building would still be standing when the battle was finished.

All of the Mechs disembarked and formed a circle around the General to ready themselves for a day of training. In the previous wars, the Marans had launched two massive landing craft from which the SCUDs began their attack. With a fleet of three warships, the General anticipated he would need to deal with six landing craft this time around. He had predicted their most likely landing spots and positioned the Mechs accordingly.

The team spent the day noting sightlines, calculating trajectories and practicing repositioning movements should the actual landing locations differ from the initial predictions. At the end of the day, the General had each Mech take their starting position and instructed each one to drop into a wait state when they were ready. At the moment of the Maran's arrival, Techs would issue the appropriate waking commands from the Operations Centre back at The Depot and the battle would begin. Confident that they had prepared as best they could, they packed up their things, readying themselves to board Scarab for the return trip to The Depot.

Orin spotted Gigahertz setting up in his assigned starting position, so he went over to wish him well.

"Hey Gig. There's going to be a lot of missiles flying around here soon. Keep your head down."

"Master Orin. How can I possibly engage the enemy effectively with my head down?"

"I just mean, try to be careful," Orin replied, trying to hide the emotion in his voice. "I'd hate to see you get hurt is all."

"I will do my best," Gigahertz promised. "Repelling the Marans is the first priority. Doing so without being damaged would be my preference as well."

Orin felt uneasy during the entire journey home. There were so many questions spinning in his mind. Would the Marans land where they were supposed to? Would the Steamers hold up during actual battle conditions? Would Gig still have all his parts the next time he saw him? And why did the Emperor seem so intent on delaying their arrival? He let out a heavy sigh. No point worrying about it now. They had done their best. Whether the war started tomorrow or three days from now, it *was* coming and they were as ready as they were ever going to be.

It was late in the evening and Orin was in the Ops Centre going over the battle plans for the twentieth time. So much thought had gone into the plans and he had faith in the General's skills as a military tactician, but there were so many things that could still go wrong. The Marans were flying a long way to start this fight, so they probably had some pretty good plans of their own. Images of Mechs flying to pieces kept popping into his head and he fought to drive them back out. He kept telling himself over and over that they were ready and everything was going to be OK.

As he sat there, trying not to worry, his father approached from behind and rested a hand on his shoulder. "Come outside Orin. I think you should see this." They walked out behind the building and joined the General who was already standing on the hill, staring out into space. Orin followed his gaze and saw what looked like three comets in the night sky.

"They're doing their deceleration burn for final approach," the Professor noted.

"They're close," added the General. "It looks like we owe the princess a big thank you. This thing starts tomorrow."

7

They were here. The weeks of waiting were over. The feeling of dread that had gripped the planet was finally realized. The Maran warships were now circling the planet and Juna had never been more afraid. She thought she would be ready for this, but the anticipation of their arrival simply did not prepare her for the reality of them actually being here. It was terrifying. The truth was unavoidable – if her father wasn't able to negotiate a truce, they would be at war within the hour.

She was sitting with Pom in a quiet corner of the dining hall, the largest room in the Summer Palace. Sunshine streamed through the windows of the elegant room, but it did nothing to brighten her sour mood. She could not stop thinking about her father's evil intentions and being surrounded by his minions was not helping one little bit. The room was filled with Cambria's most powerful people and buzzed with the sound of their incessant chatter about the latest developments in the war effort.

Everyone seemed genuinely surprised by the announcement of the Marans' early arrival. Her father assured them that it was a simple calculation error and that the people responsible would be held accountable. No one seemed overly concerned by this, acting like it was something that always happened when a planet was attacked by a fleet of interstellar warships. Juna was the only one that knew the truth. Her father kept lying and his subjects kept believing. It seemed like a cycle that would never end. Right now, his adoring subjects were milling about, talking intently and theorizing about what must be going on in the adjacent study.

Technicians had installed a remote radio system in the study her father used as an office while he was staying at the Summer Palace. The equipment allowed the Emperor to communicate with the orbiting ships from here in Alderae, but to the Marans, it would appear that all the transmissions were originating from Mount Volaris. This bit of technological trickery made her even more angry. It was her father's way of keeping himself safe while making sure the Royal Palace remained the target of the attack.

Juna had learned nothing of her father's plans over the past week. The Summer Palace did not have open rafters above all the rooms, so she had no opportunity to sneak around and listen in on all the secret meetings. And there had been many secret meetings. Her father and brother spent most of their days in the study, talking with Colonel Pavic on the new radio. The fact that the Colonel remained behind when everyone else left for Alderae had her particularly concerned. Did that mean Pom's mother wouldn't get a chance to evacuate the palace? Would all the hods be killed after all?

Juna's worst fears were finally put to rest late last night when Colonel Pavic showed up at the doors of the Summer Palace. He was noticeably upset when her father arrived to greet him. Not daring to get too close to the conversation, she somehow managed to overhear the Colonel tell the Emperor that the Mechs had arrived that morning and were already positioned to defend against the attack. Her father was devastated by the news, but Juna was elated. Mister Feathers had delivered the message!

Orin had shown it to the General and he had understood! She almost let herself believe that she would see her beautiful palace again. And best of all, with the Colonel here, all of the Elites would now be gone from the palace. Picturing a column of well-dressed hods streaming out of the building brought a well-earned smile to her face.

Juna's good mood slowly drained away as she tried to sleep that night. The Mechs were ready, but that didn't mean they were going to win. The Marans were sending a much larger force this time around. What if it was *too* large for the Mechs to turn back? There was also the small matter of explosives lining the walls of the Royal Palace. If the Mechs did win, would her father blow up the palace anyway? It was all so uncertain. Having done all that she could, she still worried about all of the things that could prevent a happy ending to all of this.

Rising with the morning's first light, she was overwhelmed by a feeling of dread that she just couldn't shake. After getting herself ready for the day, she clutched Pom's hand, stepped out of her bedroom and joined the throng of people heading for the dining hall. And now, here she was, sitting in a room full of Elites, hoping against all hope that everything was going to be alright.

A feeling of optimism was slowly growing in the room as the day progressed. The Emperor, Jakol, Colonel Pavic and Mister Nardo had been locked away in the study for over two hours talking with the Maran leadership. In the previous war, negotiations with the enemy had lasted less than half that time before the attack had begun. People suggested that this emperor might be a much better negotiator than the last one. They allowed themselves to think it was possible that the war could still be averted. Juna did not share in the group's hopes for a positive outcome. Her father's plan seemed to require an attack on the palace, so she had a hard time believing he was even attempting to avoid the inevitable assault.

The room went completely silent as the door to the study swung open. The four men emerged, dour expressions on all their faces. Mister Nardo was carrying a stack of paper, no doubt his translation of the conversation with the enemy.

"I fear the news is grave," the Emperor stated when he finally addressed the room.

The assembled group let out a collective gasp as if shocked by the news. Some of them began weeping as the reality of the situation sunk in. From the back corner of the room, Juna glowered at her father, angry at the deceit. Only she knew that the whole scene was a sham and that the negotiations had not been conducted in good faith.

"The Marans are relentless in their hatred of the people of this planet," the Emperor continued. "They will not be satisfied until every last person on Cambria has been exterminated and…, I'm sorry, Mister Nardo, what was that last part?"

Mister Nardo stepped forward and cleared his throat. "And the streets of Volara have been turned to rivers of our blood."

With that, the room released another gasp and those that had been weeping, turned to open sobbing. The Emperor raised his hands in an attempt to quiet the crowd. "All hope is not lost," he urged. "At my instruction, the Mechs have been deployed on Mount Volaris to turn back this savage invasion of our world. Right now, our thoughts should be with them and the skilled men and women who support their efforts. Our fate is now in their hands."

Tears filled Juna's eyes. Of course, he was right. As much as she loathed her father, she knew that the real threat, right at this moment, was coming from the Marans. She and Pom had been holding hands for the duration of the announcement, squeezing so hard their fingers turned white. Turning to her friend, she tried her best to look hopeful.

"Oh, Pom. They have to win. They just have to."

At that moment, the royal guardsman who was monitoring the communication link with The Depot approached the Emperor. "They've launched, Your Highness. The attack is underway."

Plumes of smoke trailed the Maran landing craft plummeting towards the surface. There were six of them, just as the General had predicted. The whole team was assembled in the Operations Centre back at The Depot. From here, they would watch the battle unfold on eighteen monitors, each one connected to the camera and microphone mounted on every Mech. The Mechs had been woken from their wait state when the Maran fleet entered orbit and were now staring skyward at the six fireballs streaking towards them.

As the monstrous cylindrical landing craft got closer to the ground, they fired rockets to slow their descent. The sound coming through the Mechs' microphones was deafening as each enemy craft settled onto the plateaus of Mount Volaris, sending dirt and debris flying hundreds of feet into the air. Orin was amazed by the accuracy of the General's projections. Every one of the landing craft set down within a few feet of the predicted location.

When the dust finally settled, the size of the craft became immediately apparent. They were enormous! Each of the cylinders was close to a hundred feet tall and fifty feet across. The scale of the attacking force was alarming. Orin ran some quick calculations in his head and figured each one could hold over two hundred SCUDs. Would the Mechs be able to deal with over a thousand of the enemy's war machines? A large square sat near the bottom of each craft, which he presumed was the door from which the SCUDs would emerge. They would know very soon.

The Ops Centre was deathly quiet, each person's attention locked on the monitors. The wait was agonizing. When it happened, it happened suddenly. All six of the craft reacted in unison, as if controlled by a single mind. The top edge of each door threw itself away from the cylinder. Hinged at the bottom, the door created a ramp that slammed to the ground with a thunderous crash. Within a heartbeat, SCUDs began pouring out onto Cambrian soil.

As soon as the SCUDs appeared, the Mechs began firing. SIMs and TRIPs flew through the air, locking themselves onto shields, draining them of their strength. The SCUDs were firing too. The Mechs' incredible reflexes allowed them to avoid many of the incoming missiles and those they couldn't, seemed to bounce harmlessly off their shields. The battlefield filled with fire and smoke, but so far, none of the Mechs appeared to have sustained any damage.

The SCUDs were not faring nearly as well. The revisions Orin and his father had made to the Mech's targeting systems were proving to be devastatingly effective. Every missile launched resulted in a direct hit. That, combined with Diara's frequency modulation revision making the missiles so much more powerful, was overwhelming the invading force. Soon shields were failing and SCUDs were flying apart, turning into harmless piles of well-armoured debris. But for every one that was destroyed, another took its place – the stream of emerging SCUDs never slowed.

Only a minute into the battle, Orin experienced his first true moment of panic. Diara stood up from her station and yelled over the sounds of the battle.

"Orin. I'm receiving a personal message for you from Spanner."

Orin rushed to Diara's station, trying to think of what he might have forgotten, what mistake he might have made.

"What does it say?" he asked, trying to hide the concern in his voice.

Diara hit a button on her console and listened to the message on her headset. A slight smile appeared at the corners of her mouth.

"It says: Orin, thanks for the shields. It has made the entire battle experience much more pleasant."

Orin couldn't hide his grin as he returned to his spot at the back of the room. Refocusing his attention on the bank of monitors, he settled in to watch the continuing action. Mounted on the top of every screen was a small placard with the name of each Mech. He tried to keep track of how all of them were doing, but his attention was clearly focused on the monitors for Gigahertz and the Steamers. Gig was a beast! Launching SIMs at an astonishing rate, he scored a direct hit with every shot. After a minute of non-stop destruction, he would pause for a moment to reload and then restart the barrage. It was breathtaking to watch.

All of Orin's optimism about the progress of the battle was instantly erased when his attention cycled back to Clank's monitor. Up until now, Clank had been performing well, definitely holding his own against the enemy onslaught. But right now, he was just standing there, staring at a single flower growing in the battle-ravaged turf. As Clank's arm moved into the frame, Orin realized what was happening, but was powerless to stop it. He wanted to throw himself through the monitor and yell "No!", but it happened anyway. Clank reached down, picked the flower and tucked the stem into a small exhaust grill on his chest plate.

Orin was feeling many emotions at that moment with embarrassment being the obvious front-runner. He scanned the room to see if anyone else had noticed and was pleased to see no one reacting to the odd episode. Now, the emotion he was feeling most was relief. It looked as though he got away with it this time, but his mind was already formulating lines of code he could include in a Distraction Avoidance algorithm that would be included in Clank's next software upgrade.

When Orin returned his gaze to Clank's monitor, he was happy to see that he had rejoined the battle as if nothing had happened. A battle that was clearly being dominated by the Mechs. At one point, the SCUDs were starting to make a small advance in the southwest quadrant of the battle-field, but the General repositioned Fallout to assist on that front and the advance was quickly thwarted. Scanning every monitor, he noticed each one showing the same thing – SCUDs being blown apart by a torrent of Mech-fired missiles.

Orin had been kept well away from the Ops Centre during the previous war with the Marans. He had only been a child, after all. This was his first real opportunity to observe a battle first-hand so he hadn't really known what to expect. He was certainly no expert, but things seemed to be going very well.

She was certainly no expert, but things seemed to be going very well. Juna was huddled together with all of the Elites around the single monitor that was their window on the battle. The images they were viewing were pro-vided through a direct link to The Depot. Apparently, there were eighteen Mech-mounted cameras and the monitor in Alderae was cycling through the views provided by each one in thirty-second bursts.

To Juna's eye, the view from every Mech was the same. Outgoing mis-siles destroying the unmanned Maran fighting machines and incoming missiles missing their target or doing no damage if they did manage to hit something. Unfortunately, one of the Mechs had been disabled. It spent its entire thirty seconds just staring at the ground. She hoped it wasn't Helion. Right at the end, she did notice its arm moving – maybe it was going to be OK.

The mood in the room was joyous. Every time one of the Maran machines exploded, the room erupted in a chorus of cheers that made Juna's heart swell. Being a hod, Pom was not allowed near the monitor, but she cheered along with everyone else from the back of the room, caught up in the excitement of the crowd. The energy was infectious. The people of Cambria had been fearing the Maran invasion for so long and now it seemed that a decisive victory may be within reach.

Juna's attention was not focused solely on the scenes playing out on the monitor's screen. She was also keeping an eye on her father. He was sitting off to the side, his expression unreadable. He did not look unhappy, nor was he joining in the revelry. He looked calm. Distinguished. Calculating. Despite his relaxed demeanour on the outside, Juna knew he must be miserable on the inside. For some reason she still didn't understand, he was hoping for a different outcome than everyone else in the room – one in which the Marans prevailed and were able to overrun the palace. Watching his plans fall apart before her eyes was almost as satisfying as seeing the Mechs' domination of the battle.

At one point, Juna noticed her father's gaze shift from the monitor to something on the other side of the room. She turned to see what had grabbed his attention. Colonel Pavic stood there, holding a small black box with a big red button. He lifted the box slightly and raised an eyebrow. A question. Yes or no? Push it or don't? She realized this was the moment that would decide the fate of the Royal Palace. Yes, the palace is gone. No, it lives to see another day. Staring at her father, she tried willing him to say no. Unable to breathe, her heart pounded like it was going to leap from her chest. And then, the answer. An almost imperceptible shake of the head. No.

"Ha!" Juna said only to herself. "Wouldn't be able to explain that one, would you?" Looking across the room, she saw Pom in the back corner. Showing her a big thumbs-up, she received a beaming smile in return. A resounding cheer in the room returned her attention to the monitor. Another one of the attacking machines had been turned to rubble in particularly impressive fashion. Her internal discussion with her father continued. "Those crazy robot guys really messed up your day, didn't they?"

⚙   ⚙   ⚙

The Mechs were doing great but the flow of SCUDs out of the landing crafts seemed endless. The piles of disembowelled machines forming at the ends of the exit ramps were becoming so large that the SCUDs were struggling to even make it to the battlefield. The Mechs would begin firing on them the moment they rounded the top of the pile. By the time they made it halfway down the other side, they were covered in SIM's. Before they could reach the bottom, they had shattered into a thousand pieces, adding more debris to the pile. Orin didn't need to be an expert to see that this was a one-sided fight weighted heavily in favour of the Mechs.

Out of the corner of his eye, Orin noticed the General waving him over to his station.

"Hello General," Orin began. "It's going really well isn't it?"

"That it is, Orin. That it is. I just wanted you to know how impressed I am with the work of the Steamers today. They have been very effective additions to the team. You did some fantastic work getting them ready."

Those words made Orin feel amazing.

"I noticed they even managed to get a little landscaping work done," he added with a wink and a smile.

Those words made Orin feel slightly less amazing, but he knew it was all in fun. Preparations had been so stressful, that it was only natural to joke around when all of that pressure was finally released. All the planning, designing, programming and assembly was done in hopes of getting to this moment, and now that it was here, it felt like an enormous weight had been lifted off of them all.

But was it really over? It couldn't be. Orin looked at the clock. The whole thing started less than an hour ago. Could it possibly have been that easy?

He hadn't noticed until just now, but the battlefield had become nearly silent. The Mechs were crouched, waiting for the next wave of SCUDs to come rushing out to join the battle. But there wasn't a next wave and there was no battle to join.

The Mechs stopped looking at the landing craft and started looking at each other. Questioning. Was that really it? You could now see all the Mechs through the eyes of their comrades and there wasn't even a scratch on any of them. For all of the missiles they fired, the Maran's assault hadn't even managed to knock the flower off of Clank.

The only motion that remained on the battlefield was a single SCUD, one of its tracks blown off, spinning in an endless circle. Not wanting to waste a missile, Carnage marched over to it and smashed it repeatedly until it was scrap metal. He tore off its remaining track, held it high over his head and released a victorious roar.

Balko, the young Tech who had been monitoring orbital telemetry, stood and addressed the General. "The Maran warships are breaking orbit, sir. They're leaving."

The room erupted in a chorus of cheers.

Just like that, the war was over. And, the best news of all – they had won.

8

A feeling of euphoria had swept over the planet and it showed no signs of relenting, even two weeks after the Maran retreat. The people of Cambria were happy again and Volara felt alive for the first time in months. Orin decided to spend the morning in the city to share in the energy of the moment. The boards that had been covering store-front windows had all been removed, the street vendors were back on their favourite corners and the streets were, once again, teeming with activity. Normal life had returned at last.

There was only one person on the planet with cause to complain about how the war had turned out. During the Maran's assault, only one stray missile had managed to leave the battlefield. It soared over the city, arcing far to the east, and ultimately landed directly on top of Leaping Lano's Furniture Emporium, completely flattening the back half of the building. Lano, however, took it all in stride. He was now offering a liquidation of "partially-undamaged" furniture in what his advertisements were proclaiming the "Worst. Mystic. Ever." sale.

The Mechs had certainly been kept very busy for the past two weeks. The battle with the Marans had left the plateaus of Mount Volaris in a bit of a mess, meaning a major clean-up was urgently required. The fields were littered with the remnants of exploded SCUDs and the once pristine fields were now scarred with scorch marks and craters. The Mechs' job was to clear the area of all the debris that had been created by their own dominating victory.

The whole team was in action. The Hydros and Solars were collecting all of the pieces, creating huge piles of scrap metal which the Diesels and Steamers were pounding into compacted cubes. The Atomics had been outfitted with laser cutting torches that they were using to cut the enormous landing craft into small pieces and the Bios were transporting everything to the train station where it would be taken back to The Depot for recycling.

Cambria was not a planet blessed with an abundance of natural resources. The constant surge of ocean water sweeping over most of the planet's landmass made mining very difficult. Much of the useful ore on the planet was found in "The Wash," the areas of the planet that cycled between wet and dry with the tides. Recovering anything from there was dangerous work and required considerable planning, so finding the metal required to keep the planet's industrial operations running was often a struggle. The thousands of tons of scrap metal left behind by the Marans was an unexpected gift – yet another reason to celebrate the victory in the war.

Once the Mechs had cleared an area, the local farmers would till the soil and replant it with native grasses and wildflowers. Soon, new life would spring from the ground trying to erase the memories of the vicious conflict that had occurred there. By this time next year, there would be no signs that a war had ever been fought on the plateaus of Mount Volaris.

The work of clearing the fields had been non-stop. Well, almost. It was decided that one day be set aside to celebrate – a chance for the people of Cambria to show their appreciation to the Mechs and all of the people that helped in the war effort. Apparently, Princess Lacee organized the whole thing. It was a wonderful day. It all started with a magnificent parade. The Mechs marched down Main Street, which was lined with people as far as the eye could see. It appeared to Orin that every citizen of Volara had come out to watch. Everyone screamed their thanks and enthusiastically waved signs and banners. Orin spent the entire parade riding on Gig's shoulder, waving back at the raucous crowd. He couldn't remember the last time he had so much fun. His only concern was that there were so many photographers lining the route yelling "say cheese" that he was afraid Clank was going to shake himself apart.

After the parade, everyone from The Depot was escorted through a reception line to meet the Royal Family. The emperor was not in attendance, but his wife and the three royal children were there to offer their thanks. Orin was so excited he could barely breathe. Weeks ago, when he had returned to his room after deciphering Juna's message, Mister Feathers had already flown away through the open window, so he never got a chance to send a reply. This would be his first chance to say anything to her since he was a love-struck kid that told her to have a nice life.

Not that he had any idea what he was going to say. All day he had been trying to think of the perfect words, but nothing had come to him so far. Maybe he just wasn't very good at this sort of thing. Finally deciding to just wing it, he hoped the perfect words would find their way to his lips when he saw her.

Orin finally arrived at the front of the line. The Empress thanked him for his service with the practiced grace of a politician's wife. Prince Jakol seemed a little grumpy, but he managed a tight smile and shook Orin's hand. Princess Lacee, wearing the tallest hat he had ever seen, hugged him with an enthusiasm he thought might crack a rib. She gushed about how wonderful it was that all of their hard work had saved the planet from those dreadful Marans.

Next came Juna. Without even realizing he had moved, Orin found himself staring into her eyes, seeing the smile he had seen a thousand times in his dreams. She was about his height with a slim, athletic build. Wearing a flower in her long dark hair, her eyes were so green they seemed to glow. She was beautiful, but it was more than that. There was a strength about her he could almost feel. She was amazing. Those words he so hoped would show up right about now still eluded him. In fact, he knew any attempt to speak at all would end in failure. All he could manage was to mouth the words "thank you".

With that, her smile shone even brighter. She took his offered hand in both of hers and whispered back, "thank you, too," as a small tear rolled down her cheek.

And just like that, the moment was over. Princess Lacee had given up trying to hug Dorel, her arms unable to fully wrap around his immense frame. The line moved forward and Orin was swept away by a royal guardsman and escorted off the stage.

Orin was jolted from his recollections by the sound of a car's horn reminding him he was standing in the middle of a crosswalk. Waving an apology to the driver, he continued on his way. He couldn't help but smile as he walked through the streets of Volara, enjoying the sounds of a city at peace. Knowing, deep down, that his attempt to make a good impression on Juna had been a dismal failure, he still smiled every time he thought about their brief moment together. All he hoped for was another chance to see her. Maybe he would do a little better the next time.

Soon, his wandering found him back at his hoverbike. Thinking of all the work still to be done, hit him with a wave of guilt, so he hopped on his bike and started the trip back to The Depot. Once again, he stopped at the valley's rim to look out over the city. The view was the same, but somehow, everything felt different. Better. The dread he felt the last time he was here was now gone. The city was safer, the future brighter.

When he got back to The Depot, Orin sat down with his father to go over plans for some possible enhancements to the Mech program. The Professor was very excited for what lay ahead for the entire team at The Depot. Without the threat of an imminent Maran attack, it was possible to rethink everything they knew about what could be done with this amazing technology. He saw an opportunity to convert the Mechs from weapons of war to tools for peace.

"Just think of it, Orin," he began. "These are the most powerful machines on the planet. Imagine what we could do to help the people of Cambria by using them to build rather than destroy. The horrible mistreatment of the hods, forcing them into a life of back-breaking labour. It could all end."

"It sounds great, Dad."

"Orin, this is what I meant when I told you that you were destined for bigger and better things. I have always been hesitant to let you get too involved in the Mech program. But it wasn't because I thought you couldn't do it – it was because I didn't want you to waste your genius on figuring out new ways to blow stuff up."

Suddenly it all made sense. His dad had never questioned Orin's abilities – he was just trying to protect him from living a life full of destruction and violence. Orin was feeling an overwhelming sense of gratitude towards his father so he reached out and pulled him into an embrace. He had so many things he wanted to say, but before he could put his thoughts into words, they were interrupted by a knock at the door. It was General Zatari.

"Sorry gentlemen, but there's a royal emissary at the gate," the General informed them. "He wants to talk to us."

"I thought we'd be done with them for a while," the Professor replied. "I wonder what the emperor wants with us now?"

"Maybe he wants to give the General a medal," Orin offered excitedly.

"If that man tries to pin a medal on me, I'll stick it so far up his. . ."

"General!" the Professor interrupted. "Perhaps we should just listen to the emissary before jumping to any rash conclusions."

"Of course, you're right Darin. Let's go see what the man has to say."

The meeting with the emissary was a short one. They were informed that the emperor, along with the rest of the royal family, had returned from Alderae and were once again living in the Royal Palace. The General and the Professor were instructed to appear before him there at eight o'clock the following morning.

"I wonder what he wants?" Orin asked as soon as the man was gone.

"I don't like it," the General said. "We still don't know what the emperor's true intentions were during the war. That man is a schemer and I do *not* trust him."

"I, for one, welcome the opportunity to speak with him," the Professor countered. "I have plans that provide for more productive uses for the Mech program. I think when he sees them, he will understand the true benefit that a non-military function for the Mechs can offer the people of Cambria."

"I hope you're right," the General said with a sigh. "But my gut tells me he has something else on his mind."

The next morning, Orin, the Professor and the General were preparing for their journey to the Royal Palace. Orin had spent the previous evening lobbying to join them on the trip. He argued that, because the goal of their meeting was to talk about the future, it only made sense to include someone from the next generation of Cambrians. Of course, his true motivation was hoping for another opportunity to see Juna, but he decided not to mention that part. His father finally relented and Orin was invited to join them.

The group rode inside Scarab as she sped along the rails to the train station at the Royal Palace. After departing the station, they walked through the courtyard towards the main entrance and stopped for a quick visit with Helion. The General ordered him to extend the range of his sensor sweeps and report back if he noticed any suspicious activity in the area. The General wasn't exactly sure what he was looking for, but he wanted as much information as he could get about what was really going on out here.

When the group arrived at the front door, they were immediately escorted to the emperor's office. As they progressed through the building, Orin scanned every hallway in hopes of spotting Juna, but he didn't see her anywhere. They finally came to a stop outside the biggest wooden door Orin had ever seen. As it swung open, he felt a lurch in his stomach, just now realizing the reality of the moment. He was about to meet the emperor. It was extremely intimidating. Sweat began to form on every part of his body and he immediately regretted his decision to come.

They were ushered towards the emperor's desk near the large window at the far end of the room. As they approached, he looked up briefly, then returned his attention to the papers on his desk. When he finally spoke, he did not lift his gaze.

"Gentlemen, we have matters to discuss of the utmost importance. Why is it you felt it necessary to bring a child to this meeting? Is it 'Bring Your Kid to Work' day at The Depot?"

Orin's heart sunk. The most powerful person on the planet had just called him a child and made it quite obvious his presence here was not appreciated. All he wanted to do at that moment was run out of the room and hide. Oh, why did he have to talk his dad into letting him come here today? But, before he could act, the General jumped to his defence.

"I can assure you, your Excellency, that Orin is an integral member of our team. His attendance here is warranted."

The Emperor finally raised his head, looking squarely at the General. "Very well, General. Just make sure he doesn't become a nuisance."

With that, Orin's level of panic dropped enough that he could actually breathe again, but he *really* didn't want to be here anymore. Even seeing Juna again wouldn't make up for how horrible he was feeling right now. As far as he was concerned, this meeting could *not* end soon enough. As they were shown to their seats, he noticed for the first time the other attendees of the meeting. Colonel Pavic and Prince Jakol were there. Also present were another man and a woman, neither of whom he recognized.

The Emperor stood to make introductions. "Professor Umbra, General Zatari. This is Mister Nardo, the Royal Interpreter," he said, pointing to the man. "And I don't believe either of you have had the pleasure of meeting Professor Oletta."

The woman stood and walked towards his father, extending her hand and offering a smile. "Professor Umbra. How nice to finally meet the second smartest person on Cambria."

The introduction was somewhat rude, but Orin noticed a playfulness in her eyes when she delivered it. His father had obviously picked up on it as well.

"That's funny Professor," he replied, returning her smile. "I was just about to say the very same thing." The two professors shared a laugh. Then, after shaking hands with the General, she returned to her seat.

"Enough pleasantries," the Emperor grumbled. "We must get on with the business at hand." He returned to his chair behind the desk, shuffled some papers and started into a well-rehearsed speech. "General Zatari,

Professor Umbra. We were all very impressed with your efforts in repelling the Maran attack on our world. The entire planet owes you our undying gratitude. Today, I would like to start planning the next phase in our battle with the Marans. I believe the time has come to take the fight to them."

"Excuse me, Your Highness," the General questioned. "Are you suggesting that we make plans for an attack on Mara?"

"That is exactly what I am suggesting."

"But, my liege, surely you realize that we possess neither the knowledge nor the equipment required for interplanetary space travel. All of the design work for the Starchaser expedition was destroyed decades ago. It would take us years to redevelop that kind of technology."

"I am aware of that," the Emperor snapped. "Fortunately, your point is irrelevant. As you know, Professor Oletta developed a portal technology that allows us to open a window through space to observe what is going on at any location in the galaxy. As my first official act as emperor, I opened a research facility allowing her to develop this technology even further. I informed her that a window was insufficient – I wanted a door. I do not want to merely see what is happening on the other side of the portal, I want to be able to step through and be on the other side. I am pleased to report that these efforts have been successful and we now possess the ability to simply walk out onto the surface of Mara."

There was a shocked silence in the room. No one could believe what they had just been told. Everyone turned and focused their attention on Professor Oletta, waiting for her to confirm the existence of this amazing technology.

"There are limitations, of course," she finally said. "Based on their mass, I believe it will only be possible to move four Mechs through the portal. There would then be a recharging period required before we could send more."

"And what exactly are they going to do when they get there?" Professor Umbra challenged.

"They are going to level the place," the Emperor jumped in, aiming a piercing stare in the Professor's direction. "They are going to do what the Marans have been trying to do to us for the last twenty years."

The Professor stood to meet the Emperor's gaze. "We can't just wipe out another civilization," he objected. "Surely, we're better than that."

"Really, Professor Umbra," the Emperor countered. "You, of all people, should welcome this plan. The Marans killed your wife, didn't they?"

Orin could see his father was too angry to reply. He feared that the next words out of his mouth would be his last if he continued to anger the Emperor like this. When his father finally did speak, his words were measured, his voice soft and controlled.

"They won't do it."

"Who won't do what?" the Emperor seethed, his rage barely contained.

"The Mechs. They won't just kill innocent people."

"They are machines!" the Emperor thundered as he pounded his fists on the desk. "They will do whatever we tell them to do!"

"They won't," the Professor replied calmly. "Do you really think I would build something with that much destructive power and not give it the ability to tell right from wrong?"

"They don't need to!" the Emperor screamed. "I know the difference between right and wrong!"

"Do you?"

The Emperor stared at the defiant man facing him for nearly a full minute, his face flushed with anger. He sat back down behind the desk, obviously attempting to reclaim his composure. When he finally replied, his voice was steady and commanding.

"Professor Umbra. Your team's recent contributions to the people of this world have bought you some leeway here, but that does not give you the right to commit treason. This is what is going to happen. You will find whatever it is that is giving these machines a conscience and you will turn it off. You will then get them to attack Mara and bring those people to their knees so that they can bow before me. Do you understand?"

Before the Professor could reply, General Zatari jumped to his feet. "Of course, your Excellency," the General offered. "We will begin planning the assault immediately."

"Good answer," the Emperor replied smugly. "Now leave me. You have a great deal of work to do."

Two royal guardsmen appeared from the back of the room and escorted Orin, the General and the two professors out of the room. Orin felt sick. The whole exchange between his father and the Emperor had been terrifying. He was grateful that the General jumped in to save his dad, but agreeing to plan an attack on Mara? Was that really what they were going to do? The whole thing left him feeling hollow inside. Throughout the entire meeting he had an uneasy feeling, like the whole world was watching the evil plans unfold. His paranoia ran so deep, that at one point, he actually thought he sensed something moving up in the rafters.

9

Juna took in a deep breath and exhaled slowly. She looked at her hands. Still shaking. Closing her eyes and trying to focus, she drew in another couple of breaths. If she wasn't able to calm down, she was going to get herself killed.

When Juna had heard that the team from The Depot was coming for a meeting this morning, she just knew she had to be there. Sneaking through the rafters in the light of day was risky, but she had to try it anyway. Getting up with the sun, she zipped up to her quiet place and slipped into her shadow suit. The trip through the rafters to her father's office took longer than usual. Several times during her journey, she was forced to stop and wait for the hallways below her to clear of people. She finally arrived at her destination just as her father was making introductions.

It was nice to see Orin again, even if it was from thirty feet in the air. The emotion she'd felt when she saw him on parade day surprised her. They had really only spent that one week together when they were kids, but seeing him again, made her realize that she missed him. The fact that the two of them had managed to thwart her father's plan and save the planet from an alien invasion certainly added to the emotion of the day. It didn't hurt that he turned out kinda cute too.

As the meeting below her progressed, she was gripped by an uncontrollable sense of fear. She could almost feel the heat of her father's rage from up in the rafters. At one point, she was afraid for Professor Umbra's life. Had General Zatari not jumped in and calmed the situation, the outcome may have been disastrous. An overwhelming sense of relief washed over her when everyone was excused and allowed to leave the office unharmed.

After the meeting was over, Juna decided to stick around a little longer to see what else she could learn. The amazing technology that Professor Oletta had developed was a huge surprise and the idea that there was an actual attack on Mara being planned was completely unbelievable. Was her father really considering taking over their planet and making them his subjects? How was that going to work? Most importantly, she needed to know how all this fit in with his master plan.

The Emperor, Colonel Pavic and Jakol began discussing the results of the meeting. They were all very concerned about the reactions of Professor Umbra and were worried that he may not cooperate when it came time to attack Mara. They didn't trust General Zatari either. Worried that one of them might need to be replaced to successfully execute their plan, they started considering other possible options.

At one point in the discussion, her father made a statement that made Juna's heart stop. At first, she thought she must have misheard or simply misunderstood what was said. As the men below her continued their conversation, she realized that she had heard perfectly well and there was no room for misunderstanding. Her mind was simply unable to process what was being discussed. How was this even possible? That's when the shaking started. She had to get out of there.

Somehow, she managed to start moving and get herself away from her father's office. Her brain was trying to make sense of this new information, but the more she thought about it, the more she struggled to maintain her composure. Her foot slipped off a beam and she had to catch herself to stop from plummeting to the ground. Hanging from a beam with both arms, her feet were dangling over the floor thirty feet below. Using all her remaining strength, she managed to pull herself back onto the beam. That was close. Too close.

So now, here she was, sitting in the rafters, paralyzed by fear, trying to get herself to calm down. All she needed was a plan. She must talk to General Zatari. Mister Feathers wasn't going to be good enough this time – she needed to get to The Depot. Taking one more deep breath, she checked her hands. Steady. She could do this. Releasing her grip on the rafter, she started moving again.

It took over an hour, but she finally made it back to her quiet place. She changed back into her clothes, but this time she threw her shadow suit onto her mattress thirty feet below, thinking she may need to take it with her. Swinging through her obstacle course, she dropped to the bedroom floor with an urgency unlike anything she had ever felt before. The need to keep moving was overwhelming.

Her first stop was Mister Stotz's office. Knocking on his door, she crossed her fingers, hoping he wouldn't be there. Fortunately, there was no answer so she slipped inside and closed the door behind her. Juna knew that Mister Stotz kept a box full of coins in the bottom drawer of his desk. Opening the drawer, she lifted the lid of the box and peered inside.

Juna didn't know very much about money. Her life of privilege meant that people would just bring her anything that she needed whenever she needed it. Realizing that she had never actually purchased anything before and had no idea how many coins might be required, she grabbed a handful and slipped them into one of the drawstring bags lying in the bottom of the drawer. Cinching it up tight so it wouldn't rattle, she tucked it into her pocket. Closing up the money box and sliding the drawer shut, she quietly left the office.

By the time she got back to her room, Pom was there waiting for her. "And where have you been my dear princess," Pom said, a playful smile on her face. "Skulking about the palace again?"

"Pom, I have to leave."

"Juna, what is it?" her smile now replaced with a look of concern.

"I can't tell you. I just have to go. Cover for me as best you can, OK? I'll get back as soon as I can."

Both girls knew what this meant. A personal servant's primary responsibility was the safety and well-being of their Elite. If anything were to happen to Juna, Pom would be held personally responsible. Pom's life was likely at stake if Juna didn't get back before her absence was discovered.

"This must be important," Pom said, forcing her smile to return. "Fate of the world, that sort of thing?"

"I think it is," Juna replied, tears rolling down her cheeks. "Oh, Pom. I will do everything I can to get back for you."

"Don't you worry about me," Pom reassured her, trying her best to hide the fear she was feeling. "You go do what you need to do. I'll be fine."

Juna felt her best chance was wearing a disguise, so the girls exchanged clothes. Juna slipped on her shadow suit and then pulled Pom's clothing over top. It was a burlap tunic with a large "H" embroidered on the front, the same outfit that was worn by all the hods. She slipped her coin pouch into the pocket and turned to face Pom.

"I will come back," she said, the tears still flowing. "I love you."

"I love you too," Pom sobbed, somehow still maintaining her smile. "Just do me a favour. If you don't make it back and this does end up saving the world, make sure they spell my name right in the history books."

"Pom, it's three letters." They shared a laugh neither one of them felt.

Knowing if she didn't leave now, she wouldn't be able to leave at all, she gave Pom a hug and scampered up to the rafters. Nimbly moving from beam to beam, she started heading in the direction of the loading dock at the back of the building. When she got there, she dropped to the floor and darted out to the fence that surrounded the palace. The fence was over ten feet high, but she scaled it quickly and dropped to the ground on the other side. Racing across the plateau, staying low so she wouldn't be seen, she started making her way down the slopes of Mount Volaris.

It had been two hours since her hug with Pom when Juna finally arrived at the edge of the city. She was just beginning to grasp how ill-prepared she was for life in the real world. Somewhere along her journey, the realization hit her that she did not have an actual plan. Knowing that she needed to get to a highway that could take her to the desert was one thing – actually figuring out how to get there was another. Paying someone to drive her was not an option because hods weren't allowed to have money. And what if someone recognized her? She would be dragged back to the palace with no rational explanation as to why she had left in the first place. No. Stealing a car and driving herself to The Depot was the only reasonable alternative.

Juna didn't know how to drive. The gardener at the palace had let her drive the tractor a few times, so she understood the basics. There would be a couple of pedals on the floor, one to go and one to stop. There would also be a steering wheel she could use to get pointed in the right direction, but other than that, she had no idea. She wasn't overly concerned. When it came to driving, she was pretty sure the car did most of the work.

As she made her way through the city, she noticed a small delivery vehicle coming out of an alley. They were very common in Volara – she thought they were called tut somethings. It had three wheels; one in the front and two in the back. There was an open cab at the front with a platform for carrying things right behind it. That seemed to be the closest thing to the tractor she had driven, so she decided to get herself one of those. As she watched, another one emerged from the same alley. Perfect. This was the place to get one.

Juna set a simple trap. She placed a couple of garbage cans in the middle of the alley making it impossible to pass by without moving them. Then she hid behind a pile of pallets and waited for her target to arrive. It was only a minute before a vehicle came to a stop right beside her. Leaving the engine running, the driver got out of the cab to remove the obstruction. This was going to be a lot easier than she thought.

As soon as the driver got to the cans, Juna sprang out of her hiding spot and jumped into the cab. On the tractor, the go pedal was on the left, so she pressed that one to the floor as hard as she could. The engine roared. The vehicle didn't move. Looking up, she saw the driver staring at her, shaking his head. He finished moving the cans out of the way and calmly walked towards her, then pushed her out of the cab.

"Shove off hod," he yelled as he stepped into the cab. He then moved a small lever next to the steering wheel and drove away, leaving Juna to pick herself up and dust herself off.

Her first effort was a bit of a disappointment, but she was far from defeated. Moving that lever next to the steering wheel was likely all that was required to get the thing to go. Quickly resetting her trap, she returned to her hiding spot to prepare for the second attempt. The wait for the next passing truck was agonizing. All she could think about was Pom, anxiously awaiting her return.

Finally, another vehicle arrived. The driver got out to move the cans and Juna leapt out for another try. This time, she moved the lever next to the steering wheel before stomping on the go pedal. Juna was thrown back into her seat. The truck darted forward, heading straight for the driver. She yanked on the steering wheel to avoid the collision, but it swerved much further than she was expecting. The little vehicle scraped along the building, sending sparks flying and destroying a small mirror that had been attached to the side of the cab. She wasn't overly concerned. Already knowing what she looked like, the mirror seemed completely unnecessary.

Juna sped past the screaming driver and burst out onto the street. Horns were blaring as she veered aggressively to the right to avoid an oncoming truck. She immediately found herself at an intersection, where a turning car forced her onto the sidewalk, knocking over a garbage can and almost running over a couple of pedestrians. Everywhere she went, she was met with honking horns, raised voices and waving fists.

After a few more near collisions and random turns, Juna was starting to get the hang of it. Once the initial panic passed, she realized that she wasn't really going all that fast. Now knowing how far to turn the steering wheel and how hard to press on the go pedal, the whole thing was a breeze. She was going to do this. With a quick glance at the sun, she established her bearings. One more right turn should get her going in the right direction. As she made the turn and proceeded down the street, a man was standing in the middle of the road, arms raised, blocking her path. It was the driver. She was right back where she started.

Juna rolled to a stop, right at the opening to the same alley where the whole thing began. The driver walked up to her and stuck his head in the cab. "You are either the worst car thief ever or the dumbest hod on the planet."

"If those are my only two choices," she replied sheepishly, "I'll take the first one."

"You know, I'd be willing to forget this ever happened – just consider it a fun story to tell my kids, but you ruined my mirror. That's going to be expensive to fix, you know."

Juna reached into her pocket and pulled out her coin bag. She reached in and pulled out one of the larger gold ones. "Will this buy you a new mirror?" she said, holding it out to him.

The man took the coin and looked at it, his expression unreadable. "Yeah," he finally replied. "I could get a new mirror with this."

"Can we forget the whole thing then?" Juna asked, removing herself from the cab.

"Sure," he replied, replacing her in the driver's seat. "Let's forget all about it."

Watching the vehicle pull away, she struggled to fight back a feeling of hopelessness. This was a disaster! What was she going to do? Standing on the sidewalk, staring at the receding truck, she tried to come up with some scenario where total failure was not the only possible outcome. Her thoughts of despair were momentarily interrupted by the sound of laughter coming from the alley. Turning, she saw a young boy, maybe a couple of years younger than her, doubled-over, laughing so hard he was almost unable to breathe. She walked over to him.

"What are you laughing at?"

"I'm laughing at you," he finally managed. "I've been watching you all afternoon. Funniest thing I've ever seen. You know, you just gave that guy more money than he could make in a year."

He was dressed in torn clothes and looked like he hadn't bathed in a month. "What's your name?" she asked. "Where do you live?"

96

"Name's Skeet," he replied. "I live right here in this alley. I was going to move last week to be closer to the bakery, but I'm sure glad I didn't. This has been the best day I've had in ages."

"Are you a hod?"

"My parents were hods," he replied defiantly. "I'm just me. Where were you trying to go, anyway?"

"I need to get to The Depot."

The laughter returned. "You were trying to get to The Depot in a tut-tut. This keeps getting better and better. Hope you're not in a big hurry."

"Actually, I am in a big hurry," she answered, tears beginning to flow. "Can you help me?"

Skeet stopped laughing, noticing the obvious distress this young woman was in. "You got any of those coins left?"

Juna shook the coins into her hand and held it out to him. "I've got this."

Skeet reached out, selecting four coins one at a time. "Sure," he said. "I can get you to The Depot. Just wait here."

An hour later, Juna was still waiting. She felt like a fool. She had run out of the palace with no idea how to get to the General. She had tried to steal a car even though she didn't know how to drive. And now, she had given half her money to a street urchin who was probably still laughing about the stupid girl who had just handed him enough money to last him ten years. Thinking of Pom awaiting her return, she started to cry.

Moments later, she was startled by the sound of a horn. She looked up to see a delivery truck stopped at the entry to the alley. Skeet was at the wheel.

"Come on," he yelled. "We gotta go. I have to get this back in four hours."

It felt good to be moving again, but Juna was overcome with a feeling of sadness. Darkness had already fallen as they drove along the highway through the high desert. It was too late. There was no way she could ever make it back in time. Skeet looked so small behind the wheel of the large truck, but his driving was so much better than her effort had been. She felt like such a failure. With all of her training, she had felt so strong, but out here, away from the security of the Royal Palace, she felt weak and power-less. More than anything, she wanted to be home and know that Pom was going to be OK. She sat in her seat, quietly hoping that it would all be worth it.

Orin was sitting in his father's office, with his dad and the General. They were up late, trying to figure out what to do about the emperor's demands.

"Perhaps some sort of surgical strike that knocked out their warship factory would satisfy him," the General suggested.

"Even that would cost lives," the Professor replied. "Factories do have people in them."

"Maybe we can find a way to get the people out first," Orin added hopefully.

"Well, we have to do something," the General insisted. "If we don't, the Emperor will find someone else to do the job."

They sat quietly, hoping a solution would come to them, when they were interrupted by a soft knocking at the door. Balko was there, an apolo-getic look on his face.

"Sorry General, there's someone at the gate to see you," he said. "She claims to be a princess."

The General raised an eyebrow at the unexpected news. "Bring her here."

A few minutes later, Juna was ushered into the room. Orin noticed how tired she looked. She had obviously been crying. He wanted to run over and hug her.

"I needed to come to stop you from killing all those people on Mara," she announced as soon as she stepped into the room.

"We don't want to kill anyone," the General assured her. "We are just in the process of figuring out a way to clear any buildings that might get destroyed during an attack."

"Why don't you just make an announcement on a loudspeaker before you blow it up," Juna questioned.

"Princess, you simply do not understand," the Professor jumped in. "They are a completely different species. The odds of them understanding our language is a statistical impossibility."

Juna's temper flared. The stress of the day. Her fears for Pom's safety. It was just too much. She snapped.

"WOULD EVERYONE PLEASE STOP CALLING ME PRINCESS!"

It wasn't until she saw the expression on their faces that Juna realized she had spoken the words out loud, not just in her head like she had intended. As long as she had their attention, she decided to keep going.

"No Professor, you're the one that doesn't understand. They! Are! Us!"

The room went silent. Orin thought he saw a moment of recognition on the faces of his dad and the General – like a light turning on. He, however, had no idea what she was talking about.

"Juna, I don't understand. What do you mean?"

"Oh, don't you see?" she pleaded, her fury spent. "The Starchaser. It never crashed into the sun. It drifted through space until the crew finally found some horrible planet to live on. They've been there for generations. They don't want to exterminate us. They don't want to fill the streets with rivers of our blood. They just want to come home."

10

"Well, that explains a lot," the Professor said.

"It certainly does," echoed the General.

Orin, his father and the General were sitting around the Professor's desk, trying to process the information they had just received. Exhausted from recounting the story of her harrowing journey, Juna sat on the floor in the corner of the office, her head in her hands, obviously lost in thought.

"What do you mean, Dad?" Orin asked.

"Quite frankly, the war with the Marans never made any sense," he replied. "I love the Mechs and I worked as hard as I could to make them as powerful as possible, but they should never have been able to repel an invasion by a civilization capable of interplanetary space travel. The Marans are obviously more technologically advanced than we are. If they really wanted to wipe us out, they should have been able to do it without ever leaving orbit. The idea of sending down a fleet of remote-controlled drones to do the fighting always seemed ridiculous to me."

"Their tactics were all wrong too," the General added. "Landing their entire force on the only spot on the planet with any defensive capability? It never felt like they were at war with Cambria. It always felt more personal, like their aggression was focused solely on the emperor."

"It also explains why the emperor locked himself in a room with the Royal Interpreter whenever he talked to the Marans," the Professor noted. "That Mister Nardo is a liar and a fraud. There has never been a need for a translator because we speak the same language. The emperor couldn't let anyone know that, so he just made up the position of Royal Interpreter. The Royal Family has been keeping this secret for generations."

At that moment, Juna stood up and walked over to join them at the desk. Her look of despair now replaced by one of fierce determination.

"I've told you what you need to know," she told them. "Now, you figure out what to do about it. I have to go."

"You're leaving?" Orin blurted out, unable to hide his disappointment.

"Pom has been covering for me back at the palace. I have been gone so much longer than I should have been. If I don't get back to stop it, they *will* kill her."

With that, she turned on her heels and stormed out of the room. Orin didn't know what to do. He looked to his father for an answer. Nothing. He turned to the General. Nothing there either. He had to help her. Turning, he looked through the doorway she had just exited, drew in a determined breath and sprinted out of the room.

Juna was halfway across the assembly floor by the time he caught up to her. "Juna, what are you going to do?"

Coming to an immediate stop, she turned to face him. "I don't know, but I have to do something." She was trying to look strong, but Orin could see it was just an act. A small tear rolled down her cheek, but she steeled herself before a second one could appear. Wiping away the tear with the back of her hand, she turned and continued her walk towards the exit.

"Juna," Orin yelled after her. "You need a plan."

That stopped her in her tracks. The last time she leapt into action without a plan, it resulted in the horrible situation she now faced. Torn between moving forward or just giving up, she tried desperately to fight off the feeling of hopelessness that was threatening to consume her. Unable to stop it, she began to sob.

Orin rushed to her, taking her hand in his. "Juna, we need to stop and think about this," he said softly. "Where is Pom now?"

Juna closed her eyes and took a deep calming breath, attempting to regain her composure. Once settled, she squared her shoulders and looked Orin in the eyes. "By now, they have certainly discovered I am missing. They will have taken her to the prison in the basement of the palace."

"If you go back, can you get them to let her go?"

"No," she replied softly, her voice cracking. "No hod has ever been released from that place. They'll interrogate her and…" Unable to finish, she just stared at Orin, struggling to hold back the tears.

"We'll just break her out then," he said, projecting as much confidence as he could.

"You're kidding right," the look on her face, one of disbelief. "No one's even tried to break out of that place. Ever."

"And that's exactly why it's going to work. No one will expect it. We just need to think it through. We'll put it together one step at a time and come up with a plan." Orin had no idea how to break someone out of prison, but that didn't mean he couldn't figure it out. What was the point of being a genius if you couldn't even help a pretty girl try to save her friend? Deciding the first step was probably finding out what resources they had at their disposal, they went outside to see the truck and talk with Skeet.

"So, is she really a princess," Skeet asked Orin as soon as they arrived at the truck. "She told the guard at the gate that she was a princess."

"Yes, she really is," Orin acknowledged. "She told me you were very helpful in getting her here. Thank you for that."

"I'm not sure I would have helped if I knew she was related to the emperor," Skeet fired back. "He had my parents killed for no reason at all!"

"No one hates that man more than me!" Juna shouted. "There is nothing I won't do to stop him from hurting more people!"

"He's going to kill someone else," Orin told Skeet. "A hod named Pom will die if we don't get there in time to save her. Will you help us?"

Skeet stood quietly for a moment, staring at the ground, before finally replying. "Sure. I'll help. If it's something that will hurt the emperor, then I'm all in."

"Thank you for that. My name's Orin, by the way. I'm not quite sure what we're going to do, but the more people we have to help, the better. Let's have a look in the back of your truck. Maybe there's something in there we can use."

Juna and Skeet seemed a little disappointed as they stared into the cavernous space in the back of the empty truck, but Orin saw only opportunity. The start of a plan began to take shape, but he would need his father's help.

"You're going to do what?" the Professor demanded, springing out of his chair.

"We are going back to the palace to break Pom out of jail," Orin repeated. "We'll do it alone if we have to, but I would really like to take Rayzor with us."

Rayzor was the smallest and fastest of the Mechs. He was still over seven feet tall and weighed two tons, but by Mech standards, he was tiny. He was also able to fold himself into a cube shape, disguising himself as a non-descript piece of electrical equipment. Not exactly stealthy, but for a Mech, he was as close as you could get.

"Absolutely not!" the Professor snapped, jabbing a finger in Orin's direction. "General, tell them how crazy this is."

The General stood up and walked over to face Juna. She held his gaze, strong and steady. "We owe her everything, Darin," he said, his focus never leaving Juna's eyes.

"Go save your friend."

As Orin and Juna turned to leave, the General cautioned them. "Orin, it would be best if The Depot's involvement in this remains a secret. Try to keep Rayzor hidden and do try not to get caught."

"I'll do my best," Orin promised. Then he and Juna ran out of the room.

"Are you crazy?" the Professor yelled at the General. "They're just kids. Orin has no idea how to do this sort of thing."

"Now, don't you worry about Orin, Professor. She'll look after him," he replied with a smile. "I know a soldier when I see one."

They were back at the truck with Skeet, watching Rayzor fold himself into the back, when an idea popped into Orin's head. "I have to get Diara working on something," Orin told them as he darted off. "I'll be right back."

Ten minutes later, Orin had returned and they were all crammed into the cab of the truck, Skeet at the wheel, heading for the palace. There was a strange sense of optimism in the air. Orin had convinced them that a bunch of overconfident guards wouldn't even recognize a prison break was happening until it was too late. Maybe he was right – they would find out soon enough. Arriving at the base of Mount Volaris, he checked his watch, figuring it was about two hours before sunrise. They would need to hurry.

A half-hour later, they had all scaled the palace fence, with a helping hand from Rayzor, and were now hiding in a hedge outside the jail. Their current challenge was trying to get past the guard at the entrance.

"Maybe, if we ask nicely, he will just let us pass," Rayzor offered.

"Funny," Orin replied. "I didn't think you Solars had a sense of humour."

"It is not encouraged," Rayzor noted. "Don't tell Sol."

Orin was leaning on a large rock when the idea came to him. He instructed Rayzor to pick up the rock and toss it as far as he could past the edge of the building. Rayzor easily flung the boulder two hundred feet, crashing it into a wall around the corner. The guard heard the noise and went to investigate. As soon as he rounded the corner, the group sprinted towards the now unguarded door. It was locked. Rayzor and Skeet squeezed into the entryway to figure out how to open it, while Orin and Juna stood back to give them room to work.

"Hey, what are you doing here?" It was the guard returning from his diversion around the corner.

Orin froze. He didn't know what to do. Looking at the approaching guard, he couldn't think of a single thing to say. "I... uh..." Turning to Juna, he hoped she might be able to come up with something. She was gone. What was he going to do now? Rayzor had folded himself up in the entryway and Skeet was probably hiding in there with him. Orin felt completely alone.

"I said, what are you doing here?" the guard repeated. He was an intimidating figure, dressed all in black and wearing a helmet with a visor that obscured his face.

Orin was paralyzed. He was trying to say something, anything, but before he could utter a sound, there was a blur of motion coming from his right. It was so fast he barely saw it happen. Juna appeared out of nowhere. Her leg swung up high, hitting the guard in the side of the head. As his arm came up in a delayed attempt to block the kick, she grabbed it, swung it over her shoulder and flipped him over her body, slamming his back to the ground with a dull thud. The whole thing seemed to be over in less than a second.

Orin just stood there, his mouth hanging open. If he was supposed to be the brains of this operation, it just became apparent who was providing the brawn. "Where did you learn to do that?" Orin asked incredulously.

"Princess school!" she snapped. "Now, help me get him out of the way."

As Orin helped Juna drag the unconscious guard out of the way, he smiled as the next phase of the plan popped into his head. Stripping off the guard's jacket, he pulled it on himself and secured all the buttons. Next, he donned the helmet, dropped the visor over his face and turned to Juna.

"You're under arrest," he said to her. "I'm afraid I have to take you to prison."

Juna smiled for the first time all day. She held out her hands in mock surrender. "If you must."

Skeet wasn't having any success with the lock, so Orin instructed Rayzor to tear the door off as quietly as he could. Juna messed up her hair and smeared a little dirt on her face hoping to disguise her royal features. Then she led the way down the stairs, still wearing Pom's tunic, her hands held behind her back. Orin was right behind her, pushing gently at her shoulder. When they reached the bottom of the stairs, they met another guard sitting at a desk. Orin ushered Juna forward until she was facing the guard.

"I've got another one for you," Orin said, trying hard to imitate Dorel, but fearing it came out sounding more like Annu.

The guard stood. "Busy night, I guess. Hey, who are you anyway? You don't sound…"

Boom! Before he could finish his sentence, Juna unleashed a sweeping kick to the side of his head, dropping him to the floor like a sack of flour. As soon as he hit the ground, she rushed to the back to search the holding cells for Pom.

Orin wanted the scene to appear as if the prison had been overrun by an angry mob, so he called for Rayzor to join him downstairs. "We want it to look like there was a scuffle down here," he told the machine. "Why don't you mess the place up a bit?"

Mechs couldn't smile, but Orin knew Rayzor would be wearing one now if he could. "Carnage will be so jealous when I tell him about this," Rayzor said with glee as he flipped over the guard's desk.

Orin searched the office for keys to the cells, finally finding them on a peg on the back wall. He rushed back to join Juna, where he found her at the very back, holding hands with someone through the bars of one of the cells. Fumbling with the keys, he finally managed to get the door open.

The two girls embraced like they would never let go of each other again. Orin felt bad about breaking up their happy reunion, but he knew their mission was not done yet. Daylight was coming, so they needed to keep moving. Just as he was about to interrupt them, a voice came from down the hall.

"Hey, is this some sort of escape?"

Orin felt a wave of panic wash over him. He spun, expecting to see another guard, but the hallway was clear.

"Cause if it is, I sure would like to come along."

Orin realized that the voice was coming from one of the cells. He walked up to the bars, as Juna and Pom stepped over to join him. Inside, was the largest person he had ever seen. He looked to be only a couple of years older than Orin, but was already bigger than Dorel. His head was shaved and he wore a hod's tunic that could have fit Rayzor.

"I see you got some keys there," the giant said, pointing at Orin's hand. "You think one of them might open this thing up?"

"I don't know if I should let you out," Orin replied cautiously. "Did you do anything really bad?"

"What? Me? No. I'm as gentle as a kitten. I was just chattin' with my friends about the emperor yesterday. I may have used a couple of bad words. Next thing I know, fifteen guys with clubs are draggin' me in here."

Orin smiled at the enormous young man. "Bad words about the emperor?" Orin said as he found the key and opened the door to the cell. "You'll fit in just fine with this group. Just be quick. We're in a bit of a hurry."

"Thanks, little man. Name's Taz, by the way. No problem with the hurryin'. I'm pretty light on my feet for a big guy."

The four of them sprinted down the hallway and into the office. They were met there by Skeet, who had just rushed down the stairs. "We got trouble," Skeet exclaimed. "Another guard just found that guy the princess laid out. I think he ran off to get help."

Everyone charged up the stairs, Rayzor leading the way. Just as they emerged from the door to the prison, the sound of alarm bells filled the air. They all dove into the hedge that had concealed them earlier. Within moments, they could see the movement of guards as they took up positions along the fence surrounding the palace. They were trapped. Not knowing what their next move should be, they crouched in silence, trying to think of a plan.

Juna turned to Orin. "I'm leaving. I'm going to draw them away."

"What? Again? No! There has to be another way," he pleaded. "Rayzor could tear through these guys in seconds. We could make a break for it."

Juna gently placed her hands on Orin's cheeks and forced him to look into her eyes. She spoke softly and calmly. "No, Orin. This is the only way. You heard what the General said. They can't find out that a Mech helped with this. I'll be OK. They will kill any of you if they catch you, but they won't hurt me. You need to get everyone away from here. You need to make them safe. It's the only thing that matters. Do you understand?"

Orin spun his head to escape Juna's touch. No. There had to be another way. He looked to Pom, his eyes begging her to help him. He looked back to Juna, but she was already gone. Looking through the hedge, he saw her running towards the closest guard. She shoved him hard against the fence, then darted off towards the palace. The guard gave chase, yelling for the others to join him. Soon, every guard was running off in pursuit of Juna. Their way was clear.

Orin knew he must make sure that Juna's sacrifice meant something. "Let's go!" he ordered. Rayzor led the way towards the fence, then launched each one of them over the top as they arrived. With the last of them on the other side, Rayzor hurdled the fence easily and followed them across the field and down the mountain.

Orin saw the train station in the distance, so he began moving the group towards the tracks. They followed the rails in silence, heading in the direction of The Depot. When they were a mile past the station, he saw the outline of a large object straddling the tracks. Scarab. Right where he knew she would be. Orin had asked Diara to install a Stealth Mode upgrade in Scarab and send her out to meet them here. The upgrade would limit her power and reduce her maximum speed, but it would allow her to run completely silent.

"It's good to see you, Orin," she said, as everyone climbed into her cargo hold. "Was the mission a success?"

Orin looked at the group climbing aboard, pained by the fact they were one member short. "Not entirely," he finally replied.

The mood was subdued as they made their way back to The Depot. Scarab's hold was huge, but somehow Rayzor and Taz seemed to fill half of it. Pom was sobbing quietly in the corner, Skeet holding her hand. Taz finally broke the silence.

"So that was the princess, huh? She seemed really nice. Too bad her dad is such a jerk." That lightened the mood a bit, but everyone remained quiet for the duration of the trip.

When they arrived at The Depot, they disembarked and filed into the assembly building, where the whole team was there to greet them. The Professor rushed over to give Orin a hug. The General walked over to join them so he could get a recap of the mission. Orin told them everything that had happened, from tricking the guard to Juna's heroic dash that allowed them to escape. Afterwards, the General clasped his shoulder and told him he had done an excellent job.

"And don't you worry about that princess of yours," he added. "That girl knows what she's doing. She'll be fine." Orin could only hope he was right.

The new additions to the group seemed to be fitting in nicely. Everyone was milling about, making introductions. At one point, Pom offered to make everyone tea.

"No!"

It was the General, looking as intense as Orin had ever seen him. He had no idea the General disliked tea so much.

"She will not serve us," the General continued. "There are no hods here. In this place, we are all just people."

"But General," Pom replied softly, "it's all I know."

"I'll train her," Diara blurted out as she jumped up and walked over to face Pom. "She seems pretty sharp. I think she'll make a great Tech."

Pom had no idea what a Tech was, but she smiled back at her new teacher anyway. Then Dorel spoke up. "As long as we're talking about train-ees, what are the odds of me getting the big guy over there to join up with the Wrenches." That got everyone laughing. Orin thought how nice it was to be home again, to be back amongst his friends. His family, really. One person was missing though. He just hoped she was going to be alright.

11

Juna was walking through the halls of the Royal Palace heading for the aviary. It was a trip she had made more than a dozen times over the past two days. Time seemed to be moving so slowly. It was hard for her to believe that only two days had passed since her adventures at the prison.

When she leapt through that hedge, her only thoughts were of getting the guards away so that Pom and the others could escape. After she shoved the guard and sprinted for the palace, everything was a blur. From the sound of all the guards yelling and chasing after her, she knew that she had been, at least, partially successful in drawing them away from the fence. Maybe it was enough. She hoped so – there was nothing more she could do about it at that point.

Avoiding capture proved easy enough. In the middle of the pursuit, she threw off Pom's tunic, leaving her only in her shadow suit. Hiding in corners, doubling back a few times and keeping to the shadows allowed her to stay one step ahead of the guards through the entire chase. Before long, they lost track of her and abandoned their search. When everything was clear, she made her way to the clearing outside her bedroom and scampered up a drainpipe, slipping through the bedroom window into her quiet place. There was nothing more she could do after that but get into her nightgown and lay on the bed to await her fate.

The sun was just rising, so trying to sleep was not an option. She spent the time looking around her room, preparing herself for the inevitable encounter with her father. It was good to be back. The whole family had stayed in Alderae for an extra week after the war, so by the time they got back, all her things had been returned to the palace. It really felt like home again. Her big question was whether all of the explosives had been removed from the walls. She made herself believe that they were – it made it easier to sleep that way.

It wasn't long before there was a rap on the door and Mister Stotz walked into the room. "Ah, the wayward princess has returned," he said, not even trying to hide his contempt.

"Where's Pom?" Juna demanded.

"It is not my place to say, Princess," he replied. "Now, get yourself together. I believe your father wants to have a word with you."

Sitting in her father's office, Juna silently rehearsed everything she would say to him when he arrived. As soon as he stepped through the door, she was on her feet.

"Where's Pom?" she demanded again.

The Emperor hesitated. He seemed pleased that his daughter did not know the whereabouts of her friend. "We will get to that in a minute," he finally replied. "First, I would like to know what you were up to yesterday."

Juna began to spin her tale. She had met a boy. He was a shopkeeper's son from the city. She had been sneaking out to see him for the past two months, thinking she was in love. But yesterday, something had gone terribly wrong. He didn't want to see her again. It was over. Paralyzed by sorrow and unable to move, she just sat there crying, not realizing how late it was until darkness had fallen.

Her performance was magnificent. There were tears, sobs and well-timed pauses where she was unable to speak. At one point, her father became so moved by the story of his jilted daughter that he offered to have the imaginary boy killed to defend her honour. Juna assured him that this would not be necessary. She just wanted to forget about it and put the whole episode behind her. At the conclusion of her story, she stared at her father, tears streaming down her face.

"Just tell me what has happened to Pom," she begged, her voice a whisper.

"I'm afraid the news is not good," he replied without emotion. "There was an unsuccessful escape attempt at the prison yesterday. We believe the instigator was another hod being held there, but Pom was caught up in it. All of the prisoners involved were killed."

Juna collapsed to the floor as sobs wracked her body. Part of it was for show, but not knowing if Pom was really safe made the tears flow easily. She hoped that it was her father's pride that would not allow him to admit that the escape had been successful, but she just didn't know. The fact that he hadn't mentioned Orin or a Mech running loose was a good sign.

The Emperor interrupted her grieving with a terse warning. "Let this be a life lesson for you, Juna. Breaking the rules has consequences. Your irresponsibility cost that girl her life. I trust you will be more thoughtful in the future. Leave me now. I have much to do and I imagine you have a great deal to think about yourself. I will have a new servant assigned to you by the end of the week."

Juna pulled herself together and left her father's office, making her way straight to the aviary. Once there, she composed a short note:

Safe. I'm going to be OK. J.

Rolling it up and sliding it into Mister Feathers' tube, she sent him on his way. There was nothing more she could do but wait.

Thinking back on it now, Juna realized how lucky she had been. There were so many things that could have gone wrong along the way. But somehow, she got her message to the General and broke Pom out of jail without her father suspecting that she was involved in any way. If she could just get word that the others were safe, she could clear her mind and get back to the business of stopping her father's horrible plans.

Juna stood at the door to the aviary, steeling herself to the likelihood of another wasted trip. She swung the door open and stepped inside. Her heart skipped when she saw Mister Feathers at the entrance. Rushing over and retrieving the note, she felt the weight of the world lifted from her shoulders as she read it.

All safe but miss you terribly. P. O. S. T.

Pom. Orin. Skeet. Taz. All safe. Juna began to weep, the sense of relief too powerful to contain. Then suddenly, she felt her strength return in a rush. All her friends were going to be OK. What mattered now was stopping her father so she could see them again. It was time to get back to work.

Once again, the assembly floor was bustling with activity. Preparations were underway for the attack on Mara so everyone had a job to do. Orin went about his daily tasks, but his heart wasn't in it. The true identity of the Marans was a powerful source of conflict for him. For years, he had wanted nothing more than to see them all destroyed, but now, he wasn't so sure. They had brought a great deal of suffering to the people of Cambria, but in a way, this was their home too. It was all so confusing. For now, he was just happy to have something to do, so he didn't have to think about it too much.

It had now been two weeks since he and Juna orchestrated the escape from the prison. The first day back was miserable. Knowing his mission had been a failure by leaving her behind, left him sick with worry. When he returned to his room at the end of the day and saw Mister Feathers sitting on the windowsill, a feeling of hope surged through him. He was overjoyed after reading the note saying she was safe, causing him to pause for a moment to steady his hands so he could write the response.

Orin missed her badly and was disappointed she couldn't be here after risking everything to save them, but knowing she was going to be alright gave him the strength to carry on. Going about his work, he looked forward to the day he would see her again. Right now, he was on his way to his father's office, having received word that his dad had lined up another "special project" for him. As always, he hoped for something good, but was careful to keep his expectations low.

As he crossed the assembly floor, Orin noted the progress being made on the highest priority project currently underway at The Depot. Massive trailers were being built to transport each of the four Mechs that would be used for the attack on Mara. The assault would not be originating from The Depot. The equipment required for creating the space portal was located at a place called The Institute. It was a fair distance away, where the northern edge of the city met the high desert, making it a three-day walk for the bigger Mechs. The plan was to travel by train as far as they could and then use the new trailers to go the rest of the way.

Orin spotted Taz working with a crew that was welding axles onto one of the trailers. He waved. Taz returned the wave and started walking towards him. Taz had adjusted to life at The Depot almost immediately. He loved it here and everyone here loved him. His tunic was now abandoned, replaced with one of Dorel's old pair of overalls. Someone had torn off the sleeves and let out some of the seams, so it kind of fit him. As he approached,

Orin noticed that the name patch had been removed and "Taz" had been written on it with a felt pen.

"Hey, little man. How ya doin'?"

"Great, Taz. How about you?"

"Couldn't be better. This place is awesome. I still work like a daggit all day, but somehow it feels different without that stupid 'H' on my shirt. Thanks for bringin' me here."

"It was my pleasure. All of us are glad you're on the team."

"People here treat me like a real person," Taz said, a look of pride in his eyes. "And they're actually givin' me money for doin' all this stuff. I gotta say, my life's never been better."

"That's how it should be. Like the General said, there are no hods here – we're all just people."

Taz gave him a beaming smile and a light pat on the back that almost knocked the wind out of him. "I better get back to it, little man. They're not payin' me to stand around yakkin'."

Orin smiled as Taz walked away. Seeing how happy a former hod was here at The Depot, gave him so much hope for the future. He surprised himself by wondering if maybe, someday, there could even be people from Mara working side-by-side with them here. That thought reminded him that his father was waiting to give him his next assignment. Turning, he continued on his way.

The Professor was alone in his office when Orin arrived. He gave his son a loving smile. "Ah, Orin. Just in time. I've got something important I need done and I'm hoping you're just the guy to do it. We need a Tech Station installed at The Institute so we can communicate with the Mechs during the assault. I would like you to head up the project to get that done."

Wow. It actually was something good this time. "Sure Dad. That sounds great."

"Pick your own team, but you'll need to do it quickly," the Professor urged. "The General wants it ready to go in two days."

"Thanks Dad, I'll get right on it," he replied as he turned to go. "You can count on me."

Orin knew there was little time to waste, but he wanted to check in on Skeet before he got started. He felt bad for Skeet. There was no one his age at The Depot, so Orin worried that he may struggle to fit in. The boy was really smart and eager to help, so Orin knew that he would eventually find his place here, but right now, he worried he might be feeling a little lonely. Orin knew he was currently in the fabrication shop helping the Atomics weld couplers for the new trailers.

As he neared the door to the fab shop, Orin heard the sound of laughter coming from the room. From the doorway, he watched as Skeet and Isotope worked on one of the couplers, laughing and joking with one another.

"How are things going?" Orin called out to them.

Skeet looked up, surprised by the interruption. "Oh, hey Orin. It's going great. I was just telling Isotope what my life was like before I came here."

"This young man has certainly had many adventures for someone so young," Isotope added. "I'm afraid he might find life at The Depot quite dull."

"Oh, I'll be fine Iz," Skeet jumped in. "I'm liking it here more and more everyday. I mean, I do miss sleeping in a cardboard box every night, but I'll get over it."

That got them laughing again. Orin couldn't help but chuckle along with them. Only moments ago, he was worried about his young friend being lonely, but now he realized everything was going to be fine. No one knew better than him how wonderful it was to have a Mech as a best friend.

"Well, I'll leave you guys to your work," Orin said, as he turned to go. "I can't wait to hear about some of those adventures, Skeet."

Orin's next stop was to go see Diara. He knew that he needed a Tech on his team and, despite her youth, she was one of the best. When he arrived at her station, she was there with Pom, pointing at something on the monitor. The two girls had been inseparable since Pom arrived at The Depot and, by all accounts, Pom's training was going very well. Hods were not allowed to read, but Pom was an exception. Apparently, Juna had rushed back to her room after every school lesson to teach her friend everything she had learned, meaning Pom had more education than any other hod on the planet.

As soon as Orin told Diara about the project, she jumped at the chance to join the team. "I'll make a list of everything we need," she offered. "It'll be ready by the end of the day."

"Who else will we need?" Orin asked her.

"Well, with you and me, we already have all the young technical geniuses we need," she replied with a smile. "I'd say, one Wrench and a little muscle should do it."

The second Orin heard that a Wrench would be required on the team, he knew he wanted Annu to join. They had grown close during their time together on Team Steam, so he was really looking forward to working with her again. He considered Taz for the muscle, but ultimately decided on Rayzor. Taz was a very memorable figure, so he didn't want to risk him being recognized away from The Depot. He also thought Rayzor might take up less space in a cargo hold. Orin finished filling out the team by recruiting Tortuga to help with transporting everything to The Institute. By the end of the next day, the team had collected every item on Diara's list and had it loaded into Tortuga's massive cargo hold. They would be ready to leave first thing in the morning.

The sun was just starting to show on the horizon as the group was preparing to start out. Orin was not necessarily looking forward to the trip. When he selected Tortuga for this assignment, he realized there was a downside and knew he was about to pay for it now. Tortuga was basically a massive shell mounted on six enormous rubber tires. Despite his size, he had the heart of a race car – he loved to go fast. He was also built for off-roading, so they would be able to completely avoid the roads by travelling across the sands of the high desert. The trip would be quicker that way, but not very pleasant.

"Strap yourselves in tight," Tortuga informed them as they boarded, his excitement evident. "This might get a little bumpy."

The walls of the hold were lined with heavily padded seats equipped with sturdy safety harnesses. Orin, Diara and Annu each took a seat and pulled the straps of their harnesses as tight as they would go. Rayzor clamped himself securely to one of Tortuga's internal struts, well aware of his reputation for speed. "Wake me when it's over," he said, just before dropping into wait state.

The trip was everything Orin expected. They seemed to be at full speed in the first ten seconds and didn't slow down once. They bounced, swayed and swerved with Tortuga letting out a whoop every time he was airborne. By the time they rolled to a stop at the gates of The Institute, each passenger looked a little green. Orin descended Tortuga's loading ramp, on shaky legs, and went to talk to the guards at the gate.

Their arrival was expected, so they were granted access right away. Annu, Diara and Rayzor were now back on solid ground, so they all walked together the rest of the way. The Institute consisted of a small brick building in the front attached to an enormous white dome in the back. Tortuga was directed to enter the dome through a large access door on the side, so they all walked through with him, casually chatting about the trip behind them and all the work that lay ahead.

Upon rounding the corner and entering the cavernous building, all conversation abruptly ended as the sight before them shocked the group into a stunned silence. The space was dominated by a gigantic ring, sitting upright on its edge. It appeared to be made of a dull black metal and was at least fifty feet across. A complex pattern of grooves and ridges were etched across its surface, like it was inscribed with words from an alien language. Rectangular lights of blue and green lined its edge, bathing the entire room in a spooky turquoise glow. The massive object seemed to pull you towards it, like it possessed its own gravitational field. It was the most impressive structure any of them had ever seen. They all just stood there, mouths gaping, staring at the thing.

"We call it the Gate."

Startled, they turned to see Professor Oletta standing beside them. "You can set up over there," she said coolly, pointing to an open area at the back of the room that would give them an unobstructed view of the ring structure. "You'll see a port marked 'Comms'. Just connect to that and you should be good to go." With that, she turned and walked away, leaving them to their work.

They all stood there, just looking at each other, taken aback by the abrupt nature of their discussion with the professor.

"I can't really say I found that woman to be particularly friendly," Annu joked, breaking them from their trance.

"Well, I guess that's all the help we're going to get," Orin said with a shrug. "Let's get to work."

It took most of the day to unload Tortuga and get the new Tech station set up. When they were done, Diara ran a series of diagnostics to confirm everything was working properly. No one from The Institute had any interaction with them throughout the day, so they saw no need to say goodbye.

Packing up their tools, they boarded Tortuga and began the return trip to The Depot.

After passing through the gate, Tortuga headed straight for the desert sand. "Without all that equipment on board, we should be able to get up to full speed this time," Tortuga announced with glee. "I'll have you home in no time." Everyone groaned and gave their harness a final tug to prepare for the excruciating journey ahead.

The sun had set by the time they got back to The Depot. Orin thanked his friends for their help and went to check in with his dad to give him a report of how everything had gone at The Institute. The Professor agreed that the behaviour of the people there was curious, but he thought Orin and his team had done very well, telling him how proud he was. Despite the success of the project, Orin felt out of sorts. He needed time to think, so he wandered out to the hill. Taking his normal spot, he pointed himself to the east and stared at the stars.

Part of the reason for Orin's sombre mood was missing Juna, but it was much more than that. The planned attack on Mara had him troubled, as did the odd encounter with Professor Oletta. He was just trying to sort it all out when Gigahertz arrived and settled in beside him.

"Ah, Master Orin. I thought I might find you here."

"Hey Gig, what's up?"

"I am afraid you will need to be more specific. There are many things that meet that criteria: the sky, the moons, the stars…"

"Yeah, any of those is fine…Wait. What? Sorry, Gig. I wasn't really listening."

"You do seem distracted, Master Orin. May I ask what is bothering you?"

"It's this whole thing with the Marans, I guess. It was so much easier when they were a bunch of terrible beings that kept attacking us. I always thought of us as the good guys. Now, I'm not so sure. I asked you once why they hated us. Now I know the answer, but it doesn't help. In fact, it's made it even harder."

"I still think they may *not* hate us. They are angry we will not let them come home, but the way they fight tells us this anger is focused on the emperor. If the people of Cambria knew the truth, I'm sure every person here would welcome them home with open arms. The emperor may have evil intent, but that does not mean we all do. What is important, is who we are as a people, our very heart and soul. I think the Marans realize that."

"Maybe you're right, Gig. I just hope we don't mess it all up when *we* attack *them*."

12

It was happening today. Within the hour, a team would be making their way to The Institute to launch an attack on an alien world. To Orin, the whole situation seemed almost surreal. For years, everyone always thought of the war with the Marans from a defensive point-of-view – the Marans attack, Cambria defends. Going on the offensive and mounting an attack on Mara just felt wrong. It seemed like the whole world had been turned upside down.

The plan was set. After days of strategizing, arguing and compromising, the General and the Professor had finalized their course of action. Four Mechs would pass through the portal and find a building instrumental to the Maran war effort. They would ensure the building was cleared of any people and then level it to the ground. A visual recording would be taken so that proof of the devastation could be shown to the emperor, hopefully ending any need for future aggression.

The General hoped that this demonstration, combined with their overwhelming victory in the recent war, would persuade the Emperor that the Marans no longer posed any threat to the people of Cambria. The

Professor came up with the next part of the plan. He felt it was imperative to convince the Emperor that Mara was a prize not worth winning. They would bring back reports of a planet so barren, an environment so hostile, that there would be no reason to conquer it.

It was *not* a great plan and everybody knew it. The true motivations of the Emperor were completely unknown. Whether or not he could be convinced that an overwhelming invasion of the planet was not required, was something they would find out after it was all over. For now, all they could do was execute the attack, hope no one got hurt and see how everything played out in the end.

The whole team was at The Depot's train station preparing for the trip. Scarab was at the head of an eight-car train. The first four cars were reserved for the four Mechs involved in the attack and the last four cars each carried one of the new trailers that would carry them on the final leg of their journey. The four Mechs chosen for the assault were Gigahertz and the three Diesels: Carnage, Mayhem and Havoc. The General wanted Gigahertz there to provide leadership and rational decision-making. The Diesels were going because there was destruction required and they were really good at that sort of thing.

All of the Mechs were there to see them off. Torque was in a circle with the Diesels giving them a pep talk while Gigahertz walked amongst his friends, receiving words of encouragement. Clank walked up to Gigahertz and gave him a big metallic hug. Orin considered developing another software upgrade that might limit these public displays of affection, but decided against it. Seeing Gig return the embrace made Orin realize that Clank may have a few quirks, but he was perfect just the way he was. He only hoped the Diesels would be as accepting of Clank's affection as Gig had been.

The General arrived, flanked by the Professor and Diara, and they boarded Scarab to get ready for the trip. Each Mech took their place on the train while Orin jumped on with Gigahertz. Scarab's engine roared to life and they were on their way, rolling along the rails towards Volara. After an hour, they reached the edge of the city, where Scarab came to a stop. Each Mech disembarked, went to the back of the train and retrieved their trailer. Scarab dismounted the rails and the trailers were connected to her so they could continue the journey along the streets of Volara.

Orin chose to ride inside Scarab for the last half of the trip rather than outside with Gig. The streets were lined with people, cheering the procession as if they were heroes. Orin didn't feel like a hero. He felt like a bully, attacking people just because the Emperor told them to. He couldn't wait for this whole thing to be over.

It was midday when they finally rolled through the gates of The Institute. The entire group was escorted through the dome's side access door. Orin and Diara had tried to prepare them for the magnificence of the Gate, but everyone was astonished when they first saw it with their own eyes. Even Orin, seeing it for the second time, just stood there staring at the remarkable structure. Professor Oletta walked over to greet them.

"It's quite something, isn't it," she said, her pride obvious.

"It most certainly is," the Professor replied, unable to conceal his sense of awe. "When do we get to see it in action?"

"If you want to get to your station," she instructed, her voice now businesslike, "we can get started right away."

Orin and Diara led the General and Professor Umbra to the newly installed Tech Station as the four Mechs took their positions directly in front of the massive ring.

"I don't see Colonel Pavic or any of the emperor's men," the General commented. "That's probably a good thing. It will be easier to convince them how unpleasant Mara is if they're not here to see it for themselves."

"That wouldn't have been a problem anyway," Diara jumped in, sporting a devilish smile. "I installed filters in the camera feeds from the Mechs. When they're activated, they distort the images coming back. They should make the whole place look quite dreary."

"Excellent work," the Professor said as he nervously scanned the room. "We might be able to pull this off after all."

Diara busied herself getting the Tech Station powered up and bringing each of the Mechs' camera feeds online. They were soon looking at four views of the Gate on the four monitors installed on the station. She sat in the console's command chair with Orin, his father and the General standing in a semi-circle behind her. "We're ready to go here," she informed them.

Professor Oletta had finished talking with members of her team and was now walking towards the Tech Station at the back of the room. "We're all ready at our end," she told them. "Let's get this over with."

Just as she finished speaking, there was a deafening clunk and the lights in the building dimmed momentarily. The Gate came to life. The centre of the ring began to glow with a swirling pattern of ambers and yellows. It was absolutely beautiful. The room was filled with a low humming sound and Orin could feel a vibration through his feet that made his entire body buzz.

"It will take about five minutes for the portal to establish itself," Professor Oletta told them. "Once it's done, there will be a physical connection between this building and the surface of Mara. We chose a spot behind a small rise on the edge of the valley that holds the entire population of the planet. They should be completely unaware of your arrival."

After about five minutes, there was a sudden change. The humming stopped and the swirling pattern was replaced by an image of what appeared to be a small colourless hill. They all looked to Professor Oletta. "The portal is established. You may proceed with your attack."

"Gigahertz," the General commanded. "Take point. Let's see what's on the other side."

Gigahertz stepped forward cautiously. When he was directly in front of the Gate, he reached out his arm and tentatively touched the surface. A yellow glow appeared around the tip of his finger and a soft hum returned. A series of concentric circles rippled across the Gate like he had touched the surface of a large vertical pond. As he began to step through, the humming intensified and the building's lights dimmed noticeably. After he completed his passage through the Gate, the humming stopped and the building's lighting returned to its normal level.

Orin could hardly believe it – his friend was standing on another world. He could still see Gig through the Gate as he walked around on the surface of Mara, his movements slow and cautious. "I see no signs of the Marans," he reported. "I do not believe my presence here has been detected."

"Carnage," the General ordered. "Lead the rest of the team through."

As each Mech passed through the Gate, the humming returned and the lights dimmed. By the time Havoc finally crossed the barrier, the lights of the building dimmed so much, they were in almost total darkness. Just as he completed his passage, the lights returned to normal and the Gate appeared to shut down. There was another deafening clunk and the view through the ring showed nothing but the far side of the dome.

"What just happened!" Orin blurted out.

"The maximum capacity of the portal has been exceeded," Professor Oletta replied calmly. "The Gate now needs time to recharge. We can re-establish the portal in about thirty minutes."

Everyone refocused their attention on the Tech Station monitors. Everything seemed to be working fine. All four Mechs were now on Mara, surveying their surroundings.

"OK. Let's see what we're up against," the General said. "Gigahertz. Get the team to the top of the hill. We need to know what's on the other side." He then turned to the Professor and whispered in his ear. "Darin, I know you probably want to watch this, but it's important we control the information that gets back to the emperor. See if you can distract Professor Oletta. Try to get her away from this station."

He nodded at the General and slowly walked over to face his fellow professor, but before he could speak, she interrupted. "I have little interest in this," she began. "Call me when it's over and I will re-establish the portal so you can get your machines back." Then she turned and walked away.

Professor Umbra rejoined the group, giving the General a shrug and a thumbs-up. Everyone returned their attention to the monitors. The Mechs had reached the top of the hill, where they knelt down to peer over the rim and scan the valley below. It looked desolate. The sun was high overhead and huge in the sky, but it seemed to give off little warmth. What light there was had a red tinge, but no other colour could be seen. The whole landscape was gloomy greys with a hint of pink. Diara was right – everything did look quite dreary. Orin leaned in to whisper in her ear. "Good job. Your filters work great."

She turned to face him, a look of disbelief on her face. "I haven't turned them on yet."

Wow. Mara really was a terrible place. Orin checked the environmental data returning from Gig's sensors. The oxygen content in the air was quite low and the temperature was well below freezing. A strong wind whistled through the valley, coating everything with a thin layer of dirty snow. It was awful. He wondered how anyone could possibly live in a place like this. It was no wonder they were trying so hard to get back to Cambria.

There was no sign of people in the area, so the General instructed Gigahertz to stand up and move closer to the edge of the valley to give him a better view. Their target became immediately obvious. The building closest to Gig's current position was the largest one in the valley. It was, no doubt, a factory of some kind with smoke billowing from the multitude of stacks on the roof. Outside were piles of the frames, shells and tracks of unassembled SCUDs.

"That's the one," the General informed Gigahertz. "Clear it out and take it down."

The four Mechs marched down into the valley and made their way to the doomed building. Just as they were nearing the floor of the valley, an alarm started ringing on the Tech Station's console.

"Sensors are picking up activity around the west side of the building," Diara warned. "I think some trouble might be on the way."

Gigahertz turned to face the area just as a dozen SCUDs raced out to turn back the Mechs' attack. Before the General could even issue the order to fire, SIMs were being launched by all four Mechs. A couple of the SCUDs managed to fire a missile or two before they blew apart, but that was the extent of the counterattack. Each of the SCUDs was turned into a pile of scrap metal before they could inflict any damage on the invading force. The Mechs crouched and readied themselves for another wave of defenders, but it never came. It was obvious that the Marans had put everything they could into the attack on Cambria and had nothing left to defend their own planet.

Confident that no more SCUDs were on the way, Gigahertz calmly walked over to the main entrance of the ill-fated building and activated his loudspeaker. "The building you are currently occupying will soon be a pile of rubble," he boomed. "Please vacate it immediately."

Within seconds, alarms were blaring and people began streaming out of every door. Orin felt horrible watching it all unfold. Everyone looked cold and scared, wondering why this huge machine was threatening to tear their world apart. When it appeared everyone had left, Gigahertz issued a final warning. "This is your last chance. Ensure the building is clear. There will be no survivors." One last person emerged through the front door, hopping on one foot as he struggled to pull on his boot.

As soon as the last Maran cleared the area, the Diesels went to work. They began peeling away sections of the walls, exposing the building's metal frame. As each girder became visible, a Mech would clamp onto it and tear it from the ground. Soon, sections of the roof began to collapse as the walls that held it in place were torn apart. The Mechs moved from one end of the building to the other until the entire structure was reduced to a pile of twisted metal and broken glass.

Most of the workers that fled the building had collected a safe distance away to watch the devastation unfold. Gigahertz moved in their direction and reactivated his loudspeaker. "Cease your attacks on Cambria," he warned. "There is no place for you there." All of the Mechs then turned and began climbing the valley walls back to their starting point. The mood back at The Institute did not match the euphoric response to their victory over the Marans on Cambria. Everyone watched quietly, just wanting to get the whole thing over with.

"We're all done here," the General announced. "We'll need that portal back."

Professor Oletta seemed to appear from nowhere and was now standing beside them. "Reactivate the Gate," she ordered. "Let's get those things back where they belong." Then she turned to address the General. "Was the attack a success?"

"Success is difficult to define with something like this," he replied. "I believe we have eliminated the possibility of further attacks on Cambria."

Professor Oletta nodded, but provided no response. She just turned her back on the General and began walking away. She stopped for a moment and spoke without turning. "Your machines will return shortly. I'm sure you'll want to get them back to The Depot as soon as possible." With that said, she walked away.

Soon, the Gate was powered-up with the hypnotic swirling pattern, once again, filling the interior of the ring. Five minutes later, the scene was replaced by the image of the hill with the Mechs standing there awaiting their opportunity to return. Orin felt relieved as each Mech stepped through – first the Diesels and finally Gigahertz. Professor Oletta seemed quite anxious to have them gone, so the whole team filed out of the dome and rejoined Scarab for the return trip to The Depot.

The mission had been a complete success, but there was no celebration during the journey home. They all felt sick about what they had just done. All four of them were sitting in Scarab's hold, lost in their thoughts. Orin finally broke the silence. "What a horrible place. And we just made it worse. We have to find a way to help those people."

"There are people on our planet we need to help first," the General responded. "But I agree. We may need to alter our plans to include assisting the people of Mara."

Orin wasn't exactly sure what the General was talking about, but it made him feel better knowing he might consider helping the Marans. He wanted to ask more questions about the General's plan, but he felt Scarab roll to a stop and realized they were already home. By now, word of their victory had reached The Depot, but there was no hero's welcome waiting for them. He was glad for that. The last thing he felt like doing right now was celebrating.

The only person waiting for them at the station was a royal emissary demanding they appear before the emperor first thing in the morning.

It was now early the following day and everyone was exhausted. Orin, his father and the General were sitting across the desk from the Emperor as he watched the video of their assault on Mara. They had stayed up all night editing the video to exclude any details they didn't want him to see. Their attention was focused on the Emperor's face, trying to gauge his reactions, but his expression gave away nothing. When the video was over, he switched off the monitor and turned to face them.

"So, tell me," the Emperor began. "Did you actually see any Marans while you were there?"

"No, Your Highness," the General lied. "As you can see, Mara is a truly horrible place. The visibility was extremely limited."

"That's a shame. It would have been nice to know what the scoundrels actually look like. So, might I ask, what is the next phase in your plan?"

"I'm not sure a next phase is required, your Excellency," the General countered. "The Maran military has been decimated. They no longer possess the ability to wage war against Cambria. There really is no need to continue the attack against them."

"It is not your place to determine what is needed!" the Emperor bellowed. "Only I know what is best for the people of this planet!"

The room fell silent as the Emperor regained his composure. When he finally spoke again, his voice was calm and controlled. "The people running the Mech program have done a wonderful job protecting the people of Cambria. We are forever in your debt. However, times have changed. I believe new leadership may be required to fully realize the true potential of these wonderful machines."

The Emperor turned to face the Professor. "Professor Umbra. The time has come for Cambria to once again, fully embrace the fields of science and technology. I would like you to take a position at the university to prepare the next generation of Cambrians for this bold new path."

"But, Your Highness…"

"Enough!" the Emperor snapped. "The decision has already been made. I have ordered Colonel Pavic to deploy a company of royal guardsmen to The Depot. He is there now, securing the facility and taking command of all the resources there."

Orin was stunned. The Emperor was taking control of The Depot? What would happen to the Mechs? To his friends?

The Emperor trained his gaze on the General. "And what shall we do with you?"

"If I might make a suggestion, my liege," the General offered. "I have dedicated my life to protecting Cambria from the Maran threat. I believe that threat no longer exists. It might be a perfect time for me to retire. I've had my eye on a plot of land west of the city. I thought I might try my hand at farming."

The Emperor eyed the General suspiciously. "Alright General, or should I say Aldin. I suppose I owe you that much. Go buy your farm. Now, all of you go. You have new lives to plan."

Orin felt lost as they filed out of the emperor's office. They weren't returning to The Depot? What would happen to everyone there? Would he ever see Gig again? Tears were streaming down his face as they emerged from the palace. Suddenly, his sorrow turned to anger and he directed it at the General. "How could you just give up like that!" he screamed. "We've lost everything!"

"All is not lost yet, Orin," he replied calmly. "Agreeing to his terms was the only way I was leaving that room with my life. Don't worry, I haven't given up. I don't really see myself as much of a farmer. Now was not the time, but the emperor will be hearing from me again. Always remember, Orin – never pick a fight you can't win. It's better to plan for one that you can."

13

The wind whipped Juna's hair as she leaned into the curve, the accelerator pedal of her tri-racer pinned to the floor. The speed was exhilarating. She smiled to herself, thinking how different this was from her first attempt at driving. Looking to her right, she saw Gimbal, pushed back in his seat, trying desperately to hide the terror he was feeling. Gimbal was her personal servant now. She was so used to his constant presence, she hardly noticed him anymore. It was hard to believe that more than a year had passed since she had last seen Pom.

And what an eventful year it had been. The biggest change in her life was having the loving friendship of Pom replaced with the overbearing supervision of Gimbal. She remembered her surprise when Mister Stotz first brought him to her room and introduced him as her new servant. He wasn't even a hod. Gimbal was one of Colonel Pavic's goons and he made it very clear, right from the start, that he had no interest in performing any sort of "servant" duties. His sole function was to keep an eye on her and prevent her from causing any trouble.

As soon as Juna saw him, she knew they weren't going to get along. The first problem was that they had met before. Years ago, when Sergeant Danto had allowed her to train with his cadets for a week, she had numerous encounters with the young Gimbal and they usually ended with him flying through the air and landing with a thud. Juna never mentioned their shared history and he certainly didn't bring it up either.

As far as Juna was concerned, the biggest problem with Gimbal was that he was always there. What he lacked in personality, he more than made up for with an unwavering dedication to his duty. Unfortunately, his duty was to never let her out of his sight. There were no more trips to the aviary, no visits with Helion and no clandestine trips through the rafters. This all made her feel completely isolated. Her sole focus was still doing anything she could to thwart her father's plans, but all her access to information was gone. Realizing this, she decided her only chance to continue the fight was to deceive him and get herself invited into his inner circle.

Juna was aware that gaining her father's trust would be a long process, but she knew what the first step had to be – she needed to start acting more like a princess. Deciding the best way to begin was to learn from someone really good at it, she began spending more time with her sister.

Much to Juna's surprise, time spent with her sister was actually quite enjoyable. Lacee was really sweet – all she wanted was to make everybody happy. She was always surrounded by servants, but she treated them more like friends. With most hods, you could see a resentment in their eyes as they went about their tasks, but Lacee's servants were eager to do things for her. By all appearances, they adored her. Those feelings were mutual as Lacee sincerely cared for them too. Seeing them all together, always made Juna miss Pom so much.

The first thing Juna learned about being a princess was how important it was to ask for things. All Elites, especially the Royals, expected to have everything done for them and to be given anything they asked for. Lacee was constantly asking her father for presents, parties or favours. He would grumble at first, but she always got everything she asked for. Ultimately, most of what she received would be given away to others who needed it and then she would simply ask for more. Lacee was quite convinced that regularly asking for things was the key to being a good princess.

Juna decided to put her sister's theory to the test. One day, she marched into her father's office and demanded that she be given a car. And not a tut-tut either – it had to be something fast. The next morning, a package was delivered to her room that contained a small key and a note from her father that read "Go look in the courtyard." Rushing outside, she saw a bright red tri-racer with a large pink bow. A tri-racer was a small sports car with two wheels in the front and one in the back. It had an open cockpit with two side-by-side seats, no doubt so Gimbal could accompany her wherever she went. Juna didn't know much about them, but she knew they were fast. She couldn't wait to try it out.

Applying what she learned on her first day as a car thief and adding in a few tips from Gimbal, Juna soon mastered the art of driving. She spent the first day speeding around the courtyard, but soon grew confident enough to venture out into the city. Although not technically old enough to be driving on the streets of Volara, she refused to let it bother her. The odds of encountering a police officer with the courage to give a ticket to the emperor's youngest daughter seemed extremely low. Her new mobility gave her a level of freedom she had never experienced before. This was exactly what she needed.

Juna was still embarrassed about her failure to function effectively in her first adventure in the real world and was determined to never let that happen again. Every day, she and Gimbal would put on their helmets, strap themselves into the tri-racer and tear through the streets of Volara. These trips allowed her to learn every road, every alley and every turn. Stopping in all the shops, meeting the shopkeepers and buying countless things she didn't need just to support them, made her the most popular customer on the planet. She was determined to learn every square inch of the city and meet as many of its citizens as she could.

When she was done with Volara, Juna expanded her scope to include the entire planet. She and Gimbal would take to the highways and drive to the cities on the coast and stop in all the small towns along the way, often camping out and sleeping under the stars. Visiting as many places and meeting as many people as she could kept her busy from dawn until dusk, every day of the week. The pampered life of a princess was now gone forever, replaced by an appreciation of, and a true connection with, the people of Cambria.

Soon, her reputation was spreading across the empire. "There may actually be a Royal who isn't horrible," someone would say. "She really seems to care about us," another would add. "Maybe our next emperor should be an empress," was the conclusion of most. Juna didn't care what people were saying. Her goal was simply to learn everything she could about the world and all of the people in it.

Today, Juna didn't expect to meet anyone new. They were speeding along the highway through the high desert that led to The Depot. She had purposely avoided this route in the past. For reasons she was still unaware, almost all of the resources of the planet had been poured into The Depot over the past year. Not knowing exactly what was going on out there was a problem, but she wasn't going to find out anything by snooping from the outside. If she was going to learn anything, it would be by earning her father's trust and getting invited inside.

As The Depot came into view, Juna rolled to a stop on the side of the road and got out to have a look. She had only seen The Depot once before, and that was at night, so she didn't really remember what it used to look like. Her initial impression was that it was much bigger now. The facility was dominated by two huge rectangular buildings that looked liked warehouses. There was also an enormous white dome she didn't think had been there during her last visit.

"I don't think we should be here." Gimbal had joined her by the side of the road, looking noticeably uncomfortable.

"You're probably right. I've just never seen it before," she lied. "I really just wanted to try out this highway – what a perfect road for driving fast. Let's go home."

The ride back was as exhilarating for Juna as it was terrifying for Gimbal. Her mind was spinning during the entire trip, trying to think of any way she might be able to get inside The Depot and find out what was really going on. For all she knew, Pom was still in there somewhere. She absolutely had to get inside, but every scenario she considered always came back to the same thing – needing to become a member of her father's inner circle.

They were back in the city now, so Juna stopped letting her mind wander and focused solely on her driving. There were a lot of pedestrians out this evening and she really didn't want to hit any of them. As she was rolling to a stop at a traffic light, she took note of the vehicle that was stopped beside her. It appeared to be a small motorcycle, but it didn't have any wheels and it wasn't touching the ground. That was strange. She looked over to see who was driving such an odd machine.

Juna let out a small gasp and jerked her head to the front. It was Orin. Resisting a powerful urge to jump out of the car to go see him, she kept her eyes focused straight ahead. All she wanted to do was run over there and ask him a million questions: Is Pom OK? What about Skeet and Taz? Do *you* know what's going on at The Depot? But she couldn't, not with

Gimbal here. All of her plans depended on gaining her father's trust and that would all be ruined if she even acknowledged knowing who Orin was. Now was a time to be strong.

When the light finally turned red, Juna stomped on the accelerator and sped away. Her hands were shaking for the remainder of the drive, but she managed to make it home without incident. The sun was setting as she pulled into the driveway of the Royal Palace. Gimbal had fallen asleep in the passenger seat, so she risked a quick wave to Helion as they passed. Helion's bright yellow eyes flashed a greeting in return. How she wished she could sneak away and talk with him. Maybe *he* had some idea about what was going on back at The Depot.

As they came to a stop, Gimbal awoke from his nap. "Great, we're finally here," he said, rubbing his hands together. "Let's get some food. I'm starving."

As they made their way to the dining hall, Juna was startled by a collision to her right and a yelp of pain from Gimbal. "Watch where you're going you little punk!" he raged at the hod who had just slammed into him. "That's hot! I could have been burned!"

As Gimbal crouched to check the mess that had been made of his clothes, the hod turned to Juna and gave her a quick wink. Skeet!

"A thousand apologies, Master," Skeet begged. "I saw the Princess and wanted her to have some of this lovely hot chocolate. I'm so clumsy. I certainly meant no harm."

Juna saw the rage boiling in Gimbal's eyes, but she interrupted him just before he could exact his revenge. "Gimbal, why don't you go get yourself cleaned up? I'll take care of this little runt."

Gimbal muttered a few obscenities as he headed to his room for a change of clothes. Juna turned to Skeet. "How did you get in here?" she asked in a whisper.

"I just snuck in," he replied with obvious pride. "The guards here really are a joke. I've dropped by a few times this year hoping to see you. I guess today's my lucky day."

"I never thought I'd see you in one of those," she said, pointing at his hod's tunic.

"It's OK if it's just a disguise," he answered with a wink and a smile. "I just needed a way to get in to see if you were all right and let you know that we're all fine."

"I'm alright, but I miss you all so much," she replied, resisting the urge to reach out and give him a hug. "Where is everybody now?"

"Orin and his dad spend most of their time at the University," he informed her. "It's a long story, but Pom, Taz and I are living with the General on his farm just west of the city. Boy, my life sure did take a turn the day I met you."

Juna's heart skipped a beat when she heard Pom's name, so it took her a moment to process the rest of what he'd said. "Wait! The General has a farm?"

"That's a long story too," he replied with a shrug. "We just wanted you to know we're OK and we haven't given up the fight."

"I'm afraid I haven't learned anything, but I keep trying every day," she assured him, as she peered around the hall to see if they were being watched. "I haven't given up either."

"We knew you wouldn't. Just find out what you can and try to get word to us at the farm. Listen, I've got to go, but I brought you something," he said as he slipped a small heavy object into her hand.

Juna opened her hand to reveal a metallic blob attached to a long leather cord. It was made of several different types of metal, creating a swirling pattern of silvers, golds and coppers. It was the most beautiful thing she had ever seen.

"Orin's been working on his alchemy skills," Skeet informed her. "He wanted you to have it."

Juna's eyes clouded with tears. She looked up to thank him, but he was already gone. Slipping the loop over her head, she slid the metal bauble beneath her blouse. "Thanks Orin," she whispered to herself as she smiled and headed to her room to get changed for dinner. As she was leaving, Juna noticed someone staring at her from across the hall. It was that horrible professor woman. Had she seen the whole thing? Were all her plans ruined? A wave of panic pulsed through her body. Knowing there was nothing she could do about it now, she ignored the woman and continued on her way.

Juna awoke the next morning with an energy she hadn't felt in months. Seeing Skeet again and learning that her friends were OK and still needing information from her was invigorating. The more she thought about it, the less she worried about Professor Oletta seeing her yesterday. All she really did was talk to a hod. She could easily explain that one away. Getting herself dressed, she headed for the dining hall for breakfast. As always, Gimbal was there at the bedroom door, waiting for her to emerge.

"You look chipper this morning," he noted. "What will we be up to today?"

"Nothing special," she replied with a devilish grin. "Just another day playing princess."

After breakfast, Juna started into her daily exercise routine. Her training had changed significantly since Gimbal came into her life. Using the obstacle course in her room or battling imaginary Marans was no longer an option, so she was limited to callisthenics, a little weight-lifting and running laps around the palace grounds. Gimbal always joined her for the first lap, but he just sat on a bench for the last three. It was the only time in her day when she could be alone with her thoughts.

After the workout, she set out to see her father. During her fourth lap around the palace, she came to a decision. The time for simply waiting to be invited to join his group was over – it was time to force the issue. Knocking gently on the door to his office, she stepped inside, leaving Gimbal waiting in the hallway.

"Hi Daddy," she began. "Have you got a minute?" The "Daddy" thing was another tip she got from Lacee. "Just call him Daddy and he's wrapped around your little finger," she often told her.

"For you, always," he replied with a smile. "What's on your mind?"

"I just wanted to apologize," she said, trying to sound as sincere as she could. "I know I've treated you unfairly over the years and I wanted you to know how sorry I am."

"It warms my heart to hear you say that," he beamed. "You know, I have been watching you very closely this past year and I am very impressed with the things you have been doing. Travelling the country. Meeting the people. It's splendid! And everyone loves you – I can use that."

"I'm just trying to do what's best for the family, Daddy."

"I knew you would come around eventually, my dear. I was hoping that getting rid of that first hod of yours might be just what you needed to see how the world really works."

Juna was seething on the inside, but managed to hold a pleasant smile on her face. "Yes, Daddy. Losing Pom was a very important moment for me. I think I see things much more clearly now."

"You probably don't realize this Juna, but you have always been my favourite. My first two children have always been a disappointment to me. They're soft like your mother. But I have seen a fire in you since the day you were born. I always hoped it would be you, standing by my side, ruling this empire."

"I would like that," she replied, almost too shocked to speak. "If you think I'm ready."

"I do, I really do. And there's no time like the present. I, along with my closest confidants, am going for a tour of The Depot today. I would like you to join us."

Juna could hardly believe how well this conversation was going. "It would be an honour to be included in something like that – of course I'll go."

"There is something you will need to know first, my dear. It's a secret that has been kept by our family for generations. Can you promise me you will never mention this to anyone?"

"I can," she lied. "I promise I won't tell anyone."

"It's about the Marans," he said, as he shuffled some papers on his desk, obviously trying to collect his thoughts. "It seems that, many years ago, the Starchaser managed to avoid crashing into the sun. Somehow, all those Cambrian scientists and trouble-makers survived, started calling themselves Marans and are now causing us all this trouble."

"What? No!" Juna exclaimed, covering her mouth with both hands. She was proud of the shock she was able to convey, thinking her efforts today might be even more convincing than her fake boyfriend performance.

"It's true," her father continued. "And now that you know the truth, you can join me in the effort to conquer them." The Emperor stood and walked around the desk. Juna stood to meet him as he threw his arms around her for the first time in years. Trying not to cringe, she returned the hug as best she could.

"Now, go get ready for the trip," he urged. "I can't tell you how happy it makes me that you are going to be a part of this, at my side, right where you belong."

As Juna exited the office, she smiled and softly muttered to herself. "That's right Daddy. I'm right where I need to be."

An hour later, Juna was sitting in a plush rail car, speeding towards The Depot, observing the other passengers. She received a dirty look from Jakol who was not at all happy to see her there. He had been very upset when their father announced that she was now a part of his inner circle. As she scanned the car, her eyes locked onto those of Professor Oletta. It was still troubling that this woman had seen her with Skeet yesterday, but she was thankful no one else seemed to be aware of it. Just as she was about to look away, she saw the woman mouth the words "help me." Juna wasn't sure she had seen it correctly. She looked again. The professor's eyes were now pleading. "Please help me," was her silent request.

Juna had no time to think about the odd encounter before the train rolled to a stop at The Depot's station. They all disembarked and were escorted into one of the large buildings in the centre of the complex. As soon as Juna stepped into the expansive space, her eyes scanned from one end of the building to the other. She was suddenly engulfed by an overwhelming sense of horror.

Oh, this was bad. This was really bad.

14

This had been the worst year of Orin's life and there were no signs of things getting better anytime soon. Two days after the emperor's men overran The Depot, a truck delivered all of his and his father's personal possessions to their apartment in the city along with a note that said if either of them ever set foot near The Depot again, they would be shot on sight. Since then, they had not heard a single thing about what was going on out there. At least he had his hoverbike back, but that felt like the only thing remaining from his old life. He missed Gig so much and didn't know if he would ever see him again. The fate of all his other friends was a complete mystery too. All he thought about, day after day, was what he could change to make everything go back to the way it used to be.

He missed Juna too. Several times over the past year, he saw her driving around the city in her fancy red sports car with some guy, but he never got a chance to talk to her. Just yesterday, he'd been stopped at a traffic light when she pulled up right beside him. But she either didn't notice him, or chose to ignore him, and then sped away when the light changed. Deep down, he knew she couldn't risk being seen with him, but it made him a little sad just the same.

Now, Orin was spending most of his time at the university. His dad was teaching there and had set up a private lab so Orin could spend his days working on his inventions. Orin could tell his dad missed life at The Depot too, but the Professor tried to highlight the positive side of their new life.

"Just think about it, Orin," he would say, "we don't have to spend our time building weapons anymore. I can teach the next generation of scientists all the wonderful things technology can do and you are free to create amazing inventions that can help the people of Cambria live better lives."

Orin always agreed with his father when he said things like this, but he had no interest in making the best of their new situation – his sole focus was on getting things back to the way they were before. The story Orin always told his dad was that he was working on a high-frequency radio that would revolutionize the planet's communication systems. The truth was, he had completed that project months ago and now dedicated his time to developing tools to help him break into The Depot to find out what had happened to Gigahertz and the rest of his friends.

The first tool Orin created was a handheld laser for cutting and welding, knowing he would need something like that to get through the metal fence that surrounded The Depot. It was based on the larger units installed in the Atomics. Next, he built a universal key card that could be used to open all the doors of the facility by cycling through every code combination until it found one that worked. Then, he built a jamming device that could intercept any alarms that might be set off before they could be reported back to Security.

The project Orin was currently working on was, by far, his most complicated. It was a large blanket made of glass fibres rather than cloth. It had sensors on the back that could detect the physical appearance of its surroundings and then mimic that view through the fibres on the front. By covering himself with the blanket, he hoped it would make him almost invisible to any guards or cameras that he may need to pass unseen. The blanket was now lying over his workbench, ready for final testing. Hearing someone opening the door to his lab, he quickly turned it on and watched it vanish before his eyes.

"Ah, Orin," the Professor said as he walked into the room. "I hope I'm not interrupting anything important."

"No. Nothing special happening today, Dad," Orin replied, trying to hide his excitement over the successful test.

"Don't worry son," his father said encouragingly. "That's the life of an inventor. Some days are filled with one disappointment after another, but when something finally clicks, it all becomes worthwhile in an instant."

"I'll keep working on it, Dad," Orin replied with a smile. "I think someday soon, it's all going to come together for me."

"That's the spirit," his dad said, clapping Orin on the back. "But sometimes, the best thing you can do to get the creative juices flowing is take a little break. The General invited us to dinner at the farm this evening. Why don't we both take some time off and go have a little fun?"

"That's perfect, Dad. I have some gear I want to take out to Diara anyway."

Diara was one of the few lucky enough to escape The Depot during the emperor's takeover and find a new home hiding out on the General's farm. Orin told his father that Diara was helping him with the testing of his new radio, but what they were really doing was building a fully operational Tech Station in the General's basement. He felt bad lying to his dad, but he knew for a fact that his father would never allow him to do anything as crazy as breaking into The Depot, especially with the emperor's threat to have him shot if he ever showed up there again.

At the end of the workday, Orin packed all the equipment he needed to finish Diara's station into his father's car and they set off for the farm. It was a beautiful evening, the amber sky slowly drifting to a deep orange as the sun neared the horizon. Orin sat back in the passenger seat, enjoying the view of the passing countryside. As they approached the General's farm, he noticed unmanned machinery tending to the fields. Having the crew from The Depot at his disposal significantly reduced the amount of manual labour the General needed to perform on his farm. Every piece of equipment had been fully automated, so he basically just sat back and watched all of the work get done for him.

As they pulled up in front of the quaint little farmhouse, Diara and Pom rushed down the steps to greet them while Skeet, Taz, Dorel, Annu and the General sat on the porch enjoying the view of the setting sun. This was all that remained of the old team from The Depot. All of the rest were likely still there, possibly being held captive by Colonel Pavic and his band of thugs. This group of survivors had Skeet to thank for their current state of freedom.

Skeet had been out in front of the assembly building playing with Isotope when he saw the convoy of military vehicles approaching from the highway. Fearing they were coming for Pom and Taz, he sprinted into the building to warn them. He found Pom and Diara in the Ops Centre, so the three of them went to the assembly floor to collect Taz. While they were searching for a good hiding place, they ran into Dorel and Annu who ushered them down into an underground service tunnel that virtually no one knew about. All six of them stayed hidden down there until whatever was going on up top ran its course.

Throughout the day, they heard the stomping of soldiers' feet and the rumble of heavy equipment roaming the halls above them. Terrified, they remained completely silent to avoid detection. When night fell, the building went quiet, so they carefully lifted the tunnel's access panel and slipped out to investigate. The building felt abandoned. There were no signs of people or Mechs anywhere. Realizing something had gone terribly wrong, they collected some supplies and snuck out a side door to escape. Dorel used bolt cutters to cut the fence and they all slipped through to begin the long journey across the desert.

Travelling only at night, it took them three days to get back to the city. Dorel and Annu kept a small apartment on the eastern edge of the city, so they went there to lay low while deciding on their next move. Skeet spent his days roaming the city streets, talking to his contacts, trying to find someone who knew what was going on at The Depot. For the first two weeks he learned nothing, but one day he heard a rumour that the mighty General Zatari had retired and bought a farm west of the city.

Skeet used his elite scrounging skills to borrow a truck and go looking for the General's new place. Two days later, he tracked it down and by the end of the following day, the whole group joined the General on the small farm they now called home. It was safe for the time being, but they all longed for a future that would see them reunited with the Mechs and the rest of their friends from The Depot.

The meal was delicious and the conversation was wonderful – it was so good to see everyone again. When the food was gone and the dishes were cleared, Orin, Diara and Pom zipped down to the basement to work on the "radio" project while everyone else cleaned up. They worked furiously, adding the final pieces to the Tech Station and powered it up the second they were done. Diara began flipping through all the standard Mech frequencies to see who she could contact.

"I found Helion," she reported. "He's on guard duty at the palace, but I'm getting nothing but static on all the other frequencies."

Orin felt his heart sink. He knew it was a long-shot, but he so hoped today would be the day he found out Gig was OK. "That's alright," he said, trying his best to hide his disappointment. "Just keep checking whenever you get a chance."

"You know I will," Diara replied, sounding as sad as Orin felt. "I miss them too."

Orin went back upstairs and found his dad chatting with the General. "Ah, Orin, just in time," the General said, waving him over. "I was about to tell your father that I'm having another little get-together two days from now. I really think both of you should be here."

"Certainly, Aldin," the Professor replied. "What's it all about?"

"There's a group of people wanting to see some big changes on this planet," he told them. "We call ourselves the Underground. The way the hods are treated in this empire is unacceptable and we mean to change that. We fear that all of the recent activity at The Depot may be strengthening the emperor's position, but we have no idea what's going on out there. What we desperately need is more information. This meeting will be to discuss possible ways to get it. I'm hoping that you two might have some suggestions."

"We'll be there," the Professor assured him. "You can count on us to help in any way we can."

On the drive back to the apartment, all Orin could think about were their parting words with the General. The hods did deserve a better life. Meeting Pom and Taz and knowing what wonderful people they were, made him realize how important it was to help them. The General required information and Orin knew he was in a position to get it. He had spent an entire year preparing to break into The Depot and now had all the tools he needed to do it. The decision was made – he would go tomorrow.

Spending the next day running all of his inventions through a final series of diagnostics, Orin's optimism slowly grew. Maybe this plan wasn't so crazy after all. Maybe he could break into The Depot without getting himself killed. He would know soon enough. When all the tests were complete, he stuffed his tools into a backpack and went to find his father.

"Hey Dad, I think I made a breakthrough on the radio today. I'm heading over to see Diara to install some new equipment at her end."

"That's excellent news son, I knew you'd figure it out if you just stuck with it."

"I'll probably be working late so I'll just stay over and stick around for the General's meeting. I'll meet you there tomorrow."

Orin felt bad about lying to his dad, but he knew he couldn't tell him the truth. There was no way his dad was going to let him risk his life on such a dangerous quest. He was scared about it himself, but knew it was the only way to get information to the General and find out what had happened to Gig.

Hopping on his hoverbike, he pulled out of the university parking lot. Making his way out of the city, he stopped at the valley's rim to wait for darkness to fall. Sitting there, feet dangling over the edge, thinking about the mission ahead, he wished Juna could have been there with him. He thought back to the prison escape and realized that if he encountered a guard tonight, it would end much differently without her there to save the day.

Orin watched the sun set and then remounted his hoverbike to continue the trip to The Depot. His anxiety built with each mile as the reality of what he was about to do started to sink in. When he rounded the final curve and saw the facility come into view, he was shocked to see the changes since the last time he had seen it. There appeared to be a second assembly building and it now had an enormous dome, just like the one at The Institute. The number of barracks was ten times what it was – there must be a thousand people living out here now.

Not wanting to get too close on his hoverbike, he pulled off the road and hid it in a gully behind a large hill before starting the long walk to The Depot. It was completely dark by the time he reached the perimeter fence. Opening his backpack, he pulled out the laser, activated the cutter and sliced through the metal fence like it was made of paper. Slipping through the opening, he sprinted for an access door around the back of the original assembly building.

Orin searched his backpack and pulled out the jammer and the key card. He flipped on the jammer so any alarms he might set off would not be reported to Security and then placed the key card in the slot by the door. The key's display began flickering through a series of numbers, finally stopping at a successful combination. The lock clicked open. Pushing through the door and letting it close silently behind him, he crouched, listening for any sign that his intrusion had been detected.

It was dark inside the building, but enough light was coming through the windows to allow him to see where he was going. There had been no sign of a guard yet, but he kept to the shadows just to be safe. As he rounded a corner to step onto the assembly floor, he saw a sight that made him so happy he had to force himself not to yell out. In the first assembly bay, standing under one of the huge gantry cranes, was Gigahertz. It appeared he was powered-down, so Orin rushed over to turn him back on.

When Orin reached his friend, he went straight for the comm panel on his left leg where he knew he would find the on switch. It wasn't there. Caught completely off-guard by this unforeseen development, he paused a moment to think. Someone had removed his comm panel. Why would they do that? He ran his hands along Gig's shin plate. Nothing. Something was wrong. The spot that should have been carved up by a love-struck little kid was as smooth as glass. Orin stepped back and looked over the huge machine from top to bottom. He looked the same, but somehow different. Everything was new and shiny without the little dents and scars Orin knew so well. This may be *a* Gigahertz, but it certainly wasn't *his* Gigahertz.

Orin just stood there, confused. Was this really a different Mech than the one he had grown up with? And where were the others? The rest of the assembly floor was completely empty. Perhaps they were being kept in the new building next door, but he was reluctant to go there without knowing the layout. Trying to think of some other place you could hide a bunch of enormous robotic fighting machines, he suddenly remembered the first time he met the Steamers. The archives vault!

Racing across the assembly floor, he had to stop abruptly when he heard someone in the hallway moving in his direction. Leaning against the wall at the entrance to a hallway, he wrestled his invisibility blanket out of the backpack. Holding it up in front of him, he turned it on. At that moment, a guard emerged from the hallway, no more than ten feet away, but passed right on by without even noticing him. When the guard finally disappeared around the next corner, Orin let out a breath he hadn't realized he was holding. Lowering the blanket, he returned it to his backpack and continued towards the vault.

When he arrived, he used his key card to open the door and crept inside. Dashing through the office area, he turned the corner to see a vault crammed with Mechs. Gigahertz, his Gigahertz, was right at the front. Rushing over, he ran his hand along the carved-up shin plate and reached for the comm panel. Throwing the power switch, his heart soared as Gig came to life.

"Master Orin. I am so pleased to see you unharmed."

"I'm fine Gig. What happened here?"

"Colonel Pavic arrived with many soldiers and informed us that you and your father had been taken hostage and would be severely injured if we did not proceed to this vault. I believe they deactivated me after that. Thank you for coming for us so quickly."

"Yeah Gig. That was over a year ago."

"Ah, I thought you looked a little taller. So, what has happened in the last year? Has the emperor continued his assault on Mara?"

"We just don't know Gig. We've been locked out of everything."

"What can I do to help?"

"For now, I need you to stay here while we come up with a plan. I'll power everybody up and you can all drop into wait state. Diara has a Tech Station – we can talk to you with that. Just sit tight and I'll let you know when we're ready to go."

"Alright Master Orin. I will remain right here."

Scampering around the room, he powered up Mechs as he went and had them all drop into wait state. By the time he was done, he noticed more light was now coming in through the windows. If he wanted any darkness to help cover his escape, he would need to get moving. Dashing through the outside access door, he sprinted for the perimeter fence. There was too much light for Orin to safely hide in the shadows, so he pulled the invisibility blanket over himself and started crawling along the fence line. When he finally reached the gap he had made in the fence, he slipped through and used the laser to weld it back together as best he could. Tucking himself under the blanket, he began the long crawl back across the desert.

Orin was exhausted by the time he got back to his hoverbike. The trip across the desert had taken him most of the day so he was going to be late for the General's meeting. As he sped along the highway, he considered what he would tell everyone when he arrived, but realized immediately that his only option was to tell them the truth. It was totally dark when he finally pushed through the door to the General's farmhouse. There were about a dozen people in the room and every eye turned his way as he entered.

"Orin!" his father exclaimed. "Where have you been? We've been worried sick."

"I've been at The Depot."

"The Depot? What are you talking about?"

Orin went on to recount his harrowing journey. All of it. His new inventions. The trek across the desert. Hiding from the guard. Finding the Mechs. The second Gigahertz. Everything. When he was done, he received a scolding and a hug from his dad and then went to sit quietly in the back corner of the room to observe the rest of the meeting.

Everyone had broken into small groups and were talking intently about how to use all this new information. Orin couldn't help but feel a little disappointed. It just looked like a room full of regular people chatting about everyday things. The only person from the group that Orin recognized was, surprisingly, Leaping Lano. It was hard to believe this was the group of people that was going to change the world. Orin's thoughts were interrupted when the General sat down in the seat next to him.

"So, this is the Underground, huh?" Orin asked, sounding a little doubtful.

"Yes Orin. Or some of us at least. We're just a group of average people that would like to see things change. We're doctors, carpenters, ..."

"Furniture salesmen," Orin interrupted.

"Yes Orin, even furniture salesmen. You don't have to have an important job in this world to try to make a difference."

Orin didn't know what to make of this information. He just sat there, staring at the ground. "Do you think you can win?" he asked softly.

"I know we have to try. And I know the information you gathered gives us a better chance. That was very brave what you did. Foolish, but brave. I think that princess of yours must be rubbing off on you."

Orin continued to stare at the ground. "Yeah, maybe," he finally replied.

"This is important, Orin. In many ways, this is far more important than our battle with the Marans. We are now fighting for the very heart and soul of this planet."

"That's funny," Orin chuckled to himself. "Gig said almost the same thing."

The General patted Orin on the back as he stood to leave. He began walking away, but paused and turned back to face him.

"You know, Orin. When your father is building a new artificial intelligence, he sometimes uses the brain scan of a real person as a baseline. I think you will find that your friend Gigahertz and I will agree on a great many things."

15

Juna felt as though she had been walking in a fog for the past two days. The tour of The Depot had really shaken her. All she wanted was to know what was going on in that place and now, having learned the truth, she was terrified. When she walked into the building and saw row after row of Mechs, her first thought was of what her father could do with all that firepower at his disposal. The feeling of terror hit her when she realized the answer to that question – anything he wanted.

The rest of the tour was a blur. People were talking about SIM's and TRIP's and Gates, but Juna struggled to take it all in. All thoughts of wanting to learn more about what was going on evaporated from her mind. Her only intention at that point was getting out of there. Wanting to shout out to the world what was really going on, she knew that, at least for now, remaining silent was her only option.

Juna found the train ride home even more challenging than the tour itself. Colonel Pavic, Jakol and her father were so excited about the progress that had been made at The Depot and couldn't wait to put the next phase of their plan into action. It was all she could do to pretend to share in their enthusiasm. It was important to alleviate any doubts they may have about her, so she had to be strong. Her brother still watched her constantly, clearly not trusting that she was truly a willing member of the team. She would laugh along with their jokes and smile whenever they mentioned their inevitable victory over the Marans, but on the inside, all she wanted was to curl up and go to sleep to dream of a world where none of this was really happening.

Settling into her bed for the night, Juna scolded herself for not doing a better job of spying during her visit to The Depot. She needed to be better than that. The General needed information and she had allowed her emotions to get the best of her and squandered a perfect opportunity to get him some. As she drifted off to sleep, her thoughts were of how to get back there and do what she needed to do.

Now steeled with a new sense of determination, she walked through the halls of the Royal Palace, Gimbal at her side, on their way to another meeting in her father's office. Professor Oletta was going to be there to update them on the status of the project. When Juna and Gimbal arrived, everyone was already seated, awaiting the professor's report.

"Work is progressing on the new Gate," Professor Oletta informed them. "If things continue to go well, it should be possible to open a portal to Mara sometime next week."

"Splendid! Splendid!" the Emperor beamed. "Just make sure things continue to go well."

Everyone agreed that the first wave of Mechs would be unleashed on Mara as soon as the Gate was operational. Juna's mind was spinning, trying to think of some way she could stop this from happening, but her thoughts were interrupted by a question from her father.

"So, tell me Juna. What do you think of all this?"

"It's all very exciting Daddy," she responded cautiously. "But what I don't understand is why any of this is necessary. I mean, haven't we already defeated them?"

"It's simple, my dear," he replied without hesitation. "The future of Cambria depends on our conquest of Mara. I love this planet, but it is simply too small. We are running out of everything. We lack the natural resources to build what we need and even the space we require for our families to grow. Just think of it Juna. With the technology and resources of the Marans, imagine all the things they can build for us – all the wonderful machines we could have to make all our lives easier."

"So, you're talking about enslaving them?"

"Well, that's an ugly word, but yes, that's exactly what I'm saying. I think they deserve it for all the grief they have put us through for the last twenty years. The time has come to expand our reach so that I can finally reign over a true empire."

"Well, when you put it like that, I guess it makes sense," Juna lied. "If it's the best thing for Cambria, then I suppose that's what we should do."

"I'm so glad you finally see how important this is. Now, everyone leave me be. I have an invasion to plan."

As they were filing out of the office, Juna noticed Professor Oletta heading for the exit. It was the first time she had seen her since that silent plea for help on the train and she really wanted a chance to talk to her in private.

"Hey Gimbal, I feel like going for a drive," she announced. "Why don't you go fetch the helmets from my bedroom?"

"Anything for you, Your Highness," he replied sarcastically. "I am always at your service."

When he was gone, Juna sprinted down the hall to catch the professor. When she caught up, she grabbed the woman's shoulder and spun her around to face her. "So, what exactly is it you want me to help you with?" she demanded.

The professor looked her in the eye for a moment, clearly trying to decide if she could be trusted. "Do you agree with everything your father is doing?" she finally asked.

The look on the woman's face made Juna believe that they shared the same feelings about this attack on Mara. "No. I think it's horrible."

"Well, I do too," Professor Oletta replied softly, tears shimmering in the corners of her eyes. "I created that portal as a tool for exploration, not as a weapon. Some of my ancestors were on the Starchaser. That's my family he's talking about conquering. I want no part in this, but they have threatened my life if I don't help them. I just don't know what to do."

"If I can get you out of here," Juna asked urgently, "will you help me defeat them?"

"Of course," she replied, looking around to make sure no one was eavesdropping. "If you can get me away from here, I'll do everything I can to stop them."

"OK, I'll get you out," Juna assured her. "I have friends that can help, but I'll need more time. Do everything you can to slow things down. Sabotage something if you have to – just don't finish that Gate. I'll come for you. I promise."

Juna noticed Gimbal approaching in the distance, so she spun away from the professor and went to meet him before he could see them together. "Thanks," she said, snatching her helmet from him. "I feel like a little excitement today. Let's hit the back roads again."

"Great," Gimbal responded, donning his best fake smile. "Just try not to get us both killed."

Gravel flew from the rear tire of the tri-racer creating a cloud of dust as far as the eye could see. Gimbal gripped the armrests so tightly, Juna worried they might be ripped free. She had been out travelling the country roads west of the city everyday for the last week, hoping to see some sign that would show her which of these farms belonged to the General. As she leaned into a curve that swept past an endless sea of grain, she noticed huge harvesting machines that appeared to be operating without a driver. Not being aware that this sort of technology even existed, she slowed slightly to get a better look.

As they passed the small farmhouse, she noticed a young man working in the front yard – a man so large it could only be Taz. She found it! It took all of her self-control not to slam on the brakes and pull into that driveway. Pom was in that house. All of her friends were there. But this was not the time. She knew that someday soon, she would be able to join them here, but not today. For now, she was more valuable at her father's side, learning everything she could about his plans.

Juna's efforts to dig up information about the impending attack on Mara finally took a turn for the better three days after finding the farm. Her father was storming about the palace, slamming doors and yelling at people for no reason.

"What's wrong Daddy?" she asked softly, faking a level of concern she certainly didn't feel.

"Professor Oletta has just informed me that there has been a setback at The Depot. It seems something has gone wrong with the Gate and it will take her at least three weeks to get it running. I'm not sure I even believe her," he bellowed, pointing a finger right in Juna's face. "I do not trust that woman."

Juna felt this lack of trust may have something to do with him threatening to kill her, but she kept that thought to herself. "Why don't you let me go over there, Daddy," she offered. "I can see what's wrong and maybe speed things up a bit."

"An excellent plan," he replied, his mood suddenly brightening. "Go there today and sort this mess out for me."

An hour later, Juna and Gimbal were standing before Professor Oletta at The Depot. "This is unacceptable!" Juna yelled, as she pounded on the professor's desk. "My father gave you very simple instructions. Get this thing working. Is that task too difficult for you?" She noticed Gimbal wasn't paying attention to the conversation, so she gave the professor a quick wink to let her know she was just kidding.

"I'm doing my best," the professor pleaded. "I've got everyone working to resolve the problem. There's really nothing more I can do."

"Show me!" Juna demanded. "I want to see everything!"

Professor Oletta took them for a tour of the entire facility. Juna was determined not to make the same mistake she did the last time she was here. This time, she paid attention to every detail. Counting every Mech and every missile. Memorizing the layout of the building and the location of every item in it. When they were done, she barked out a few more threats and stormed out of the building.

It was on the train ride home that Juna realized she had learned all she could by remaining with her father at the palace. She knew what they were planning to do and what weapons they possessed to do it. The time had come to get all of this information to the General and join her friends in the fight to make things right. She would leave tonight.

Later that evening, Juna was in her room planning her escape. As always, Gimbal was there with her, keeping watch over her every move. This was going to be difficult. She knew Jakol and Colonel Pavic still didn't trust her, so she would certainly need to avoid them. And then there was Gimbal. The first step was going to be ditching him, so she decided to start with that.

"Gimbal, I'm bored."

"What do you want me to do about it?" he replied, not even shifting his gaze from the comic book he was reading.

"Hey, I know what we can do," she suggested, flashing him a mischievous grin. "Do you remember the first time we met?"

"Yeah. Mister Stotz brought me here and I told you I wasn't going to help you with anything."

"No, I mean the very first time. With Sergeant Danto. That was fun." She walked over to him and gave him a playful pat on the shoulder. "We should fight."

"Yeah, right. Like I'm going to beat up a princess. I don't think they'd give me a promotion for that."

"You're not scared, are you?" She gave him another playful pat on the shoulder. "As I recall, you didn't do very well the last time."

Gimbal stood to face her. "That was a long time ago and I was just a little kid. I'm sure things would go much differently now."

Juna assumed a fighting stance. "You are scared," she teased. "I don't think things would go differently at all."

"Alright Princess, let's do this," he said, mirroring her stance. "But I should probably warn you…"

Boom! Juna's kick landed on Gimbal's jaw, dropping him to the floor in a heap.

"Yup. Pretty much the same as the last time," she chuckled to herself, as she grabbed his feet and dragged him into her dressing room. Using some of her belts in the closet, she tied him up and left him in a corner. Locking the door behind her as she left, she raced to her bedroom door and slowly stepped out into the hallway. Not wanting to draw any attention to herself, she moved as discreetly as she could, but it still felt like every eye was on her as she made her way to the rear exit of the palace.

Once outside, Juna crossed the large driveway leading to the garage. As she reached for the handle of the door that would open to her tri-racer, she heard footsteps behind her on the driveway.

"Where do you think you're going, sister?"

Juna turned to see Jakol standing there, a smug smile on his face.

"I thought I would go for a quick drive," she replied innocently. "It's such a beautiful evening."

"Without Gimbal? You know that's not allowed," he said, the look on his face unwavering. "Where is he anyway?"

"He was tired. He's having a nap back in my room."

Jakol shook his head slowly, obviously unconvinced by his sister's story. "You're not fooling me Juna. You have no intention of helping us. We should have gotten rid of you a long time ago. I told Father you couldn't be trusted. Why don't we go back and tell him about this little outing of yours? I'm sure he'd be very interested in finding out who you're going to see."

"I'm not going back with you brother," she replied, assuming her fighting stance. "I have to stop Father from hurting those people. Can't you see what he's doing is wrong?"

Jakol laughed. "You're kidding right. *You* want to fight *me*? Do you really think you can beat me with one whole week of cadet training back when you were a little girl? Oh, yes. Don't think the boys in the barracks haven't had a good laugh about that one."

He stepped forward and reached out to grab her, but before he could get a grip, Juna launched a kick to his stomach, grabbed his arm and flipped him over her shoulder. As he landed, she stomped down on the side of his knee, shattering the joint with a sickening crunch. He let out a scream and laid there, whimpering on the ground.

Juna bent down and whispered in his ear. "Now the boys in the barracks have something new to laugh at. And make sure you tell Father I'm going to stop him."

Juna returned to the garage door, but a chill ran down her spine when she heard a slow clap coming from behind her. Colonel Pavic stepped out of the shadows.

"It would appear we have underestimated you, Princess," he said calmly. "It's not a mistake I intend to make again." He raised his arm and pointed a gun at her. "Your father really does love you, so I can't give you a chance to talk your way out of this one. We need to end this here."

There was an explosion of sound and Juna was flung back as she felt the impact. As she lay on the ground, a thought occurred to her that she was not in as much pain as she would have expected. She suddenly realized that it wasn't a bullet that had hit her – it was a spray of gravel. Looking up, her heart surged when she saw that Helion had leapt into the space between her and the Colonel. His massive metal arm swung out and swept the Colonel away like he was a leaf in the wind.

"Jump on!" Helion yelled. "There are soldiers everywhere." Juna went to climb on his back, but he turned to face her. "No. On the front – they have guns."

Juna gripped his chest plate and he lifted her, cradling her in his powerful arms. Shots rang out as Helion sprinted for the open field. She could hear the bullets ringing off his armour as he hurdled the fence and raced down the hill.

"Head for the river," she instructed him. "We can lose them there."

They travelled for nearly an hour before they dared to slow down. Helion changed course continuously and crossed the river several times to make tracking them more difficult. When Juna was sure they were safely away, she asked Helion to stop so she could get her bearings.

"Oh, Helion, thank you so much. I thought I was done for back there. How did you know I was in trouble?"

"I monitor you constantly," he replied, as if this was the most obvious thing in the world. "The necklace Orin gave you contains a small transmitter, so I always know where you are."

Juna didn't know what to make of this new piece of information, but she didn't have time to think about it now. "We have to get to the General," she told her mechanical friend. "He's on a farm west of the city."

"I know the place," he replied. "I will get you there safely."

Orin sat with his father and the General in the farmhouse's small dining room. They had decided to get together this evening to plan their next move. Two large pieces of paper had been taped to the wall which they were using to make lists for organizing their thoughts. The first list was for the things they knew and the second was for things they didn't know. Everyone was a little discouraged by the length of the second list. The item they were discussing now was how many Mechs the emperor had built for himself.

"How is it even possible?" the General asked. "Is it just Gigahertz or could he have made copies of all of them?"

"All of the plans and moulds are at The Depot," the Professor replied sheepishly. "There was no need to hide anything – our enemy doesn't even live on this planet. Theoretically, he could build as many as he wanted. Especially with all that scrap metal the Marans left behind. I don't think he could install AI's in them, but I think it unlikely he would want those anyway."

"That makes sense," Orin added. "The Gigahertz clone I saw didn't even have a comm panel."

Their discussion was cut short when Diara burst into the room. "I just got an emergency call from Helion. He's on his way here," she reported, hands on her knees, trying to catch her breath. "The Princess is with him."

Everyone was waiting outside to greet them when Helion and Juna arrived at the farmhouse. Pom rushed to greet her friend and the girls locked in an embrace.

"I'm a Tech now," Pom informed her excitedly as they separated. Juna didn't know what a Tech was, but she didn't really care. Pom was safe and happy and that was all that mattered. It felt so good to finally be back among her friends. Moving through the group, she hugged everyone, even the ones she had never met before.

When she came to Orin, she looked at him sternly. "Hello Orin," she said, no warmth in her voice. "Do you realize the first gift you ever gave me was a tracking device? That's a little creepy, don't you think?"

"Ah… But…I just…"

Juna's face lit up with a radiant smile. "Orin, I'm kidding," she said, throwing her arms around him. "That little transmitter of yours just saved my butt. It's the most beautiful thing I've ever owned – I'll never take it off."

The relief Orin felt at that moment was almost as wonderful as the feeling of her arms around him. He wanted it to last forever, but she broke the embrace and walked over to the General.

"I have information for you, sir," she told him. "We need to get to work."

They hid Helion in the barn and then assembled in the dining room where Juna began to tell them everything she had learned. Her father's plans to enslave the Marans. The army of Mechs and the massive stores of SIM's and TRIP's. Professor Oletta's situation. All of it. It was amazing to hear all the information she had acquired and everything she had gone through to get it. As she spoke, the General crossed off items on their list of things they didn't know and added items to the list of things they did. Orin noticed the General circling the entry noting Professor Oletta's willingness to help. When Juna concluded her report, the General stepped back to review everything he had written.

"You've done amazing work Juna," he finally said. "Two worlds owe you their thanks. There's still a lot to do, but we finally have enough to put together a decent plan. I don't see it all yet, but I know what our first step is going to be."

"What's that, General?" Orin asked.

"It's simple," he replied. "We get our Mechs back."

16

The General decided that the first thing their little group needed to do was move to a safer location. Knowing that Juna's escape, particularly because it involved a Mech, would eventually bring the emperor's men here in search of her, he felt it best to abandon the farm before royal guardsmen started showing up on the doorstep. First thing the next morning, a large delivery truck pulled up in front of the farmhouse. Orin was not surprised to see the side of the truck emblazoned with the logo for Leaping Lano's Furniture Emporium. Everyone packed up their things, including Diara's Tech station, and loaded them into the truck.

Their biggest problem was what to do with Helion. Being significantly larger than the truck, he certainly wasn't going in there. Hiding a giant fighting robot in the middle of an endless expanse of farmland was going to be a challenge. Ultimately, it was decided that he would lay low in the General's field for the day and then travel by night, making his way to the high desert. He would try to find a good hiding spot near The Depot where they could meet up with him later. After receiving an emotional goodbye from Juna, he stomped into the field and settled in amongst a field of high grasses to wait for nightfall.

The scene was hectic as belongings were packed and loaded into the truck. Seeing everyone working together, laughing and joking as they went about their tasks, warmed Orin's heart. It was really starting to feel like a team. Just as they were finishing up, he noticed the General standing on the porch, staring off into the distance, so he went over to check on him.

"Is everything OK General?" he asked.

"I'm fine, Orin. I didn't expect to enjoy it out here, but I really did. There is something to be said for living a simple life that doesn't involve blowing things up. I'm going to miss this place."

"Maybe you can come back some day."

"Maybe I can," he responded as he locked the farmhouse door and descended the steps. "But there is too much to be done to even consider that possibility right now. I'm afraid it might be quite some time before any of us have a real home again."

Orin and the General climbed into the back of the truck and pulled the doors shut behind them. The truck's engine fired up and they began their long trip to the city. The ride was rough and the confines were dark and cramped, but there were no complaints. Everyone was quiet, not really knowing what to expect in this next phase of their journey.

The truck made a quick stop at the Umbras' apartment so Orin and his dad could run in and grab a few things. As he was leaving the apartment, Orin wondered if he would ever come here again. This place never felt like home the way The Depot did, but it felt strange to think he may never see it again. The reality of life on the run was beginning to sink in.

Orin threw the hoverbike and the rest of his things into the truck and they continued on the long trip to wherever it was they were going. When the truck finally pulled to a stop and the doors swung open, everyone rushed out just to get a deep breath of fresh air. They emerged into a huge, well-lit room lined with rows of empty shelves. Everything looked bright and new, like the space had never been used before.

"Where are we?" Orin asked.

"We are in a hidden basement under Lano's warehouse," the General informed them. "I knew that the Underground would need a base of operations, so I secretly told Gigahertz to fire a missile at Lano's old warehouse while we were fighting the Marans. It gave us the perfect excuse to build this place."

Orin was surprised by the news – it seemed it wasn't the mystic's fault after all. He always found it remarkable how the General was able to plan things so far in advance.

"So, what do we do now?" he inquired.

"Nothing too difficult," the General responded with a smile. "We come up with a plan to defeat the emperor, free the hods and save the Marans. So, let's get to it."

The first step was setting up the Tech Station to re-establish communications with the Mechs. The General asked Diara and Orin to develop software upgrades to enhance the Mechs' sensor capabilities. He wanted to know everything he could about what was going on in The Depot.

The next step was to figure out a way to rescue Professor Oletta and get her to join them for the planning of the next phase of the operation. The General was convinced that gaining control of the Gate was going to be the key to extracting the Mechs from The Depot, but he didn't know enough about how it actually worked. He assembled the entire team around a large conference table to discuss how to get her here.

"So how do we rescue someone from the most secure building on the planet?" he asked the group.

"We could just get one of our Mechs to storm in and grab her," Orin offered.

"We have to remember that they have a lot more Mechs than we do," The General countered. "We're lucky they didn't decide to destroy the original group when they first took over. No. This needs to be something quiet. We have to sneak her out before they even know she's missing."

"There must be delivery vehicles going to The Depot," Juna chimed in. "Maybe we can get her out in one of those."

"Excellent!" the General responded. "Diara, what would we need to do to access their computer systems?"

"There's a network running through the entire facility," Diara responded. "There would be access points in the archives vault. If we could connect a cable from one of those to one of our Mechs, I should be able to hack into their system."

"Then that's what we'll do." You could see the details of a plan forming in the General's mind. "Orin and Juna. Get your stealth gear together. You're going to be making a little nighttime raid on The Depot this evening."

The plan was simple enough. Orin and Juna would break into The Depot the same way Orin had done it earlier. They would then connect one of the Mechs to the building's network and hide out in one of the Bios' cargo holds until they were needed to assist in the rescue of Professor Oletta.

That evening, Orin and Juna collected everything they needed and stuffed it into their backpacks. Orin packed up his handheld laser along with the key card, alarm jammer and invisibility blanket. They also took a network cable and two small radios that could be clipped to their ears, so they could stay in constant contact with Diara. Lastly, they packed enough food and water to last them a few days while they waited in the archives vault for the plan to come together. Orin was worried about breaking into

The Depot again, but the thought of spending a few days alone with Juna made all the risks seem worth it.

Hugs and well wishes were exchanged as Orin and Juna hopped on the hoverbike for their journey to The Depot. Night had already fallen and the moons weren't out tonight, so the hoverbike's headlight provided the only illumination of the pitch-black highway. The trip went well except for Juna's constant ribbing about what a slow driver Orin was. They pulled off the road when The Depot came into view and hid the hoverbike in the same gulley Orin had used before. Clipping on their radios, they began the long hike to the fence line.

Orin found the same spot on the fence he had cut before and used his laser to recreate the opening. They both slipped through. It was unlikely they would be leaving the same way they came in, so Orin decided to weld the gap closed now. He slid the invisibility blanket out of this backpack and threw it over them to conceal their activity. His welds were not very precise. He was having difficulty concentrating while trapped under the blanket with Juna – she even smelled beautiful.

When the repair was completed, they checked in with Diara. Gig was using his sensors to track the position of all the security guards and then relaying that information to her. When they were given the all-clear, they dashed across the field for the door at the back of the assembly building. Orin turned on the alarm jammer and used his key card to open the door. Just as they stepped inside, an emergency call came in from Diara.

"Move to your left and hide there for a minute," she warned them. "There's a guard coming."

Orin and Juna crouched behind a large crate and waited for the guard to pass. When he was gone, they emerged from their hiding spot and sprinted across the room in the direction of the archives vault.

"Wait!" Diara shouted over the radio. "The General wants you to do something first."

Slipping in and hiding behind another crate, they waited for Diara to give them further instructions. "The General thinks you might need to go see Professor Oletta sometime during the day and you'll need to blend in. See if you can find a locker room and get some overalls for yourselves to use as a disguise."

"I know where that is!" they said in unison, smiling at each other as they zipped across the assembly floor to the locker room at the back of the building. When they got there, Orin used his key card to gain access. None of the lockers were locked, so they each opened several until they found something that fit.

Emerging from the locker room, they each wore a pair of blue overalls and a grey cap – the standard uniform worn by every Wrench at The Depot. With guidance from Gigahertz every step of the way, they managed to arrive at the door to the archives vault without encountering a single guard. Orin used his key card to open the door and they quietly stepped inside.

"It's good to see you, Master Orin," Gigahertz said as they rounded the corner. "You too, Princess."

"It's just Juna, if you don't mind," she replied. "Thanks for your help. I didn't feel like fighting any guards tonight."

"The pleasure was mine."

They both searched the walls of the vault for a network access point, finally finding one near the back of the room. Isotope was the closest Mech, so Orin recovered the network cable from his backpack and ran it from her comm panel to the access point on the wall. Before they could even report their progress, their radios sprang to life.

"I'm in!" Diara reported. "Their security is really bad." There was a pause as Diara had a conversation with someone on the other end. "OK," she finally returned. "The General says that's all we need for now. You guys sit tight while we come up with a plan. We'll get back to you first thing in the morning. Great job you two."

They were both too wired to sleep, so Orin led Juna around the vault, introducing her to all the Mechs. When they were done, they climbed into Armorat's cargo hold to find a place to sleep.

"Well, this is cozy," Juna said when she got inside.

Orin didn't know if she was being sarcastic or not, but he assumed she was. "Yeah, I guess you're used to something *a lot* more luxurious than this," he guessed.

"No, I'm serious," she replied, somewhat offended. "A year ago, I would have agreed with you, but not anymore. That day I first came to see you at The Depot was the worst day of my life. I felt so useless, not being able to do anything in the real world. I spent the last year learning to be a survivor. I travelled the back roads, slept outside and even learned to make fire by rubbing two sticks together."

"Wow," Orin said, genuinely impressed. "I've never done any of those things. I guess I had the wrong idea about the life of a princess."

"Oh, I'm not a princess anymore. Literally. I would imagine I've been officially thrown out of the family for all the things I've done the last few days."

Orin sat there listening as she recounted her recent adventures, including her harrowing escape from the palace and the fight with her brother and the Colonel. Then he told her all the details of his last adventure at The Depot. He had never found anyone he could talk to as easily as he could with Gig, but sitting here chatting with Juna felt so natural. It was like nothing had changed between them since they were kids.

"We need to get some sleep," Juna finally said as she stifled a yawn. "The General might have big plans for us tomorrow. Thank you, Orin. I'm glad we got to do this together. It's been really nice."

"I had fun too," he replied. "We should do it again sometime."

Juna laughed at that, then rolled herself onto one of Armorat's benches to go to sleep. Orin laid down on another bench and thought about everything they had done today. He knew he wouldn't be able to sleep, but he closed his eyes anyway. What seemed like a moment later, he was startled awake by a squawk on the radio.

"Rise and shine everybody," came Diara's cheerful voice. "We've got a big day planned for you two."

Orin checked the time and realized he'd been asleep for hours. He looked over to see Juna slowly rising to her feet, rubbing the sleep from her eyes.

"We have a plan," Diara continued. "There's a laundry truck coming to The Depot this afternoon. The General has pulled some strings with his contacts in the Underground. We're going to get you and the professor out on that truck."

"What do you want us to do?" Orin asked.

"You need to go find Professor Oletta and get her working on the Gate. Have her repair it, but then take something important out and hide it. We want to leave it so no one will be able to fix it while she's gone but she can get it running right away when she gets back. Then the three of you need to be in the locker room in the dome at 4 o'clock."

Excited to have a plan, they ate a quick breakfast and began packing up to start the search for the professor. They left most of the food and water behind, bringing only enough with them for lunch. Putting everything else they had brought in a large cardboard box they found in the office, they got ready to set out. Orin took the box and Juna grabbed a toolbox that had been left behind by Team Steam and they quietly stepped out into the hallway.

Orin worried about running into someone who might recognize him, so he stayed in constant contact with Diara so she and Gigahertz could guide them along a path with as few people as possible. The best route appeared to be one that would lead them outside, so they headed for the nearest exit. It was such a beautiful day. They let the heat of the sun wash over them, thankful to be breathing outside air again. Seeing the immense dome in the distance, they set off in that direction.

When they reached the dome, Orin pulled out his key card and used it to open one of the doors on the side of the building. Inside was a Gate that appeared to be identical to the one he had seen at The Institute, except the lights lining its edge were red and orange rather than blue and green. Three people were working on the massive structure – one of them was Professor Oletta. They quietly walked up behind her.

"Is there somewhere we can talk?" Juna asked, tapping her shoulder.

The woman was startled by the sudden appearance of two strangers. Juna had tucked her long hair into her cap, so she was not immediately recognized. When the professor finally made the connection, a look of relief swept across her face.

"Oh, yes," she said, ushering them into a nearby office. "We can talk in here."

Closing the door behind them, she rushed over to Juna and threw her arms around her. "Oh, thank you for coming," she said, her relief evident. "I've been so worried they would discover what I've been doing."

Juna returned the embrace, then explained to her exactly what the General needed them to do. The professor mulled over the task at hand. "It will be close," she finally replied. "But if you help me, we should be able to get it done."

Stepping out of the office, Professor Oletta informed the people working on the Gate that their services would not be required for the rest of the day. When they were gone, she walked over to an access panel, removed the cover and pulled out a large piece of paper from deep within the open cavity. Spreading it out on a nearby table, she showed them schematics for the Gate's control system.

"This is what it's supposed to look like," she told them. "I have incorrectly wired almost every cable on this control board. I have broken some other things as well. I'll work on those while you fix the control board wiring. Do you know how to use a soldering iron?"

"What's a soldering iron?" Juna asked.

"Don't worry," Orin jumped in. "We've got this. You go do what you need to do."

They worked at it all day. Orin read the schematic and operated the soldering iron while Juna used a pair of pliers to hold each wire steady as he worked on it. They made quite a team. Just as they completed the last cable, Professor Oletta joined them at the control panel.

"I'm all done," she informed them. "How are you doing?"

"Just finished up," Orin replied. "Let's give it a test."

Professor Oletta powered up the control board and ran it through a series of diagnostics. Orin kept his eye on the clock during the entire process – they were running out of time. After half an hour of testing, the professor powered down the unit and declared it fully operational. Walking over to a large parts cabinet, she pulled out a small black component with four silver terminals on it.

"It's the dynamic field regulator," she informed them. "This is the last spare we have left." She snapped the cover off and started cutting components out of it and throwing them in the garbage. She replaced the cover and proceeded to disconnect an identical unit from the control board. She replaced it with the newly-damaged device and hid the good one deep inside the cavity from which she had recovered the schematics.

"It will take them a month to figure that one out," she said with a devilish smile. "I, however, will be able to fix it in less than a minute."

Orin checked the time – it was 4 o'clock. Looking across to the far side of the massive room, he saw a large laundry cart being pushed by an even larger man. Taz. He grabbed the attention of Juna and Professor Oletta and, within seconds, they were sprinting for the locker room. All four of them arrived at the door simultaneously, so they piled inside. Taz removed the laundry from the cart and directed the professor to get inside. She eyed him suspiciously.

"It's OK," he reassured her with a beaming smile. "I'm one of the good guys."

Professor Oletta climbed into the cart and they covered her with a heap of dirty overalls. Orin grabbed the box with all their stuff while Juna took the toolbox and they set out for the building's loading dock, Taz following closely behind. With some helpful guidance from Gig and Diara, they managed to reach the dock without interruption and rolled the cart into a waiting truck. Orin and Juna buried themselves in a pile of stinky laundry as Taz slammed the truck's door shut. Seconds later they began to move.

The truck came to a stop at The Depot's main gate. Hearing the guards questioning the driver, Orin held his breath when the back door of the truck swung open.

"See. Dirty laundry, just like I told you," he heard Taz say.

Orin remained perfectly still and didn't allow himself to breathe again until the truck door closed and they were moving again. When they were safely away, Orin dug himself out of the pile and helped Juna do the same. Together, they pulled the laundry off of the professor and helped her out of the cart.

A huge grin emerged on Orin's face. "We did it!" he exclaimed.

Professor Oletta's relief was obvious as they all embraced, barely able to believe that they had pulled it off.

After a short trip, the truck rolled to a stop and they all got out at the laundry's loading dock. Transferring to an almost identical truck, this one sporting a picture of Leaping Lano's smiling face, they continued their journey. Twenty minutes later, they emerged, unscathed but smelling bad, in their new hiding place under Lano's warehouse. The whole team was there to greet them.

Professor Oletta was introduced to the group as they made their way to the conference room where the General was going to fill them in on the plan.

"Congratulations everyone on a successful mission," the General began. "Let's hope it is the first of many. Here's what we need to do next. We will sneak into The Depot with all our equipment, grab the Mechs and as many missiles as we can get our hands on and then use the Gate to escape to a secure location that is yet to be determined. Oh, and the Gate will have to come with us."

Everyone turned their gaze in the direction of Professor Oletta to gauge her reaction to the plan. She looked like she was going to be sick. "But, that's impossible," she finally replied.

"Impossible?" the General countered, an amused look on his face. "We have just gone to great lengths to put the two smartest people on the planet in the same room. I shouldn't think anything was impossible after accomplishing that."

17

The work began immediately. The General worried that the disappearance of Professor Oletta would enrage the emperor and feared they only had a few days to execute their plan. The last thing he wanted to see was a platoon of royal guardsmen scouring the city in search of her. His goal was to recover the Mechs and steal the Gate as quickly as possible to give the emperor something much bigger to worry about than the mere inconvenience of a missing professor.

The General had the whole team assemble in the conference room. He had taped a large piece of paper to the wall and written "The Great Mech Heist" at the top. Under that, he had listed the major obstacles they would need to overcome to accomplish their mission:

- Where do we go after the heist?
- How do we get into The Depot?
- What do we need to take with us?
- What do we steal when we get there?
- How do we take the Gate with us?

Orin looked around the room and saw the eleven people that would be tasked with solving all of these problems. They were seated around a large conference table, waiting for the meeting to get started. None of them appeared to be brimming with confidence. He realized that the General put up the list to help them organize the mission, but he found the whole situation very discouraging. Sensing a lot of other people in the room were feeling the same way, he sat quietly, trying not to look too depressed. Thankfully, his father spoke up to break the silence. "I think I can help with the first one," he offered.

"You know of a secret hiding place big enough to fit eighteen Mechs and a fifty-foot tall space portal gate?" the General asked skeptically.

"In fact, I do," The Professor replied confidently. "Years ago, my father started an ambitious project trying to bring water to the high desert. He built a facility on the eastern edge of the desert near the coast. It's nearly a thousand miles from The Depot. I'm probably the only person on the planet that remembers it's there. It has huge underground caverns that were dug out by the Steamers – it's why they were built in the first place. When the Marans showed up, the emperor changed his priorities and the whole project was abandoned."

"But Darin, do you think it will still be intact?" the General asked.

"I don't see why not," he replied. "Everything my father built, he built to last."

The General clapped his hands together and stood to add a checkmark to his list. "You see," he proclaimed triumphantly. "Things are starting to come together already. I believe the next three things on the list are just a matter of careful planning. We can do that. The big one is going to be taking the Gate with us. The professors will focus on that while the rest of us break into teams to organize everything else. Time is of the essence everyone, so let's get to work."

Orin and Juna were assigned the task of making a list of all the things they would need to survive in their new home in the desert. For each item, they needed to decide whether to take it with them to The Depot during the heist or whether it made more sense to steal it when they got there. The list of things to take with them included items like food, clothing and the Tech Station, while things like missiles, tools and spare parts would have to be taken from The Depot during the mission.

As they were working, Orin noticed Dorel and Annu pacing the floor, taking measurements and drawing up plans. The General knew that surviving in an isolated location on the edge of the desert would require a way to restock their supplies as they ran out. His proposed solution was opening portals right here under Lano's warehouse. Currently, the space was too small, so he had Dorel and Annu designing the changes that would be required to make it happen.

"So, is it going to fit?" Orin called over jokingly.

"Oh, it'll fit," Dorel called back. "We're going to have to move some stuff around, but we'll get it in here."

"I sure hope so. We're all going to be awfully hungry if you don't figure it out."

"Not missing a meal is all the motivation I need," Dorel replied, patting himself on the stomach.

Their banter was cut short when the sound of a truck entering the building drew Orin's attention to the loading dock. Skeet and Taz were back. The General had sent them out this morning to recover Orin's hoverbike from its hiding spot in the desert. "No sense leaving clues lying around if we don't have to," he had said.

Orin walked over to the loading dock to greet Skeet and Taz and give them their next assignment. He handed over the list of things required for the heist. "Here's all the stuff we need," he told them. "The General wants you guys to collect it and get it packed into boxes."

"That's a lot of stuff," Taz noted as he ran his finger down the list. "It's gonna take us a while."

"Yeah, well we might be there for a long time," Orin replied. "Lano has offered to help if you need it."

"Don't worry about a thing," Skeet jumped in, snatching the list from Taz. "This is exactly the kind of stuff that I do best."

Just as they turned to begin working on the list, Diara burst into the room. "Conference room, everybody!" she shouted. "I think I have a way in."

When everyone was assembled, Diara told them what she had come up with. "There is a scheduled delivery for a company called Empire Equipment on the day after tomorrow. It's a large truck that will be going directly to the Central Assembly Building."

"That's perfect," the General noted. "If we can intercept that delivery, it will give us the perfect opportunity to get inside. Skeet. Taz. You two are going to arrange for some mechanical problems with the delivery trucks over at Empire Equipment. And find out what those trucks look like – we'll have to repaint one of Lano's to look just like it." He clapped his hands together and scanned the room to make sure he had everyone's attention. "So that's it everyone. The plan is set. We go the day after tomorrow. Let's make sure we're ready."

Having a deadline energized everybody in the building. Dorel and Annu finished their plans for enlarging the warehouse while Skeet and Taz continued to collect everything the team would need for the mission. Orin and Juna were busy drawing up a floor plan for The Depot and marking the locations of everything they would need to grab during the heist. They were interrupted from their work when the General walked up to speak with them.

"You two, come with me. I need you to work with the Techs on something."

Orin and Juna joined Diara and Pom at the Tech Station. The General addressed them in a quiet voice. "There is one major obstacle that I didn't include on the list," he informed them. "I really didn't want to scare everyone on the first day."

"What is it?" Orin asked, his concern obvious.

"We will try to be as quiet as we can when we invade The Depot, but at some point, they're going to know we're there. They have an army of Mechs at their disposal. We need to figure out a way to avoid an all-out battle with them. That is *not* something we would survive. Disabling those Mechs before anyone is aware of what we are doing is imperative."

"They appeared to be turned off when I saw them," Juna offered. "Maybe we can stop anyone from trying to turn them on."

"The one I saw didn't even have a power switch," Orin added. "Without the AI's, I'm not even sure how they work."

"If they can't think on their own, there must be a central command centre somewhere," Diara proposed. "If we could hack into that, we might be able to keep them from powering up."

"OK, work on that," the General instructed. "This is priority one. If we can't figure out a way to stop those Mechs, this whole operation is in jeopardy."

Orin felt his anxiety rising as he wandered back to his work area. As if they didn't have enough to worry about already. He hadn't thought of it before, but a pack of rampaging Mechs would definitely add to the difficulty of this mission. The General was right – this was priority one.

The rest of the day proved busy for everyone. Orin and Juna finished marking up their floor plan mapping out the best route through The Depot, then went to help Diara and Pom work on hacking into the Mechs' control system. Taz and Skeet started painting one of Lano's delivery trucks to look like it belonged to Empire Equipment, while Dorel and Annu continued to work on the warehouse revisions. Nobody saw the professors for the entire afternoon as they were locked away trying to figure out some way to steal the Gate.

At the end of the day, the General brought everyone together in the conference room to see how everything was going. He started by getting Taz and Skeet to update him on their collecting activity. They had more than half of the list accounted for and were confident they could finish it by tomorrow. They thought the truck would be repainted by then too. Next, Orin and Juna showed everyone the floor plan and how they would need to move through the building to gather everything they required. Dorel and Annu updated everyone on their proposed changes to the warehouse to allow a portal to be opened there. Professor Oletta made a couple of suggestions, but thought, in the end, the new space would be large enough.

"We'll need some help building it," Dorel added. "There's excavation work required and walls to be moved. Even part of the floor to the warehouse above us will have to be cut away. This is a big job, so we'll need some heavy equipment to get it done."

"We'll leave a couple of Mechs behind and get them over here to help," the General stated. "I'll make sure I work that into the plan." He paused for a moment and stared at the professors, looking almost afraid to hear the answer to his next question. "How are things going with the Gate?" he finally asked. "Are we going to be able to take it with us?"

Professor Umbra spoke first. "Right now, Aeva is teaching me the science she used to build it. So far, the only thing I know for sure is that I am *not* the smartest person on the planet."

"We're making progress," Professor Oletta interrupted, smiling at her fellow professor and patting him on the hand. "And Darin is doing just fine. We have a theory we're working on. I think it's possible – we just need to keep at it."

"That's good," the General replied. "Do your best. If you can't figure out a way to make this work, we can still escape to the desert, but I'm not sure what we'll be able to do when we get there."

There was a brief delay before the General continued – he was obviously considering his next words carefully. "There is no way to put off this discussion any longer," he finally said. "I am very concerned about all of the unfriendly Mechs in the building we are breaking into and I'm afraid of what might happen if someone decides to turn them on. I've asked our young technical geniuses to see if they can find a way to stop that from happening. So, Diara, do you have an update on that?"

"I have some good news and some bad news," she reported. "The good news is that there *is* a master power-up command broadcast from a central control system. If I can block that frequency, we should be able to prevent the Mechs from turning on, at least for a while."

"What's the bad news?"

"I don't know what frequency to block," she replied with unconcealed frustration. "Until the command is sent, I won't be able to see what frequency they are using and by then, it will be too late to block it."

"So, we need them to power up those Mechs early," the General suggested.

"But, why would they do that?" Orin asked.

"Maybe, if there was some sort of emergency," Juna proposed. "What if they thought they were under attack?"

"That's good," the General said, a plan coming into focus. "Darin, what sort of weapons is Helion carrying right now?"

The Professor smiled, seeing what the General had in mind. "He's currently configured for perimeter guard duty. That means he'll have a dozen conventional missiles onboard."

"So, we have a plan," the General concluded. "Tonight, we will get Helion to simulate an attack on The Depot. Something small enough that they won't get too suspicious, but big enough to get them to power up those Mechs."

Later that evening, everyone prepared for Helion's attack on The Depot. Diara and Pom sat at the Tech station while the rest of the group stood behind them to watch the action on the monitors. Pom instructed Helion to emerge from his hiding spot about a mile from The Depot. He swept the area with his camera and sensors and fed the information back to the Tech Station.

"There!" The General exclaimed. "That fuel truck parked behind the dome. If we can blow it up, they should get spooked enough to call an emergency. If nothing happens after that, they might think some sort of electrical problem sparked an explosion and not investigate any further."

On the General's command, Helion locked onto his target and launched one of his missiles. The resulting explosion was spectacular, the truck transforming into a monstrous fireball that illuminated the entire facility.

"I'm getting a report from Gigahertz of alarm bells ringing inside The Depot," Pom reported.

"I've got it!" Diara exclaimed. "They're powering up the Mechs. I have the frequency."

"Excellent," the General acknowledged. "Let's hope their search into the cause of all this mess is not too thorough."

For the next three hours, the Mech clones patrolled the grounds of The Depot. Helion had returned to his hiding place and dropped into wait state so he would be impossible to pick up on sensors. The whole group watched the proceedings using only the sensor read-outs provided by Gigahertz from inside the archives vault. They were all so nervous, there was hardly a word spoken during the entire ordeal.

Finally, the search was called off and the Mech clones returned to their storage building next to the dome. The room let out a collective sigh as they realized the search for the source of the attack was over. The General had been correct – they must have concluded that the truck exploded because of a mechanical failure.

"Well, that's it for tonight," the General said, wiping sweat from his brow. "We should all try to get some sleep. Tomorrow is our last day to get ready so we need to be at our best."

The morning brought with it the best news they could have hoped for. The professors had stayed up all night and came up with a plan to take the Gate with them to their new home in the desert. They were all assembled in the conference room while Professor Oletta explained the details.

"There are still a few technical problems we'll need to address, but I think we can do it," she began. "If we can send a power surge through the Gate's induction coil, the portal should push out past the opening of the Gate and completely surround it. If we power it down at that moment, the Gate should emerge at the other end of the portal. That means it will physically move to the underground cavern in the desert."

The General was stunned. "That's amazing," he said. "What are the technical problems we need to address?"

"The first one is that this process will melt the Gate's induction coil, so we need to take another one with us if we ever want to get it running again."

"Orin, add that to your list," the General ordered. "In fact, grab as many as you can. We may need to move this thing again sometime. Hope for the best, plan for the worst, I always say. What else, Aeva?"

"The generator in the dome is not going to be able to provide us with enough power to produce the surge we need. We'll have to find a second power source and run a feed to the Gate's induction coil."

"Dorel and Annu, you've got this one," the General instructed. "Go through The Depot's electrical drawings and find a way to run a second power feed."

"As long as we're talking about power," Professor Umbra chimed in, "we may have a serious problem when we arrive in the desert. There is a large generator there, but it hasn't been turned on in over twenty years. I'm sure we'll be able to get it running again, but it may take us a few days. It will be impossible to live out there without any power. When my father first started the project, he ran a super-conducting power cable all the way from The Depot. That cable will still be there, but I'm sure it was disconnected years ago. It's buried very deep, so I don't think they'll be able to track us with it, but we *will* need to figure out where it is and get it reconnected."

"Dorel and Annu, you've got that one too," the General instructed as he paced back and forth, surveying the room to assess the mood of the team. "Is there anything else I need to know about?" No one had anything to add – they all just sat there fidgeting in their seats. "Good," he concluded. "Our heist just got a little more complicated, but I'm sure it's nothing we can't handle. Let's get to work people. Tomorrow is going to be here before we know it."

The whole team kept up a frantic pace all morning. Skeet and Taz finished painting the truck and were busy loading it with boxes full of the things they had collected for the mission. Dorel and Annu were building large crates with wheels on the bottom that would be used to sneak members of the team into the building. Right now, they were drilling holes in the top of them so everyone inside could breathe. Diara and Pom were setting up their Tech Station inside one of the new crates and adding batteries so they could use it throughout the mission.

By the middle of the afternoon, the truck was packed and ready to roll. The General called everyone together for a rehearsal of the heist. Juna led them through the floor plan to show each person where they needed to be and what they needed to do at each stage of the plan. Diara kept a comm link open with the Mechs in the archives vault so they would know their roles as well. After running through it several times, everyone was exhausted, but in the end, they had all memorized every move they would need to make for the mission to be a success.

That evening, they ate dinner together around the conference table. Orin looked around the room, amazed at this odd group of people that had been brought together for this mission. There was an Elite, a military officer, academics, Techs, Wrenches and hods. It was such an unlikely group, yet it felt so natural to be together like this. Despite the dangers they would all be facing tomorrow, laughter filled the room, as if none of them had a care in the world. It felt like a family. He looked across the table and caught Juna's eye. The way she returned his smile, he knew she was thinking the exact same thing.

After dinner, Lano brought down a large box and placed it in the middle of the table. It was filled with items from a costume shop for making disguises so they wouldn't be recognized while roaming the halls of The Depot. They all tried on wigs and put on fake glasses, laughing and joking at every ridiculous combination. Everyone agreed that Juna looked incredible with a thick black moustache and frizzy blond wig. It was so much fun, no one wanted the evening to end. Finally, the General reminded them what a big day they had in store and ordered them all to get some sleep.

Orin was lying on his bed, thinking about the adventure that lay ahead. He tried to focus on what he needed to do rather than all the things that could go wrong along the way. Mostly, he thought about Gig, and all the other Mechs, and how nice it would be when they were all together again. It was these thoughts that finally allowed him to drift off to sleep with a peaceful smile on his face.

18

The Great Mech Heist was underway. Nerves were on edge as they made their way through the streets of Volara in Lano's newly repainted delivery truck. Dorel and Annu were up front in the cab with a member of the Underground who would drive the truck away when it was unloaded. The General, the professors, Juna, Diara and Pom were all packed into the back with Orin. The space was dark and cramped with the rumble of the truck's engine providing the only sound. There was little talking, each person seemingly lost in their own thoughts. Despite all their rehearsals, everyone was noticeably anxious now that they were actually on their way.

Nervous glances were exchanged as the truck rolled to a stop. Orin checked his watch – right on time. The back door of the truck swung open and Skeet and Taz jumped in, closing the door behind them. The two of them had set out before dawn to disable the delivery trucks at Empire Equipment. It was easy to tell from Skeet's beaming smile that the first step of the plan had been a success.

"It will take them all day to get those trucks running," Skeet reported. "They should be finding out very shortly that they won't be making any deliveries today."

Everyone sat quietly, watching the Tech Station. Diara had hacked into the phone system and programmed it to intercept all outgoing calls from Empire Equipment directed to The Depot and reroute them to her station in the back of the truck. Although they were expecting it, everyone jumped when the console buzzed. Pom slipped on her headset and pressed a button on the console. "Hello. You have reached The Depot. How may I help you?" There was a short pause, then Pom continued. "Empire Equipment? Oh yes, I see it here on the delivery schedule." Another pause. "A problem with your trucks? Yes, that *can* be annoying. Why don't we just reschedule for the same time tomorrow?" Another pause. "No problem at all. You have a nice day too." Pom pressed a button on the console to disconnect the call and threw off her headset.

"How was that?" she asked, an ear-to-ear grin on her face.

"You were awesome!" Juna exclaimed as Pom received congratulations for her performance and a big hug from Diara. Phase one was complete. Empire Equipment would not be making a delivery today, but The Depot was still expecting them to arrive on time. Everything was going according to plan. The General radioed Dorel to get the truck moving again and they were on their way.

During the trip, everyone took their assigned positions. Diara and Pom sat in their seats at the Tech Station in the crate as Taz replaced the removable panel to seal them inside. Then the General, the professors, Taz and Skeet climbed into the second wheeled crate so Orin and Juna could seal that one too. By the time everyone was locked in, the truck was slowing for the final turn into The Depot's driveway. There was a brief stop as the guards cleared the truck through the security gate. Everyone breathed a sigh of relief when they were moving again, knowing that their ruse had been a success.

The truck bumped to a stop at the loading dock and, moments later, the back door swung open. Dorel and Annu walked in, wearing overalls from Lano's with the patches removed and "Empire Equipment" written on with a black pen. It wasn't perfect, but it would probably be OK if no one looked too closely. They each pushed one of the large crates onto the loading dock and then started in on the smaller ones containing all of their supplies.

Orin and Juna were wearing the overalls they had stolen on their last trip here, along with wigs, glasses and a little grease smeared on their faces. They helped with a couple of boxes and then made a dash for the assembly floor when nobody was looking. Moving quickly but trying to look inconspicuous, they made their way to the locker room from which they had stolen the overalls on their last trip here. When they reached the door, Orin used his key card to open it. As he was stepping inside, he turned and passed the key card to Juna. She gave his arm a light squeeze as she took it from him.

"Thanks," she said, giving him a quick smile. "See you in the archives vault." Then she zipped back across the assembly floor.

The universal key card Orin had built was still the only one they had. One of the most complicated aspects of planning the heist had been how to move the key card from one place to another as each person needed to gain access to a different location.

Fortunately, the locker room was unoccupied, so he headed for the back corner, retrieved one of the laundry carts and wheeled it over to a bank of lockers. Not having the time required to pick out individual uniforms for each member of the team, he just started grabbing things out of the lockers and stuffing them into his cart. When it was full, he pushed it out the door and headed in the direction of the archives vault.

Orin was relieved that there weren't any alarm bells ringing. So far, their presence must not have been detected. This phase of the plan had Dorel and Annu unloading the truck and then pushing the crates with people in them to the archives vault. By the time they got there, Juna should have arrived with the key card to let them in. He pictured them having already arrived, safely awaiting his arrival. As he pushed his cart through the halls to join them, he felt himself smile – things seemed to be going quite well so far.

"Orin! Is that you?"

Orin felt a surge of panic and immediately regretted not spending a little more time on his disguise. He turned to see Balko staring at him. "Ah, no. My name's not Orin," he said, once again failing in his attempt to mimic Dorel.

"You're kidding me, right?" Balko responded, a look of disbelief on his face. "Orin. I know it's you. What are you doing here?"

"OK. OK, it's me. But no one is supposed to know I'm here," he begged. "Let's just keep this between us, all right?"

"Sure, no problem," Balko reassured him. "It sure is great to see you. You wouldn't believe what it's like here now. The Royal Guard has completely taken over the place. They threaten us if we don't help and we're never allowed to leave. It's like we're prisoners. Why are you here? Did you come to save us?"

"Not right now," Orin told him, "but we are working on something big. We're going to be gone for a while, but I promise we'll be back to help you as soon as we can. Just don't tell anyone you saw me today."

"OK," he promised. "But come back soon. It's really horrible here now."

Orin felt terrible as he turned to walk away from Balko. It was sad that his old friends were now prisoners in a place that used to be his home. He just hoped that someday he would be able to keep the promise he just made. But there was no time to think about that now. The mission he was on would require his full attention, so he refocused his thoughts and continued the walk towards the archives vault. When he got there, he knocked lightly on the door three times. The General opened the door to allow him inside.

"We were starting to worry," the General said. "Did everything go alright?"

"Balko recognized me," Orin told him. "He promised he wouldn't tell anyone he saw me, but the people here need our help. They're all being held prisoner."

"And we will help them, Orin," the General assured him. "But I'm afraid they may have to wait a while. This operation is the only thing we can think about right now. If we can get through this, we will be in a better position to start helping others." He turned to peer inside the laundry cart. "So, let's have a look at what you brought us."

As Orin stepped further into the room, he noticed that he was not the only person to encounter some trouble on the way to the vault. There was an unconscious guard tied up in the corner. His gaze immediately turned to Juna. She returned a shrug and a mischievous smile. "Yeah, I kind of bumped into someone on the way here."

Orin couldn't help but laugh. It was times like this when he was truly grateful that he and Juna were on the same side. Looking around the room, he saw that all eleven members of the team were there. Phase two of the plan was now complete. Everyone started rummaging around in the newly arrived laundry bin looking for something that might fit them. As each person finished slipping into their new disguise, they went to join the General to get their next assignment.

"Professors, you're in the maintenance shop," he began. "Skeet and Taz, you've got the armoury. Get everything on your lists and stack it near the emergency exit doors. If you can't lift something, don't worry. I'll be sending the Mechs in twenty minutes to pick everything up. Dorel, you go to the generator room, find those old electrical drawings the Professor told you about and get that buried cable to the desert reconnected. Annu will go straight to the dome to install the second power feed for the Gate."

The General paused, sensing the team was being overwhelmed by the task ahead of them. "Don't worry. We *can* do this," he reassured them. "Guards get lazy in facilities like this – we probably won't even see one until the alarms start ringing. When they do, don't panic. Just get to the dome. Never forget – we have the Mechs. If you get into any trouble, call in on the radio and I *will* send help."

He looked around the room and noticed the team looking a little more confident, so he continued with the assignments. "Orin, you'll need to use the key card to grant everyone access. When that's done, you and Juna get to the loading dock, grab a couple of forklifts and get all our supplies to the dome. I'll be here helping Diara and Pom get the Tech Station loaded into Armorat. OK. Everybody knows what to do. Let's get moving."

Everyone clipped radios to their ears and performed sound checks. Orin grabbed the key card and waited until Gigahertz told him the hallway was clear. As soon as they were given the go-ahead, the entire group spilled out of the vault as quietly as they could. Annu grabbed her tools and headed for the dome while the rest of the team made their way in the direction of the generator room. Orin opened the door for Dorel and wished him luck as those remaining set off for the armoury. After dropping Skeet and Taz at the armoury and the professors at the maintenance shop, Orin and Juna made their way to the loading dock.

Orin had been driving forklifts since he was a little kid, so he gave Juna a quick lesson on how to operate one. She picked it up easily and soon they had all their crates stacked neatly into two piles. Each using their forklift to pick up one of the piles, they started moving in the direction of the dome. Being more familiar with the newer parts of the facility, Juna took the lead.

The only way Orin could keep up with Juna was by holding the accelerator pedal pinned to the floor. Despite her inexperience driving a forklift, she certainly liked to keep it moving as fast as she could. Not wanting to hit anyone, he tried to focus on his driving, but often found himself distracted by the chatter on the radio. The General kept his microphone open so everyone could keep track of how the other members of the team were doing. Dorel and Annu were both making progress on their electrical work and Diara and Pom had finished setting up the Tech Station inside Armorat's cargo hold.

Desperately trying to keep up with Juna, he soon found himself in the large tunnel that connected the Central Assembly Building to the new storage building next to the dome. Rounding the corner into the cavernous space, he let out a gasp. There were Mechs lined up as far as the eye could see. Arranged in four long rows, each machine was standing only a few feet from its neighbour. The emperor's workforce had been very busy – it looked like they had built five or six of each model. There were over a hundred of them! Even for someone who had grown up surrounded by Mechs, it was an awesome sight.

A distress call on the radio startled Orin back to reality. It was his father. "We have a problem, General," he reported. "Carnage has arrived to help us load the equipment, but the outside door to the maintenance shop isn't big enough to let him in."

"Oh well," the General replied calmly. "We knew we were going to have to make some noise eventually. Just tell him to make the door bigger."

Orin imagined how happy Carnage was at that moment, picturing him tearing pieces of the building away so he could get inside. Seconds later, alarm bells started ringing. Everyone in the building started yelling and running frantically, trying to find the cause of the unexpected commotion. Juna almost ran over two guards as they darted out of a lunchroom. Orin nervously glanced up at the Mechs as he passed, looking for any sign that they might be coming to life.

"They're trying to power up the Mechs!" Diara's voice boomed through the radio. "I'm holding them off for now."

"Nobody panic," the General announced, his voice still calm. "We knew this was going to happen. Just continue to do your jobs. Finish up what you're doing and get to the dome, just like we planned."

Orin and Juna continued to speed past the rows of Mechs on their way to the dome. For now, everyone seemed too preoccupied to pay any attention to them. As they were nearing the end of the building, their radios rang out with the next set of orders from the General. "Diara, get Helion heading this way," he commanded. "And have him blow up a few things along the way – the more distractions the better at this point. And get Vortex and Havoc to sneak out the back of the archives vault and head for the desert. They'll need to hide out there for a while and then find their way to Lano's when the coast is clear."

Finally reaching the end of the storage building, Orin and Juna drove through the door entering the dome. It appeared they were the first members of the team to arrive. There were several workers from the dome standing around in a state of confusion, not knowing what to do about the alarms. A few of them looked to the door to watch the speeding forklifts enter the building, but they didn't seem to know what to do about that either.

Orin did notice one person still hard at work, running a power cable over near the Gate. Relief flooded him when he realized it was Annu. He steered his forklift towards her, Juna following closely behind. They both dismounted and went over to talk to her.

"Just finishing up now. We should be ready for that power surge when we need it," she reported as she scanned the room, observing the chaos. "Quite the racket, huh?"

Before Orin could respond, the sound of ripping metal drew their attention to the far side of the room. They saw a large door had been torn off and Gigahertz was racing through the new opening with Armorat following right on his heels. All of the dome's workers began to scream in terror as the Mechs entered, so Gigahertz went over to calm them.

"We mean you no harm," he tried to reassure them. "We are taking control of this facility. If you would all please leave in an orderly manner, no one will be hurt."

They all stared at the monstrous machine for a moment, then sprinted for the door to the storage building in a very unorderly manner. By the time they were gone, Armorat had rolled to a stop near the Gate and his massive loading door swung open. Inside, the General, Diara, Pom and the Tech Station were crammed to the front of the cargo hold. The rest of the space was filled with SIMs.

As the General emerged, he stretched his arms, drew in a deep breath and surveyed his surroundings, a broad smile forming on his face. "I think things are going quite well so far," he yelled, hoping to be heard over the alarms. "We might just pull this off after all."

Moments later, Tortuga and Scarab rolled into the building with all of the other Mechs walking in right behind them. As soon as Scarab came to a stop, her side door popped open and both professors jumped out and bolted over to the Gate. Professor Oletta opened up an access panel, reached inside and pulled out the dynamic field generator she had hidden there earlier.

"Give me a moment and I'll have it ready to go," she announced as she went to install the new device.

"I could use a little help here!" It was Dorel's voice coming through the radio. "The power feed to the desert is reconnected, but the building is crawling with guards. I don't think I'll be able to get out of here without being spotted and these guys are carrying some pretty big guns."

"Solitaire, get to the generator room and pick up Dorel," the General ordered. Then, he calmly spoke into the radio. "Sit tight, Dorel. Help is on the way." Next, he ordered Carnage and Mayhem to guard the two doors leading into the dome to prevent any guards from entering.

Suddenly, a familiar hum filled the room. Everyone looked to the Gate and saw it filled with hypnotic swirls of colour. Professor Oletta approached the General. "This Gate is more advanced than the one at The Institute," she informed him. "The portal to the desert will be open in one minute instead of five. Even better, the recharge time is now down to fifteen minutes."

The General started running some calculations in his head. "With Vortex and Havoc on their way to the desert, we have sixteen Mechs. That means we need about an hour to get everyone through," he said as they all walked over to check in with Diara. "Do you think you can hold them off for an hour?" he asked her.

"They know what I'm doing to block the power-up frequency, so they keep changing it," Diara informed them, her hands were a blur as they flew across the keyboard. "I don't know how much longer I can stop them."

"Carnage," the General bellowed, "those Mech clones might be powering up soon. See what you can do to slow them down."

As Carnage walked through the door to the storage building, bullets from a hundred guns rang off his armor as he approached the sleeping giants. He paused for a moment, then walked over to the guards who were firing at him. "Can't you see this is not hurting me?" he boomed through his loudspeaker. "Now, drop your guns and leave before I lose my temper."

With that, every guard dropped their weapon and sprinted for the other end of the building. Carnage walked over to the first column of Mechs and pushed the first one over, dropping the entire row like a game of dominos. He proceeded to the next two rows and did the same. At the fourth and final row, he paused and looked into the eyes of his twin. "You will never be me!" he wailed as he gave the machine a mighty shove, sending the last of the clones tumbling to the ground.

Orin thought the next hour felt more like a week. Helion had arrived from the desert and Solitaire had returned from his rescue of Dorel. There were now twelve Mechs, most of the team and all of their stuff at the other end of the portal. Anxious seconds ticked down as Orin waited for the portal to open one last time. A wave of relief washed over him when the swirling pattern of colours was replaced by a clear view of the desert facility that would become their new home. That feeling was replaced by one of dread when he heard Diara yell out.

"I've lost it, General! The clones are powering up!" The sound of scraping metal could be heard in the building next door, no doubt the Mechs trying to pick themselves up off the ground.

"We need that power surge now!" Professor Oletta screamed.

Annu flipped a switch and the Gate began to howl with the loudest sound Orin had ever heard. It felt as if the entire planet was shaking itself apart. Slowly, the image at the Gate's centre began to expand outward, like a soap bubble forming on its surface. As it grew, the four remaining Mechs and the rest of the team stepped into the area directly in front of the Gate. Orin could feel a tingle through his entire body as the bubble's surface washed over him. He looked at his feet and noticed he was no longer standing on the tiled floor of the dome, but on the dusty rock surface of the cavern in the desert. When he looked up again, he saw the Mech clones entering the dome, rushing towards them. He turned to check the progress of the bubble. It now encased the Mechs, the Tech Station and all remaining members of the team and, just now, it became large enough to envelop the entire structure of the Gate itself. Professor Oletta threw a switch. Instantly, the whole world went quiet. The ear-splitting shriek of the Gate was replaced by silence. The dome full of attacking Mechs was gone. They were on the other side.

Orin looked up to see the friendly confines of their desert cave and the faces of all his friends. Everyone was staring in silence, still not really believing that they had pulled it off. Suddenly, the room erupted in a chorus of laughter and cheers. They did it! The Great Mech Heist was over and it had been a rousing success.

19

A week had passed since their arrival in the desert and it was finally start-ing to feel like home. The facility was a small brick building cut into the side of a towering mountain. Inside, a ramp led down to an enormous underground cavern that extended for over a mile. The walls were rough-cut stone in a slate grey colour with shimmering metallic silver bands running throughout. It was dark and a little cold, but at least it was keeping them safe for now.

Good news was waiting for them when they first arrived – the electric-ity was turned on when they got here. Dorel's reconnection of the power feed from The Depot had been successful, so they didn't have to spend their early days fumbling around in the dark. Even so, the General knew that it was only a matter of time before the feed was discovered and turned off at the other end, so he made repairing the generator the group's number one priority.

Next on the priority list was discovering a source of water. They had brought enough drinking water with them to last a few days, but they would need more than that if they were actually going to live here. Fortunately, the entire facility was built for the sole purpose of finding water. There were massive pumps and numerous holes drilled deep into the ground. By the end of the third day, they had access to more water than they could use in a lifetime.

The facility itself was built to house dozens of workers, so there were large washrooms, shower facilities and sleeping quarters. Everyone staked out a bedroom for themselves and moved in what few personal belongings they had. On the fifth day, Dorel announced that the showers were working with hot running water. The resulting cheer was so loud, Orin worried they would hear it from The Depot. With everything up and running, life here had become quite comfortable. Both Taz and Skeet commented that it was the nicest place they had ever lived.

Right now, the entire team was assembled in a large office, seated around an enormous conference table, discussing what their next move should be.

"Alright everyone," the General began. "We have done an amazing job getting this place working again. I think we can all be very proud of what we have accomplished so far. Now, we need to figure out what we can do from here to put an end to the emperor's plans. Professor Oletta, tell me about the Gate at The Institute. Are they going to be able to use it without you being there?"

"Yes," she replied thoughtfully. "There are enough trained people there to get it running and then use it to open a portal."

"Then we should assume that the emperor's goals have not changed," the General surmised, rocking back in his chair. "He will still be planning an assault on Mara. That means either moving the Gate to The Depot to replace the one we stole or getting his army of Mech clones stationed at The Institute."

"The Gate would be extremely difficult to move," Professor Oletta noted. "That's the primary reason we decided to build a second one. It is very likely they would choose to transfer the Mechs to The Institute."

"And what can we do from here to stop them if they do launch an attack on Mara?" he asked her.

"Opening a portal does create a powerful distortion in space. I believe Darin and I can build a scanner that will detect it from here. Their Gate will take five minutes to establish a portal, but ours can do it in one minute. Theoretically, we can determine where their portal will open, establish one of our own nearby and be there waiting for them when they arrive."

The General smiled. "I like that," he said. "Darin and Aeva, get working on that scanner. I'll organize the Mechs into teams of four so we'll be ready to go the moment the emperor tries to open a portal somewhere."

Just as he finished speaking, the lights dimmed momentarily and the generator's motor started running a little louder. "I think they just shut down our power feed from The Depot," the General commented.

"It was only a matter of time," Dorel noted. "I hid the connection as best I could and destroyed all the old drawings, but that unexplained power draw was going to be detected eventually. They probably didn't even know what it was when they disconnected it."

"That's OK," the General reassured him. "The feed from The Depot served its purpose, but now, it looks like we're on our own." He paused and scanned the room for any signs of panic. Seeing none, he continued.

"Diara, how are we doing with radio communications?"

"Great," she replied enthusiastically. "Annu used every piece of spare wire she could find to build an enormous antenna. I can now use the Tech Station to talk to Vortex and Havoc. They told me the project at Lano's warehouse is going very well. We should be able to open a portal there by the end of the day."

"Excellent news," the General responded happily, clapping his hands together. "We are running dangerously low on some things, so it will be nice to restock our supplies. Orin and Juna, get to work on a shopping list. It looks like we're going to be here for a while, so let's make it as comfortable as we can."

Orin and Juna spent the day sitting at a small table in the central cavern, working on the list. Orin really enjoyed spending so much time with her. They debated some items on the list, but mostly they laughed and joked with each other, coming up with crazy suggestions for things they should include.

"I sure do miss my tri-racer," Juna proposed. "Maybe we can get them to send us one of those."

Orin laughed. "I don't think it would be very useful in the middle of a desert," he countered. "Besides, if you really want to fill your need for speed, you can always borrow my hoverbike."

"What! That worthless piece of junk?" she joked. "I may as well walk."

Their laughing was interrupted when Gigahertz walked into the room. "Hello Master Orin. As you requested, I have surveyed the other Mechs to see if they need anything. Tortuga has a leak in one of his tires, so we should get a patch for that. Torque needs a new trigger for his shoulder cannon and Isotope requires a new lens for her laser. Also, Clank has requested a beach ball, but I don't really think we need to get him one of those."

"OK. Thanks Gig. We'll add all that to the list."

"You are most welcome, Master Orin," he replied as he turned to leave.

Juna leaned in close. "Why does he call you that?" she asked softly.

"Call me what?"

"Master Orin. Why does he call you Master Orin?"

"I don't know. That's just what he's always called me."

She gave him a puzzled look. "Why don't you ask him not to?"

"What do you mean?" he asked, leaning back in his chair and clasping his hands behind his head.

"I mean, why don't you ask him not to. When I first met Helion, he called me princess, so I asked him not to. Now he just calls me Juna."

"Hey Gig," Orin yelled across the room, "could you just call me Orin from now on?"

"OK, Orin"

Orin turned to Juna, an embarrassed look on his face. "Well, that was easy. I should have done that years ago." He added an awkward laugh.

Juna just shook her head, rolled her eyes and returned her attention to the list. Often, Orin felt like a little kid when he was around Juna. They were about the same age, but sometimes it seemed like she had grown up a bit faster than he had. But that was OK. He still loved spending time with her and hoped that, maybe someday, he might catch up.

He was snapped from his daydreaming when Diara rushed into the room. "The work is done at the warehouse," she announced cheerily. "We're ready for the portal test."

Everyone was crowded around the Gate when Professor Oletta threw the switch. The Gate sprang to life and, one minute later, they found themselves staring into the underground warehouse at Lano's. The General led most of the group through the Gate while Professor Oletta remained behind with Diara and Pom so that the portal could be re-opened when they wanted to return.

Everyone who worked for Lano was a member of the Underground, so there were a lot of people there to greet them. Introductions were made and hugs and handshakes were exchanged. Orin and Juna presented their shopping list and it was decided that Skeet and Taz would stay behind to help collect everything on it. After a short visit, Vortex sent word to Diara to re-activate the Gate and the team returned home.

The group was re-energized by the trip to the warehouse. Knowing they had a physical connection with the rest of the world made them feel far less isolated. Somehow, seeing so many other people involved in their cause, gave them hope that maybe they would be victorious in their battle with the emperor.

As the days passed, their lives settled into a familiar routine. Things had been so exciting for them over the last few weeks that this new peaceful existence seemed almost boring. At one point, Orin actually regretted not getting Clank that beach ball. It was probably the tranquillity of their new circumstances that made it so shocking when the alarms started blaring. Everyone sprinted to the Tech Station to see what was going on.

"Our new detector is picking up a portal opening on Mara," Professor Oletta informed them. "It's very close to the location we used the first time we went there."

"Mech Team 1 is ready to go," the General announced. "Let's get our portal open right beside theirs."

Professor Oletta entered the coordinates and fired up the Gate. One minute later, Gigahertz, Isotope, Mayhem and Solitaire, all of their weapons attached, were stepping onto the surface of Mara. Everyone crowded around the Tech Station's monitors to watch the events unfold.

The four Mechs were standing directly in front of another Gate. As soon as they got there, the swirling pattern of colours at its centre was replaced by an image of four Mechs on the other side. At first, Orin thought he was looking at a mirror because there was a Gigahertz front and centre on both sides, but then he noticed the other three Mech clones were all Diesels.

Before the clones could move, Gig started firing and the Mechs on the other side began flying apart. Within ten seconds, all four clones were reduced to piles of debris and the enemy's Gate vanished. The entire group watching the battle on the monitors began to cheer the decisive victory, but the celebration was cut short by stern words from the General.

"Now, now, everyone. Calm down," he demanded. "That one was easy. They had no reason to expect any resistance so they didn't even turn their shields on. That is not a mistake they will make again. It is an absolute certainty that our next encounter will be much more difficult." The room fell quiet, so the General continued. "We were just lucky that they got careless. Did you see how close we were to not arriving on time? Orin, I want you to work with Diara to come up with a way to get more warning for an impending attack. We do *not* want to cut it that close again. So, as soon as that Gate is recharged, we get our Mechs back, get them reloaded and be ready for the next fight."

Orin was glad the General had refocused everyone on the seriousness of their situation. Despite the overwhelming victory, Orin had been unnerved by watching the battle with the clones. Seeing something that looked exactly like Gig get blown to pieces had been unsettling. He imagined how terrible he would feel if his friend met the same fate. Determined to never let that happen, he rushed off to talk to Diara about building a better advanced warning system.

It was the middle of the night when the alarms rang again. By the time Orin was out of his bed and arrived at the Gate, Spanner, Helion, Geiger and Diode were already stepping through. The General was correct – this encounter was much more difficult than the first one. Watching the brutality of the battle was a sobering experience for the entire team. SIM's and TRIP's flew through the Gate from both directions, draining shields and doing damage. The clones were at a disadvantage without AI's or the tactical support of the General and the technical support of the Techs, but they *were* formidable adversaries. The decisive victory of their first encounter was long forgotten.

The battle lasted only ten minutes but it seemed so much longer to those observing it on the monitors. All four of the clones were destroyed by the time the enemy shut down their Gate and ended the conflict. It was a victory, but this time a price had been paid. When the Mechs returned, Orin noticed Geiger had suffered damage to his missile launcher and Helion was carrying his right arm, having had it blown off during the fight. Juna rushed to him to make sure he was OK, saddened and angered about the harm that had come to her friend.

The General instructed Dorel and Annu to begin repairs and had the next team of Mechs assemble in front of the Gate to be ready for the next attack. It was lucky he did because, several minutes later, Professor Oletta announced another portal was opening on the surface of Mara.

There were a total of five attacks that day. They were all turned back, but every battle was hard-fought and resulted in damage to at least one of their Mechs. Dorel and Annu were overwhelmed trying to keep up with repairs, so Orin and Taz jumped in to help. By the end of the day, the entire team was exhausted. The General broke them into two shifts and had half the team get some sleep while the others monitored for any further activity on Mara.

Five days passed and there had been no further attempts by their enemy to open more portals. The General was not surprised by this fortunate turn of events. Since the last battle ended, he had been concerned about their dwindling stores of missiles and surmised that the emperor's side was probably having the same problem. During the heist, they had managed to steal more than half of the missiles from the armoury, so it was quite likely that their enemy had simply run out of them.

"The problem is, they can make more and we can't," the General told the group. "Get ready to open a portal to Lano's. Darin, you are going to have to teach the people over there how to make missiles."

It took them a week, but they managed to turn Lano's warehouse into a weapons factory. Fortunately, during that time there had been no further attempts to attack the Marans. Not wanting to waste the opportunity this quiet time provided, Orin and Diara managed to come up with a better advanced warning system. Using Diara's knowledge of the frequencies used to communicate with the clones, they built a monitor that would tell them when the machines were being activated and what commands were being sent to them. There was nothing they could do to block the commands, but just knowing what they were did give them some tactical advantage. Everyone just hoped it would be enough.

It had been two weeks since the last attack when the new advanced warning system was put to the test. "They just fired up four Mechs, General," Diara reported. "I think they might be up to something."

Sure enough, twenty minutes later, Professor Oletta informed them a portal was opening on Mara. She opened up one right next to it and Mech Team 4 stormed through to turn the enemy away again.

This was now the cycle of their life. Open portal. Fight. Repair. Repeat. They had won every battle so far, but Orin still found the whole thing extremely frustrating. It had been five days since the last attack when he found himself sitting alone, pondering their current situation. He was startled when someone rested their hand on his shoulder.

"You look lost in thought, Orin," the General said as he sat down beside him. "What's on your mind?"

"I don't know," he replied quietly. "It all seems so pointless. The emperor attacks Mara. We stop him. He attacks again. We stop him again. When is it going to end? Why don't we just attack him for a change?"

"There will be a time for that," the General assured him. "But that time is not now. If we attack the emperor and storm the palace, we'll be no better than he is. The people of Cambria will decide when the planet is ready for real change. Remember, it's their heart and soul we have to win over. Only when that is done, will the emperor's rule come to an end."

"I guess," Orin admitted, staring at the ground and kicking some sand around. "We keep winning all these battles, but we're no closer to defeating the emperor than we were when we started. It would be nice to have a real victory for once."

"We just need to have a little patience," the General urged, patting Orin on the shoulder. "It can be disappointing not winning the whole war with every battle, but for now, just living to fight another day can be a victory in itself."

Their conversation was cut short by Pom, calling out from the Tech Station. "They're at it again," she announced. "Four Mechs powering up."

Professor Oletta typed the usual coordinates into the Gate and prepared to fire it up. "Something's wrong," she muttered as her hands flew across the keyboard. "Their portal is not opening on Mara."

"Where *is* it opening?" the General asked, obviously concerned and confused by this unexpected news.

"They're here!" she shouted. "Right outside our front door!"

"Forget the portal!" the General commanded. "All Mechs! Outside now!"

Gigahertz led the charge up the ramp to the surface, all of the other Mechs right on his heels. By the time they reached the front entrance, a portal was open and Mech clones were stepping through the Gate. Down in the control room, the entire team was huddled around the Tech Station, watching in horror as their new home was under attack.

Orin noticed that all four of the clones were Solitaires. His first thought was how unhappy the real Solitaire would be having so much help. Gig and the rest of their Mechs sprinted at the attackers, their launchers raised. Each fake Solitaire unleashed a barrage of missiles, but they were not aiming at the approaching Mechs – their target was the building itself.

The ground shook as the missiles hit their mark. Dust fell from the ceiling and racks of shelves toppled to the ground. A piece of rock dislodged from the ceiling and struck a glancing blow to the side of Orin's head, nearly knocking him to the ground. Blood trickled down his face as he watched the rest of the battle unfold. Gigahertz and the rest of his team launched their missiles in waves at the attacking force. The assault was so fierce, the clones never got off another shot. Their shields failed and they began flying apart as pieces of fake Solitaires rained from the sky.

The team was shaken. In addition to Orin's minor wound, a falling rack had broken Annu's arm and one of the monitors on the Tech station had been shattered. The General ordered half the Mechs to stay outside to defend the building and brought the rest inside in case an attack on Mara was planned. Everyone was quiet, thinking about the reality of their new situation. Orin finally broke the silence.

"They know we're here," he said, stating the obvious.

"How did this happen?" the General asked. "Could they have built a portal detector like ours?"

"I don't think that's possible," Professor Oletta insisted. "No one there would have the knowledge or technical skills to make one."

"I'm afraid I might know the answer," Professor Umbra admitted softly. "The Emperor was here once. When he was young and his father was emperor, they both came for a tour. I assumed he would have forgotten about it. I guess he didn't."

The group went silent again. This changed everything. The only advantage they had was that no one knew where they were. Now that was gone.

"Something's happening!" Pom yelled from the Tech Station. "They're doing something but using commands I've never seen before."

Diara went over to help. "They're just instructing the Mechs to move." Reaching over Pom's shoulder, she pressed more buttons. "I think they're headed this way."

"What?" the General seemed skeptical. "They're going to walk here?"

"That's what it looks like."

"How many?" he asked.

Diara pressed a few more buttons. She turned to face the General, a panicked look on her face. "All of them."

For the first time Orin could remember, there was a look of fear in the General's eyes.

"How long will it take, Darin?"

"If they move at top speed, about six days."

The original Mechs had an advantage with their AI's, but that was while fighting four-on-four. Against an army of clones, they had no chance. Everyone knew it.

"What do we do, General?" Juna finally asked.

The General paced for a moment, then turned to face them. The look on his face was that of a man who had just made a difficult decision and was about to deliver some very bad news.

"We run."

20

Running was one thing – having a destination was another matter entirely. There was really nowhere else to go. They were already at the far end of a planet with very little room to roam. No. Cambria had no further options to offer. They would have to find someplace else.

"What if we go to Mara?" Orin offered.

"That place was awful," Diara remarked. "I really hope we don't end up there."

"Mara is a poor option for many reasons," the General stated. "For one, we may not be welcome there after blowing up their factory last year. It's also a place the emperor knows about. No, I think we need to go somewhere we can't be found. Our abbreviated stay in the desert is proof of that."

"Those are the only two planets we know about," Orin mumbled, unable to hide his frustration.

"Well then, we find another one," the General said as if this was the easiest thing that had ever been done.

Everyone turned and looked at the professors.

"There's probably something we can do," Professor Oletta sighed. She turned to the Professor and forced a smile. "Let's get to work."

What they came up with was a way to reprogram the Gate to create something called "micro-portals." With these, the Gate could search an area of space to locate a planet and then scan its atmosphere, temperature and gravity to see if it might provide a suitable living environment. Once implemented, it could run automatically and work so quickly, it would be able to examine more than a hundred planets every hour. When the modifications were complete, the professors pointed the Gate at a piece of the sky and let it run.

The following days were filled with high anxiety coupled with crushing boredom. The team spent hours staring at monitors tracking the Gate's progress, but until it found a match, there was nothing they could do but pace the floor and hope that the massive device would find them a new home. Halfway through the third day, their wait finally ended when the first potential landing spot was discovered. It wasn't perfect. The air was breathable and the gravity was about right, but it did have one major problem – there were already a few billion people living on it.

Orin could not even comprehend a number that large. How could that many people possibly live on one planet? The good news was that Professor Oletta fine-tuned the search and found a secluded place where they would be able to hide. It was a huge cave hidden in an enormous canyon. There was a river running nearby to provide water, so if they took everything with them and used a portal to connect to Lano's periodically, they should be able to live there indefinitely without anyone ever knowing about it.

Right now, everyone was busy moving everything through the portal to the cave on the other side. And that did mean everything. Furniture, lights, pumps, and all of the bathroom fixtures were being pushed through the Gate. Every piece of wire, cable, hose and pipe was stripped from the walls and sent through to the other side. Even some of the walls were going. Anything that could be removed without collapsing the building was being torn away and pushed through the Gate.

The Diesels were having more fun than they had had since the war. Working alongside Torque, they would dismantle equipment, rip apart rooms, tear down walls and then throw everything through the Gate. There weren't any explosions, but other than that, it was a wonderful way to spend the day. On the other side of the portal, the Hydros and Solars were putting it all back together, trying to recreate their old home on a new world.

The only Mech not enjoying the process was Clank. He was proud of this place and all the work he put into building it for Orin's grandfather. He would happily give people tours, showing them each section he had dug out personally. It seemed he had a story to tell about every square inch of this place. Orin assured him that there was much work to do in the new cave and he could be proud of that too. That seemed to cheer him up a bit and make him feel a little better about the move.

The cycle of work was non-stop. The portal would open and items would be shoved through. When its upper limit was reached, the Gate would shut down and they would wait for it to recharge. When it was ready to go again, the portal would reopen and the whole process would start over. It was exhausting, repetitive work, but it was their only chance for survival with a horde of Mech clones slowly stomping towards them.

The biggest, and most important, item to move was the generator. It had already been removed from its mounts and been slid over beside the Gate. The plan was to slide it directly in front of the Gate for the last trip, so when the power surge came, the portal bubble would surround it and move it to the other end along with the Gate. It was a good plan with one major problem. The whole group was assembled around the conference table and were discussing it now.

"We don't have enough power to create the surge," Professor Oletta informed them. "The generator is simply not powerful enough."

"We'll have to reconnect the power feed from The Depot," the General insisted. "We must take the Gate with us – leaving it behind is not an option. A one-way trip to another planet is not something any of us signed up for."

"We could open a portal to the dome," Juna offered. "Dorel could go through and reconnect the feed and then come right back."

"They'll just disconnect it again as soon as he's gone," the Professor said. "They will know exactly why we went there and what we did."

"What if we were sneakier about it?" Orin suggested. "Why don't we attack them through the portal and make a big show of stealing something important. While that's happening, Dorel could sneak off and reconnect the feed. They might not think to look for it if we do that."

"That could work," the General considered. "But, what would we steal?"

"There's a small forge on the assembly floor," the Professor jumped in. "It's big enough to look like the target of our attack, but small enough to fit in one of the Bios. Besides, I'd love to have it. We could use it to build our own tools and spare parts."

"OK. That's a good start," the General concluded. "I'll spend the day working out the details. For now, everyone get back to work. There are still a lot of things we need to move before an army of hostile Mechs shows up on our doorstep."

Work continued non-stop for the next couple of days, but it was getting more challenging with each passing hour. As things were moved to their new home, it was becoming increasingly difficult to live in this one. It was decided that most of the team should start living on the other side full-time. Neither Orin nor Juna had been there yet, so they decided to go over together to have a look. They each grabbed their box of personal belongings and set out for the Gate.

For both of them, it would be their first time touching the surface of another planet. It was exciting and terrifying at the same time. They exchanged a quick glance and nervous smile as they took that first tentative step over the threshold of the Gate and set foot on a new world. The air was stale and dusty, the surroundings both alien and beautiful. The rock that made up the walls of the cave was layered in stone of brilliant reds and oranges. The only illumination came from a string of lights hanging from the ceiling. Orin followed the length of wire powering the bulbs and saw it was connected to Fallout, his atomic reactor providing the only source of power on this side of the portal.

Walls had been brought over and reassembled here to create a row of small rooms along one side of the cave. Orin and Juna each claimed one of them as their new bedroom and left their box of things behind. After emerging from their new rooms, they set out to tour the rest of the cave.

It was enormous. The ceiling was higher than the one in the Central Assembly Building and the numerous passageways seemed to go on forever. Massive stalactites hung high overhead, making it both the most beautiful and most terrifying place Orin had ever walked through. He wondered if a place so strange could ever truly feel like home. As they were wandering, they met up with Taz who was working on one of the massive pumps that would eventually be providing them with water.

"Quite the place, huh?" he commented. "Never thought I'd be livin' on a totally different planet."

"It is impressive, all right," Orin agreed. "How are things going over here?"

"Pretty good," Taz replied. "Skeet and Isotope just finished drillin' a big hole in the ground all the way to the river. Dorel says we should be able to get a hose down there soon. He says we'll have runnin' water in here as soon as the generator gets brought over."

Juna was scanning the massive space. "It will be just like home," she added cheerfully. "Except for all the walls being made out of rock."

Orin was so impressed with Juna. She had spent her entire life living in the luxury of the Royal Palace and now, she was being asked to live in a dusty cave on a distant planet and she still managed to keep a smile on her face the whole time. It was obvious that the year spent roughing it on her tour of Cambria and her overriding desire not to be treated like a princess had prepared her for anything that life threw her way. Orin only hoped that he would prove to be so resilient. If he was really being honest with himself, the idea of living on another planet had him a little spooked.

Some colourful language coming from the opposite side of the cave jarred Orin from his thoughts. Dorel was wrestling with a large coil of hose, clearly frustrated.

Orin, Juna and Taz rushed over to help. Just as they arrived, Annu, her left arm still in a sling, showed up to lend a hand as well.

"What I wouldn't give for a couple of the assembly drones from back at The Depot," Dorel said as he wiped the sweat off his forehead. "I'm getting too old for this sort of back-breaking work."

"Oh, stop your whining," Annu scoffed. "You're not *that* old. Besides, if I had two good arms, I would have had this done an hour ago." She directed a loving smile his way to show that she was just kidding. "Why don't we all chip in and get this done."

Orin, along with Juna, grabbed onto the hose to help lower it into the hole that led to the river a hundred feet below. He looked up at the three mountainous people surrounding him and realized he was probably wasting his time. He had never felt so tiny. He looked over to Juna. She just smiled and gave him a shrug, obviously coming to the same conclusion.

Between the five of them, they made quick work of the task and soon heard the satisfying splash of the hose hitting the water below. Orin turned to Juna.

"We better get back," he told her. "There's still a bunch of stuff to do on the other side."

Quickly winding their way back through the twisting corridors, they returned to the main cavern. The portal was just reopening as they arrived. Pom was waiting for them on the other side.

"Get everybody back," she asked urgently. "The General says it's an emergency."

The General's concern was obvious as he addressed the group after their hasty return to the desert. "The clone army has just come within range of Gigahertz's sensors," he began. "It seems they are making better time than we thought. There are sixty-two of them and they will be here in four hours."

A collective gasp filled the room and worried looks were exchanged.

"Our trip to The Depot needs to happen right now," he continued. "Orin, Juna, Dorel and Skeet, come with me. I'll need Gigahertz and Tortuga as well. Everyone else, get one more load through to the other side. When the Gate is recharged, the next portal opens to The Depot."

The team was ready. Orin, Juna, Dorel and Skeet were strapped into Tortuga's cargo hold, watching a monitor linked to his outside camera. They were facing the Gate, its mesmerizing pattern of colours filling the screen. Suddenly, the view changed to show the interior of The Depot's dome. Gigahertz sprinted through the Gate with Tortuga following right on his heels.

A couple of workers scattered as the Mechs sped through the building, but generally, there seemed to be far fewer people around than would be expected at this time of day. Orin assumed that most of The Depot's regular staff were moved to The Institute after the Gate was stolen. The storage building that once held an army of Mechs was now abandoned. Racing through the now empty space, they zipped through a tunnel, emerging onto the assembly floor.

Orin noticed two Mechs standing in maintenance bays, no doubt awaiting some type of repair. They showed no signs of life, but Gig tore them both in half anyway, just to make sure there would be no surprises later on.

Gigahertz came to a stop next to the forge that was the target of their mission. Tortuga screeched to a halt beside him and opened up his massive access door. The team spilled out and scanned the room for guards, but saw no one. Orin had an unobstructed view of the door to the generator room. The way was clear. Gig was already removing the bolts that secured the forge to the floor, so with that underway, they all made a dash for the generator room.

Orin activated the jammer and used his key card to open the door. As soon as they were inside, Dorel went to work reconnecting the power feed to the desert facility. Orin shared an anxious look with Juna. Things had gone perfectly so far, but they were still a long way from completing their mission. The thought of sixty-two Mechs speeding towards their friends in the desert filled them with a powerful sense of urgency.

"All done here," Dorel announced almost immediately. "All they did was open a circuit breaker. They didn't even try to figure this out. The people hired to do electrical work around here sure are lazy," he said with a disapproving shake of his head. "But I guess that's good news for us. It's ready to go. All we have to do is throw the switch and we'll have the power we need for the surge."

The General was not willing to take the chance that someone would discover the reconnected power feed and shut it off before they needed it. The decision was made to leave someone behind to throw the switch at the moment the surge was required. Orin removed the watch from his wrist and handed it to Skeet.

"You sure you're up for this?" he asked his young friend. "I can be the one to stay behind if you want."

"Are you kidding?" Skeet replied confidently. "I did stuff scarier than this every single day living in Volara. This will be a piece of cake."

"I know you'll do great," Orin agreed, giving him a supportive pat on the shoulder. "OK. In exactly half an hour, you throw that switch. Then, you need to get out." Orin took off his backpack and pulled out his invisibility blanket, handing it over to Skeet. "Hide under this for now." Next, Orin handed him the backpack. "When you leave, turn on the alarm jammer and go out the emergency exit. The laser is in there to cut through the fence. Hide in the desert until it's clear. Don't worry about how long it takes – there's plenty of food and water in the backpack. Then, get to Lano's. He knows you're coming. We'll meet up with you through the first portal."

"Orin, don't look so worried," Skeet reassured him with one of his typical ear-to-ear grins. "Sneaking around and not getting caught is what I do."

At that moment, the sound of gunfire erupted on the other side of the door. Orin keyed the mike on his radio. "Hey Gig, what's going on out there?"

"Several guards are shooting at me," he replied. "I think I should put a stop to it before you try to join me out here."

Moments later, new sounds emerged on the other side of the door – mostly tearing metal, thunderous crashes and booming threats from Gig's loudspeaker.

"The guards have decided to leave," Gig reported over the radio. "But I think they have gone to get reinforcements. We should get out of here very soon."

Orin, Juna and Dorel helped Skeet into his hiding spot, covered him with the blanket and said their goodbyes. Leaving the generator room, they sprinted across the assembly floor to join the Mechs. They climbed inside Tortuga and buckled themselves in beside the stolen forge. As soon as his door slid shut, they were off, following Gigahertz on his race across the building. The sound of bullets bouncing off Tortuga's armour echoed through the hold and the high-speed swerves had everyone feeling a little sick. At one point, they took a corner so fast, Tortuga was up on three wheels, but somehow, they managed to reach the dome with no serious injuries.

Gigahertz had called ahead as soon as the forge was secured, so the portal was waiting for them when they arrived. Gig flew through the Gate without breaking stride and Tortuga followed right behind him, tires squealing as they hit the hard, stone floor of the desert cave.

The General ordered the Gate closed the instant they were clear to put an end to the spray of incoming bullets that were accompanying the retreating Mechs through the portal. When the bullets stopped ricocheting around the cavern and the dust had settled, the General made his way to Tortuga's access door to meet the team as they emerged from their harrowing trip to the Depot.

"How did it go?" he asked them.

"We got the forge," Orin replied as he looked at the clock. "And we should have power for the surge in exactly twenty minutes."

"Excellent work," the General said, giving Orin a heavy slap on the back. "That should give us just enough time to recharge the Gate. We are cutting this far too close. That army of clones is almost within missile range."

Waiting for the Gate to recharge felt like a lifetime. Orin stood over Diara's shoulder staring at the Tech Station, watching the seconds tick down. Juna joined him and reached for his hand, squeezing so tight he thought his fingers might break. He glanced over and saw a worried look on her face, no doubt identical to the one he was sporting.

"Are we going to make it?" she asked.

"Absolutely," he replied, mustering all the fake optimism he could. "We're almost there."

He returned his attention to the timer to watch its frustratingly slow descent. When it finally reached zero, the Gate sprang to life. One more minute.

Just as the portal opened, the ground shook as if a giant sledgehammer had been slammed into the side of the building. Orin was knocked to the ground as a large piece of the ceiling gave way and fell only a few feet from where he stood. Debris flew through the air and the sound of alarms filled the room.

"Well, I guess we are officially within missile range of those clones," he commented as he pulled himself to his feet. Peering through the dust, he saw Juna trying to pick herself up off the ground, so he reached out to help her.

"Thanks," she said, as she rose to her feet. "That was too close. We can't take many more hits like that one."

Orin agreed. They needed to get out of here right now. He surveyed the room, waiting for the next set of instructions from the General, but terror gripped him when he looked in the direction of the ceiling collapse. Lying on the ground next to the pile of rubble, was the General. Blood dripped from a gash on his head as he lay there, motionless. As the impact from a second missile shook his world again, Orin fought to keep a feeling of hopelessness from consuming him. No. All of their hard work could not end like this. He would *not* let that happen.

21

"Gig! We need more time!" Orin yelled over the blaring alarms. "Get out there and see what you can do to slow them down."

Orin felt horrible sending Gigahertz out to face the attacking clones by himself, but he had little choice. Tortuga was the only other Mech on this side of the portal and he had been stripped of all his weapons to free up enough space to carry the forge.

As Gigahertz sprinted up the ramp towards the surface, Orin scanned the room, trying to assess the current situation and figure out some way to improve upon it. Oh, how he wished the General was the one dealing with this mess. But the General was lying in a heap on the floor, hopefully just unconscious. Looking over to the Tech Station, he noticed Diara slumped over the console, barely stirring herself.

This was a dire situation and his inactivity wasn't helping anyone. He forced himself to focus, trying to think what the General would be doing right now. Get as many people to safety as possible – that had to be the first thing. Over near the roof collapse, Dorel was just trying to lift himself to his feet, so Orin signalled Juna to join him and they hurried over to help.

"You OK there, big guy?" Orin asked as he helped his friend up off the ground.

"Just a little groggy," Dorel answered tentatively. "I took a bit of a bump on the old noggin, but I think I'm going to be OK."

"You'd better get it together pronto. This building is about to come down and I'd rather not be here when it happens." Orin took a moment to survey the area, trying to come up with a plan. "Let's get the General and Diara onboard Tortuga," he suggested, trying to project that air of confidence the General was so good at. "Then all of you need to get through that Gate."

Dorel shuffled over to grab the General while Orin and Juna rushed over to check on Diara. She was muttering to herself when they got there, obviously disoriented by a knock on the head from one of the many pieces of ceiling that had fallen on the Tech Station. By the time they managed to get her to her feet and ushered over to Tortuga, Dorel was already there, stuffing the General onboard.

With the wounded safely stowed in Tortuga's hold, Orin began making his way back through the access door. Noticing that Juna was following, he turned to tell her that she needed to get herself to safety on the other side of the portal.

"Don't even think it," she said, pointing an accusatory finger right in his face. "I'm staying."

He considered trying to talk her out of it, but knew it would be a waste of time. Besides, he was kind of glad she had decided to stay. Not knowing exactly what he was supposed to be doing over here, meant having a little help was probably a good thing.

As soon as they cleared the hatch, Orin closed Tortuga's access door and ordered him through the Gate.

"Well, I guess it's just the two of us," he said to Juna, trying hard to hide his fear. "Any idea what we're supposed to do next?"

"Not really," she admitted. "I guess we should start by seeing what's going on outside."

As they made their way to the Tech Station, Orin looked to his watch before remembering he had left it with Skeet. A quick glance at the clock on the wall only told him that neither the clock nor the wall was even there anymore. He could only guess at this point, but he figured it would only be four or five minutes until Skeet threw the switch back at The Depot to provide the power surge for the Gate. He could only hope that the building would still be standing when it arrived.

Orin swept the debris off the Tech Station and used it to access Gig's camera. The clones were still a fair distance away, lobbing their missiles in from long-range. As they arced through the air, Gig was using his missiles to intercept them and blow them out of the sky before they could do any damage. That explained why the building hadn't been rocked by any more explosions recently.

Feeling safe, at least for the time being, Orin turned his attention to their most immediate problem – the generator. If they got stuck on an alien planet without a generator, their odds of survival were essentially zero. Staring at the massive piece of equipment sitting next to the Gate, it was hard not to feel completely defeated. He and Juna weren't moving that thing in a million years and Gig needed to stay outside to hold off those incoming missiles.

"Worried about the generator?" Juna asked, obviously reading his mind.

"Yup. Got any ideas?"

"How many Mechs have gone through the portal this time around?"

Orin broke into a smile, understanding exactly what Juna was getting at. "Just Tortuga so far," he replied excitedly. "The Gate won't be anywhere near its upper limit. We should be able to bring a Mech over and still have plenty of capacity to send them back again."

Orin keyed the mike on the Tech Station. "Hey Sol. We could use a little help over here. We need you back on this side for a bit."

Less than two minutes later, Solitaire had stepped through the portal, pushed the generator in front of the Gate and squeezed back through to the other side, pulling the generator even closer as he went. The positioning was perfect. If a portal bubble became large enough to capture the Gate, the generator was guaranteed to go along with it. They were as ready as they were going to get – all that was needed now was the power surge. Orin looked at Juna and showed her his crossed fingers.

"I think we're close," he told her, knowing it was only a guess. "Skeet should be throwing the switch right about…"

WOOOOOOO! The deafening howl of the Gate engulfed them as a glistening bubble started to form on its surface. Its progress was agonizingly slow as it pushed away from the Gate and began surrounding the generator. Orin turned his attention to the Tech Station's monitor to see how the battle out there was going. He realized that their best chance at survival would be to leave Gig outside, fending off the clone assault until the Gate was sitting safely at the other end of the portal, but he knew that was never going to happen. Remembering back to how he had felt after leaving Juna behind following Pom's rescue from the prison, he knew he would never allow himself to live through that again. Leaving a friend behind, even one made out of metal, was simply not an option.

Again, keying the Tech Station's mike, he spoke directly to Gigahertz. "Hey Gig, we've got the portal bubble starting in here. Hold them off as long as you can. When I give you the word, you get down here as fast as you can."

"No, Orin. I will stay here until you are all safely away."

"Not going to happen, buddy. I'm not popping this bubble until you're in it, so when I say move, you get your butt down here."

Just as he finished speaking, Orin felt the cool tingle of the portal's bubble washing over him. Looking up, he saw the shimmering surface slowly envelop Juna. She reached out and grabbed his hand.

"You did the right thing," she reassured him. "Don't worry. We'll make it."

Orin looked up to watch the progress of the bubble. In seconds, it would be surrounding the generator, the Tech Station and the Gate.

"Now Gig!" he yelled into the mike. "You have to get down here right now!"

Ten seconds later, they could see Gig charging down the ramp and ten seconds after that, the building shook with the impact of another direct hit from an enemy missile. A large beam fell from the ceiling and crashed into Gigahertz, knocking him to the ground and severing his left arm. Gig managed to get back on his feet as his, now unattached arm skittered across the floor, coming to a stop just short of the bubble's edge. Gig sprinted towards the Gate, scooping up his missing arm as he went, just as another missile shook the building. Orin was nearly knocked to the ground when a large piece of the ceiling crashed to the floor only a few feet from where he was standing. He felt a sharp pain in his hand and realized Juna was still holding on, squeezing harder with each missile that struck the building. Noticing they were now standing on the red stone floor of their new home, he looked up to see that the bubble had engulfed everything – the generator, the Tech Station, Gigahertz and, just now, the entire structure of the Gate. Lunging for the Tech Station, he threw the switch that would power down the Gate. Silence. Sweet, glorious silence. They were away. They were safe.

The sense of relief was overwhelming. Orin's gaze swept the room, looking into the faces of his friends. His eyes caught onto Juna's. Her look of apprehension and fear slowly turned into the start of a smile. The next thing he knew, they were beaming at each other, then hugging so tightly his arms ached. It was wonderful. They stayed like that until he was interrupted by a friendly voice and a tap on the shoulder.

"Excuse me young man. Have you got one of those for your father?"

"Hey Dad," Orin said as he switched his hug from Juna to the Professor. "I guess we made it."

"We certainly did," his father replied. "Thanks to some quick thinking on your part. That was a gold star escape if ever I saw one."

"Well, it *was* a team effort," Orin replied modestly. "How's the General doing?"

"He's just coming around now. Let's go say hello – I know he wants to talk to you."

Orin looked for Juna, a little disappointed their moment together had ended prematurely. She had gone over to be with Pom who was tending to Diara's injuries, so Orin went with the Professor to talk with the General. When they arrived, the General was sitting on a large crate, head in his hands, looking like he had just been through a war. He looked up when he heard Orin and his father approaching.

"Well, there's our new commander," the General joked. "Sorry I wasn't there to help you at the end, but you obviously did just fine without me."

"I learned by watching the best," Orin offered.

"Thanks for saving my butt back there," the General said sincerely. "I would have hated to be left behind. I'm not sure the emperor would have treated me very well if he got his hands on me."

"Don't mention it," Orin replied dismissively. "You've certainly saved mine enough times."

"Well then, how about you do me one more favour and we'll call it even," the General proposed. "I'm not really feeling up to it right now, so

233

why don't you check in with the troops, make sure everyone's alright and let them know how proud I am of all of them."

"Consider it done."

Orin set out to do just what the General asked, starting with Juna, Pom and Diara, who were all still together over by the Gate. Aside from Diara having a bump on her head the size of a barcaberry, they were all doing fine, but looking forward to some well-deserved peace and quiet. Finding the professors chatting by the Gate, he relayed the General's message and left them to their enthusiastic conversation about actually living on another planet and all the exciting scientific discoveries that would likely unfold as a result.

That left only the Wrenches to talk to, so Orin wandered the cave's passageways searching for them, wondering how it could be so difficult to find three people that large. He finally found them in a huge chamber that was clearly shaping up to be the new maintenance and assembly area of their new home. Dorel, Annu and Taz were there, along with all the Mechs, setting up their equipment and tools, getting the place ready for all of the important work that lay ahead in their ongoing conflict with the emperor.

Orin interrupted their activity to pass on the General's thanks and make sure everyone was OK.

"Well, my husband is still a little loopy from that knock on the head," Annu informed him. "But, other than that, we just need to fix-up the big guy over there, and we'll be good to go."

Orin spun to look in the direction she was pointing and saw Gigahertz standing on the far side of the chamber. His left arm was missing, just like it was on the first day they met.

"Hey Gig, how ya holdin' up?" he asked as he made his way over to talk.

"I should probably avoid holding things up at all until I have my second arm attached, Orin. Just to be safe."

"That's probably a good idea, Gig, but I was really just wondering if you were OK."

"I am well. Thank you for asking. And thank you for not leaving me behind. It was not the smartest thing to do, but I am pleased you chose to do it."

"I'm certainly not going to start living on a new planet without taking my best friend along. Where's the fun in that?"

At that moment, Vortex arrived, carrying Gig's arm. Right behind him came the Wrenches, loaded down with the tools they would need to reattach it. Gigahertz readied himself for the procedure and the team set to work immediately. It was a time-consuming process and, just as he had done all those years ago, Orin stayed with him for all of it, chatting the entire time.

It was beginning to feel like home. Ten days had passed since their harrowing escape and the daily rhythm of a normal life was starting to take hold. The time was filled with hours of hard work, but there was fun and laughter as well. After the first chaotic day of their arrival, the General encouraged everyone to catch their breath and relax for a bit.

"We have just endured a lifetime of stress in the span of two weeks," he had said. "We need to build a home here, but let's take our time and try to have a little fun along the way."

The General knew that all the Mech clones back on Cambria were at the far edge of the desert, so it would take them at least six days to walk back to The Institute. They weren't sure what the emperor would do next, but knew it would be some time before he could resume his attacks on Mara.

So, they spent their time turning their cave into a home. They now had electricity, running water and plenty of food. On their third day here, they replaced the Gate's induction coil, which had melted during the move, and opened a portal to Lano's warehouse. Orin felt an overpowering sense of relief when they were greeted by Skeet's smiling face.

"I told you it would be a piece of cake," he had proclaimed after receiving a bone-crushing hug from Taz. "There's no way those guards at The Depot were going to catch me."

"I never doubted it for a second," Orin responded as he pulled his young friend into an embrace.

Dozens of members of the Underground were there to greet them, eagerly asking countless questions about their heroic escape to another planet. Orin wasn't sure if he felt much like a hero. It seemed to him that all they were really good at was running away when the emperor got too close, but the fact that they were all still alive was no small thing. Like the General said, sometimes just living to fight another day could be a victory in itself.

After stocking up on food and supplies, the group said their goodbyes, grabbed Skeet and stepped back through the Gate, returning to their new home on a distant planet. The whole team was together again. No, the whole family was together again. Orin could not remember ever being so happy.

Right now, he decided to go outside and get some air, emerging from the cave to the sights, smells and sounds of an alien world. Everything was so different here. The sky was blue! The most beautiful blue he had ever seen. He had been outside several times before, but the scene never failed to take his breath away.

Sitting down on a large flat stone, he took it all in. Below, the surging water of the river crashed over rocks. It was an awesome, almost violent sight, but he found the thunderous sounds rather soothing. The tall cliffs that formed the canyon walls created the most spectacular landscape he had ever seen. They were made up of layers of rock in reds, oranges, greys and even pinks. There were delicate green shrubs emerging from every crack and crevice and majestic trees grew out of the rock at impossible angles. It looked more like a painting than an actual place.

And the size of the canyon was almost impossible to comprehend. It was so deep, that it would take a person the entire day just to hike to the top of it. Orin was aware of how many people lived on this planet, but it felt as if he could walk for the rest of his life and never meet a single one of them. It felt safe – like they could stay here forever and the emperor, or anyone else for that matter, would never be able to find them.

As he sat there admiring the breathtaking view, he heard footsteps approaching from behind. As she often did, Juna came out to join him.

"Hey you," she said

"Hey you too."

"Mind if I join you?"

"Sure. Pull up a rock and make yourself comfortable."

They sat in silence for a while, just enjoying the beauty of it all.

"So, do you think we can do it?" Juna finally asked.

"Do what?"

"Defeat my father. Free the hods. Save the Marans. All of it."

Orin showed her his most confident smile. "Sure. The General knows what he's doing. We'll be able to keep the Marans safe from here and then, someday, we'll all go home and help make everything right."

"I think so too." She returned his smile as she tucked her knees up to her chin, hugging herself into a ball. "I like it here, but I'm already looking forward to going back. There are so many things left to be done and so many questions that need answers."

"Like why would we ever get involved in this in the first place?" Orin asked, only half-joking.

"No," she replied, rolling her eyes. "Like, why was my father trying to blow up his own palace? Or, why doesn't he just let the Marans come home? Or, how did they end up on that horrible planet to begin with?"

"Yeah. A lot of it doesn't make much sense," Orin agreed.

They sat quietly again, soaking in the beauty of their surroundings, but were startled by the sound of alarm bells coming from the mouth of the cave. It was the first time since they arrived that the alarms had rung, so they hesitated for a moment, not sure how to react. Then, instinct taking over, they stood and sprinted for the entrance, rushing over to see Pom who was currently manning the Tech Station.

"Looks like your dad is at it again," she told Juna. "There's a portal opening on Mara."

The General took his spot in the middle of the room and began shouting orders. "Mech Team 1, to the Gate. Aeva, verify the enemy's portal coordinates and open up ours right next door." He paused, annoyed by the fact he needed to yell to be heard. "Would somebody please shut that thing off!" When the ringing stopped, the General calmly addressed his team. "OK people, we've got this. We didn't ask for this life, but for now, this is what we do, so let's make sure we do it well. Always remember what we're fighting for." He smiled as he scanned the room, looking into the faces of this rag-tag collection of would-be rebels. They were in for a long fight, but he couldn't imagine a group of people he would rather have by his side.

"Our portal is open, General," Pom reported from the Tech Station.

"Well then, let's get to work."

Acknowledgements

First up, thank you to my son, Jason, whose question: "Does your game need a back story?" is what started me on this journey in the first place. To my wife, Martelle, thank you for help in ways too numerous to count, including love, support, encouragement and for being my frontline proof-reader. Many thanks to Acacia Scabar for helping me turn a decent story into something people may actually enjoy reading. Despite being no older than Juna, her advice throughout has been invaluable. She says she might like to be an editor someday, but to me, she already is one.

Others who have read early drafts of the story and provided much-appreciated and helpful advice include Leah Reynolds, Andrés Basteris, Richard Jones and Johann Preller. I would also like to thank the army of beta readers, of all ages, who were kind enough to read the earliest versions of my story including Mya, Emma, Teagan, James, Josh, Jett, Dawn, Krista, Kathy and Bob, as well as Tami Mumford and her grade 5/6 class at LBS.

WANT TO KNOW MORE?

FOR ALL THINGS:

GO TO:

www.MECHtheBook.com

Printed in Canada